UNDERTOW

Elizabeth
O'Roark

Cover Design and Formatting: Damonza

Undertow

ACKNOWLEDGEMENTS

This book would still be a sad little document sitting on my laptop shaming me were it not for the unfailing support of my family and friends.

Thanks to my parents for never once appearing to doubt that I could pull this off, and to my kids for putting up with my somewhat obsessive devotion to getting it done.

Thanks to my wonderful beta readers: Katie Meyer (sometimes a Coldplay concert and too many margaritas are a good thing, since I'd never have admitted to writing a book otherwise), Carol Ann Garner and Kate French. Your suggestions made this a much better book than it was when I first sent it out.

Last, but not least, a million thanks to the members of the Capital Grille Club: Sallye Clark, Diane Dematatis and Deanna Heaven. I can't imagine surviving the past year without you. The next round of prison-style spa treatments is on me.

CHAPTER 1

My first memories are of Nate. But I knew him even before those.

There's a picture of me on a blanket in my grandmother's yard, all dolled up in white bloomers and a little bonnet, trying to push up off chubby arms. He and Jordan sit in back of me, and Jordan looks straight at the camera, already a little cocky though he couldn't even have been five at the time. But Nate — Nate looks only at me, fascinated, as if I'm a wild animal someone has trapped and placed before him. I always loved that picture, back before it became painful to look at.

The fact that he's in the picture at all tells me one thing: my grandfather was behind the camera. My grandmother and my parents didn't want us playing with the housekeeper's kid, so they sure as hell weren't going to memorialize it on film.

I was four when I first got shipped out to my grandparents' estate at Paradise Cove for the summer. This was thanks to a seriously questionable tradition among my parents and the people they grew up with: ditch your offspring at the beach, to be poorly supervised by grandparents and maids, while you stay home, free to start on the gin and tonics at noon instead of five. Some parents visited frequently during the summer. My parents only ever came twice – the weekend they brought us in early June and the weekend they reluctantly picked us up at the end of August.

I don't remember missing my parents that summer. I don't

remember longing for Charlotte or the comfort of my own bed. I only remember Nate. He and Jordan, high up in a tree, laughing when I tried to climb toward them. Jordan shouting down that it's not for babies. It's the only memory I have that involves Nate on a side other than my own.

I remember trying to follow him into the surf once, only to be yanked out by my grandfather and dragged home. Jordan laughed. Nate said nothing, but I remember his face. Troubled and unhappy. I knew, even then, that he would have helped if he could.

A thousand memories would follow those, better ones. Nate would grow to become my best friend, my favorite person, the thing that made the beach what I dreamed about during the dull Charlotte winters. I sometimes wish I could just have that version of him back.

But even as I wish it, I know it still wouldn't be enough.

CHAPTER 2

My cell phone vibrates silently inside my backpack just as I exit the library. It's somewhere in there, probably at the bottom, buried under several textbooks, a laptop and remnants of the dinner I snuck in hours earlier.

It is bound to be one of three people: my roommate Jackie, who is probably out drinking and wants me to join her, my roommate Karen, who has likely locked herself out and wants to know when I'll be home, or my ex-boyfriend Tyler, wanting once again to hash out the demise of our relationship. We've had any number of these "talks" so far, which always involve him asking why we broke up, and arguing with my reasons. Of course, the real reason, the one I can't say, is that I just don't like him.

And right now, I really don't want to talk to any of them, so I'm not sure why I'm flinging books across the portico trying to get to my phone.

It's an unfamiliar number and I answer warily.

"This is Ethan Mayhew," says the voice. "Jordan's friend?"

I've known Ethan my entire life, so it's ridiculous that he'd think he has to qualify it by reminding me that he's my brother's best friend. "Ethan, Ethan," I muse, sounding perplexed. I tap a finger against my lip, although he can't see the gesture. "The name rings a bell but I can't really place you."

He laughs good-naturedly, and sounds sheepish when he

replies. "Well, I've been hearing how popular you are, Maura. I wasn't sure how many Ethans were calling you."

"I think my brother's been spinning a few stories on my behalf."

"Maura, you've had a parade of boys following you since you could walk."

It was just one boy, really. One boy I refuse to think about, so I don't bother to correct him.

He's coming to town for the weekend and wants to take me to dinner. I agree, feeling pleased but the tiniest bit confused. I've known Ethan forever, and he's always been unfailingly nice, but it's a brother's-best-friend kind of nice. Nice because he has to be, but otherwise maintaining a polite distance.

A few of my parents' friends have taken me out to dinner when they've come into town – adults always seem to imagine that college students are living off ramen noodles and cereal, even college students with a fairly substantial trust fund, but Ethan is the same age as Jordan. He's not really in the stage of life where you nurture and take pity on other people's kids. Then again, Jordan's wife just had a baby, so maybe Ethan's entering that phase of life too. I shrug it off. It'll be nice to see him either way.

* *

I take a final glance at the mirror just before he arrives on Friday. The dress is cute, but not revealing. Pretty but respectable. It's at times like this, the rare occasions when I've dressed like an adult and really made an effort, that I'm shocked to find my mother staring back at me in the mirror. I got my dad's height, but her dark hair, her green eyes, her tiny nose. The mouth I've finally grown into, after all those years of Jordan taunting me with Rolling Stones songs, implying I looked like Mick Jagger. I wonder if I'll look like an adult to Ethan. Probably not.

I hear him knock and briefly wish I'd picked up the

apartment, which looks like exactly what it is: a place where four college seniors who spend every free hour at school or out drinking keep their clothes, and occasionally sleep. I see Jackie's bra on the couch as I cross the room and shove it under a cushion.

I open the door and he is exactly as I remember — the sandy blonde hair, the crinkly blue eyes, the wide, confident smile. He was always good looking. Even when we were little, girls would grow stupid and dreamy-eyed when he smiled, although I was never one of them. I always preferred a little dose of bad with my good, a hint of something wild that Ethan just never had.

"You're all grown up," he says.

I laugh. "You just saw me at Christmas."

But I know what he means. It's odd to see him here, out of context. He's really an adult now. At home, around Jordan and his friends, it still feels as if I'm 12 and he's 16. Somehow, removed from the setting he's always been in, I see him anew. Maybe it's the same for him. Maybe, away from my family, he doesn't see me as a little girl.

"Maura!" calls Jackie, coming out of her room. "Can I borrow your…?" She doesn't just stop, but bounces backward as if she's hit a rubber wall, when she sees Ethan. "Oh, sorry." I can tell she thinks he's hot. Jackie's got the worst poker face in the world.

I introduce them, trying to hide a smile at her open-jaw gaping. She turns to glare at me. "I thought you were being taken to dinner by a 'family friend'?"

"I *am* being taken to dinner by a family friend."

"You made it sound like he was 60," she argues. Ethan laughs.

"I'm pretty sure you came up with that on your own," I say, though I can totally see where she'd have gotten that impression. "Borrow whatever you want," I grin as I leave, knowing from her narrowed eyes that I will be grilled relentlessly when I get home tonight.

"I think my roommate has a crush on you," I tell him as we walk to his car.

He shrugs, endearingly. "I've got my eye on someone else," he smiles, giving me a sly glance. I'm so stunned that I barely conceal the way my steps stutter. It's the first moment it's occurred to me that this might be a date. I shake my head a little. It's a ridiculous thought.

"I made reservations at Claremont's," he says. "Is that okay?"

Oh my God this really is sounding like a date.

"I've never been there," I reply. "It's supposed to be nice though."

He looks at me incredulously. "How could you have never been there? It's the most highly rated restaurant in town."

"I'm in college, Ethan. College students don't eat at four-star restaurants. We order pizza."

"You're hardly an average college student, Maura," he chides.

"I'm trying to be," I say quietly.

"Fair enough," he replies. "I guess I tried to be too. Unless I was trying to impress a girl," he adds, winking at me.

Oh my God. I may actually be on a date with Ethan-freaking-Mayhew. My brother's unbelievably hot friend, the guy that every single girl I know from the beach, from Charlotte, has fantasized about since puberty. Back home this would inspire a lot of girlish screaming, and probably some jealousy too.

"I saw the baby last week," he tells me with a grin.

I stick my tongue out at him. "So unfair. I'm her aunt and godmother and I've barely seen her."

"She's a cutie. Never thought I'd see Jordan as a dad, though."

I grimace. "As far as I can tell you still haven't seen Jordan as a dad. Mia does all the work." My poor sister-in-law. It worked well early on, her fragile, quiet beauty matched to his bombast. But since the baby was born she appears to be shrinking into herself, and Jordan appears to still be... Jordan. Out drinking every night, content as long as he's the center of attention.

He shrugs. "They seem happy enough." I keep my disagreement to myself.

Ethan is a perfect gentleman. He holds the door for me, remains standing until I've been seated. I could tell myself these are date behaviors, except that Ethan was raised to do all of these things. He'd act no different if I were 80.

"Excited to graduate?" he asks, as we look at the menus. It's the kind of question only an adult would ask. A parental question. Maybe it's not a date. That's disappointing, but probably for the best. Our families are so close that dating him would be fraught with peril. No matter how badly it went, I'd still have to see him regularly for the next 50 years of my life. And if my mother got wind of this, she'd have the country club reserved for our wedding before he even hit second base.

"Your question makes me feel like I'm at dinner with my dad," I smile.

"What's wrong with asking you if you're excited to graduate?"

I shrug. "It's just one of those grown-up questions, like 'are you excited to see your friends this summer?' or 'what did you ask Santa for?'" He looks a little uncomfortable, which makes me giggle. "It's okay! You're just always going to see me as Jordan's little sister."

He reaches across the table to graze my hand with his fingers. "Maura, let me make it clear. You are no longer little, and I'm not thinking about Jordan in any way, shape or form right now."

Oh my God. This IS a date. I am one part horrified, one part excited. Either way, I can't wait to tell the girls.

"Are you in Elise's wedding?" he asks.

I groan. "Yes." Elise has only been engaged for three months, but her wedding has already become a full-time job.

"Why the groan? I can't imagine her being a bridezilla."

"She's not," I reply. "It's her mom. She's a momzilla, if there is such a thing." Mrs. McDonald calls me every week with some new, ridiculous demand. We had to go all the way to Atlanta to look at dresses, and she's made me come back to Charlotte twice for dress fittings. She called me at 7 a.m. the previous Saturday to make sure my ears were pierced.

"She's had so many years to plan this she's bound to go a little crazy," he says. "How long have they been together?"

"Seven years," I say, and I smile, but this time the movement is stiff and sluggish. Elise and Brian started dating the year after Nate and I did. Nate and I being together wasn't even a choice. It had to happen, and once it did we were like two objects that couldn't be pried apart. But Elise and Brian began as a relationship of convenience, the inevitable result of being our closest friends, of always being thrown together because Nate and I could not stay apart, not for a minute. When I imagined adulthood, it wasn't Brian and Elise I saw walking down the aisle. It shouldn't still hurt, but it does, and all I can do is pretend otherwise and change the subject.

The night passes swiftly, something I haven't said of a date in a long time. It's not until the ride home that I grow nervous. I've known him for my entire life. I'm not sure if he'll try to kiss me, but the thought leaves me with a somewhat unpleasant mix of both fear and excitement.

He walks me to door. "Well, thank you for dinner, Ethan," I say, doing my best not to sound as nervous as I feel.

Do I wait for him to kiss me? Because if he doesn't try then I'll look like an idiot. But I kind of want him to. I search my purse for my keys, and he tips my chin up to look at him. He leans down and brushes his mouth lightly over mine. He moves closer, placing his hands on my waist and leaning into me slightly, parting my lips with his tongue.

He's a good kisser, but it went without saying that Ethan Mayhew would be a good kisser.

"Can I see you tomorrow?" he asks.

I hesitate. I have a party to go to and Tyler, my ex, will be there. He's been acting somewhat unstable since our break-up — seeing me with someone else might be the last straw. Plus, Ethan's an honest-to-God adult. I'd feel like a moron dragging him to a college party. "I have a friend's birthday party," I say apologetically.

"What time?"

"We're meeting at 9."

"I'll pick you up at 10:30."

If I didn't like him, it would be presumptuous, but I do like him, so I agree.

CHAPTER 3

I was nearly a teenager before I realized the extent to which houses don't just stay clean on their own, that there were people who had to sweep up the sand I dragged over the kitchen floor and hose off my flip flops each night. I didn't realize that the big bowl of fresh fruit had to be replenished, that the basket of warm muffins in the morning wasn't one more example of nature's bounty. My grandparents had a stunning number of people scurrying in the background to make our days seamless and perfect, and at the head of it all was Nate's mother, Mary, our housekeeper.

Nate fascinated me. He was so agile, and so free. There seemed to be nothing he couldn't do. There weren't many local kids who lived on the island – the land had grown so expensive over the years that only wealthy families from much farther inland could afford it. But Nate lived in the carriage house out back with his mother, and from my bedroom window I'd watch him sneak out at night. I was never sure where he was going, but I'd hear the dull thud of him landing on the ground after climbing out of his window, or the soft crunch of his shoes on the gravel and run to watch the mystery unfold. I wanted to know where he was going so badly that I often thought of sneaking after him, but I was scared of getting caught, scared I couldn't jump from the porch roof to the ground, scared I wouldn't be able to climb back up.

I was six when he finally stopped under my window and looked up.

"Well, are you coming or what?" he asked, as if we'd been planning this all along.

I was terrified, and at the same time I couldn't resist. So I shimmied down the side of the house and followed him anxiously into the dark night.

Down at the beach there were several more kids, giggling and stripping naked before running in the water. But I froze, standing paralyzed in the sand alone.

Nate waded back out of the water. "Aren't you coming?" he asked, standing butt-naked in front of me on the beach. I shook my head.

"Why not?"

"Sharks eat at night," I whispered.

"I wouldn't let a shark get you," he said, as if surprised I'd even think it, "and anyway, that's a myth."

I believed him because he was two years older than me, and seemed to know everything. Plus he lived here year-round, so who'd know better than him? I dropped my little nightgown and underpants in the sand and ran into the water, staying close to Nate in case I needed protection after all.

He stopped at my window from then on, and I always went. Soon our nights morphed into our days, and without discussion we became simply inseparable. We'd remain that way for years to come, because things were different when I was with Nate, as if he were a separate continent with its own rules. I felt free with him, something I never was at home, but I was also safe. And in some ways, that was different from home too.

"You're not like the rest of them," he said once. I knew who he meant – the other kids here from Charlotte. Even back then, before distinctions like age and gender and class were a factor, you could tell who was from home. A certain kind of posturing, affectation, a haughtiness when they came out to play as if they were above this place and its people.

But Nate wasn't really like the kids from the island, either. He was smarter. Silent and watchful, but kind. I didn't see it at the time. I just knew, for me, he felt *right* in a way no one else did.

The older kids played, some nights, at a big field at the end of the island. The first summer I was old enough to go, my grandfather pulled Jordan and Nate aside.

"She's little. You boys are gonna keep an eye out for her, right?"

Nate looked appalled. "Of course we are," he said, as if he couldn't believe there was another option.

"Speak for yourself," Jordan smirked.

The look Nate gave Jordan was almost identical to the one my grandfather did – disgust, disbelief. It's no wonder, really, that Nate was always my grandfather's favorite.

Nate got a canoe for his tenth birthday, and for a few summers it consumed us. We spent our days on the sound, where the calm water led to patches of tall weeds and hidden islands, undiscovered until found by us. We built a fort on one of those islands, and for a brief time it was our obsession, our secret. I assisted, but the planning, the inexhaustible dedication to making it perfect – that was entirely Nate's. I'd watched him draw before, intricate buildings and houses, more interesting and detailed than you'd ever expect from someone his age, but I'd never understood until we built the fort how much he loved to create. As soon as we woke we were off in the canoe, with lunch Mary had packed and small trinkets from home. We never told anyone about it, as if by mutual agreement we knew something special would be lost if we did.

One afternoon, on the way home, I asked him why he didn't have a father.

He was neither offended by nor interested in the question. "He left. He was one of you."

Even then, at age 8, I knew what he meant. Not a townie. His dad was one of the summer families. "In Old Cove?" There were lots of summer families, but only 15 mansions along mile-long Old Cove Road, numbered simply. The houses were famous, though I didn't know it at the time. People hours inland knew them by family name, but we just knew them by number. I lived in 11.

"He lived in 3."

"Ethan lives in 3," I told him. I was often sent down to Ethan's to collect my brother for dinner.

He nodded. "He's my cousin."

My jaw dropped. It had never occurred to me that Nate might be related to one of us. It made him seem exotic, like a foundling prince.

"So why don't you live in 3?" I asked. I was a little scared to suggest it, as if the idea hadn't occurred to him yet and might change things. Nate had always lived in our carriage house. I wouldn't want him to leave.

"They don't want me there," he said, kicking at the smooth glass of the water a little angrily.

I wanted to comfort him. "3 is a stupid house anyway."

I never looked at Ethan's house quite the same again. It took on the trappings of fairy tales I'd read. Unfair as it was, I saw Mrs. Mayhew as the evil queen, Mr. Mayhew as the gullible king, Ethan the usurper to the throne. It was wildly unfair, actually. Nate's dad had skipped town long before Mr. and Mrs. Mayhew took over the house. And Ethan was always nice to me. Nicer, in fact, than any of Jordan's other friends. I kind of wished he'd be mean just so it wouldn't tamper with my story.

"Go down to Graham's and look for your brother," my grandmother told me, pointing imperiously at the front door. "And if he's not there, look at Ethan's." With anxious excitement, I went to Ethan's first.

His mom answered, looking very pregnant and tired. Her pregnancy was another thorn in my side. She didn't much look like an evil queen, all sweaty and bedraggled, walking toward me with lurching steps and swollen feet.

"Honey, you've got to go up there and get him yourself," his mother said, sinking in a chair beside the door. "If I walk those stairs one more time this baby's just gonna fall out of my stomach." I hurried away, a little horrified by the image she'd conjured. I renewed my vow to never have children.

I went upstairs, looking at all the rooms in wonder. Thinking how unfair it was that Nate didn't live there. And how selfishly glad I was that it had worked out the way it had.

CHAPTER 4

"**D**ude," groans Jackie when she saunters out of bed at noon the next day, wearing only panties and the shirt she wore out last night. "Your brother's friend is so hot."

I grin. "He's okay."

"Shut up!" she laughs. "You totally want to bang him and you know it!"

I shrug. "Maybe." The truth is that I totally don't want that, not yet, but Jackie doesn't understand that gray area between mild interest and desperate arousal. It's all or nothing with her. And it's usually "all".

"So, what's the deal? Was it a date? It looked like a date," she says, grabbing a two-liter bottle of diet soda out of the fridge and drinking straight from it.

"Jackie, that's so gross," I scold, watching her chug.

She shrugs. "What do you care? You don't drink diet, you skinny bitch. So date or not a date?"

I smile. "He kissed me, so I guess it was."

"Yay!" she says, doing a little happy dance beside the fridge. "Are you going to see him again?"

"He's picking me up after Tricia's party tonight."

"You are totally going to sleep with him," she insists.

I laugh. "Jackie, how long have you known me? Have you ever known me to sleep with a guy on the second date?"

"I would," she argues.

"Yes, Jackie, I'm well aware of that," I grin.

For my second date with Ethan, at Jackie's insistence, I dress slightly less conservatively than I did the night before: a striped mini-dress with a flouncy little skirt and spaghetti straps, covered by a cardigan. It's more 1960s schoolgirl than stripper, which is the way I like it. I'd never admit it to my friends, but I'm looking forward to seeing Ethan. It's nice to have something to be excited about again.

When we arrive at the bar, Tricia comes over and throws a heavy arm around my shoulders, already drunk enough that odds are she will not retain a single memory of this party.

"You can't leave!" she cries. "I'm taking you back to Greenville with me!"

In a way I wish she could. I have less than three months left with these people, my closest friends for the past four years. Sometimes they feel more like family than the people who wait for me to return to Charlotte at the end of May. And I'll certainly miss them more than my family when I head to law school in the fall.

I giggle and lean my head against her arm affectionately. "I'll miss you too. You can always come visit."

"Seriously, Maura? Exactly how many planes would it take to get to BFE Michigan?"

"It's like an hour from Detroit! You make it sound like I'm going to school in the Alaskan wilderness!"

"I don't understand why you have to go so far," she whines. "Go to Duke or UVA! They've got great law schools." I stiffen at the suggestion, though she's far too inebriated to notice. There are literally a thousand words in the English language that destroy me. Innocent words, common words – ocean, canoe, UVA, beach, baseball. If I could remove them all from the dictionary I would.

I wonder how long it will take before every single reminder of him doesn't blow through me like some kind of natural disaster, taking away every vestige of happiness I was feeling the second before?

"Nope, sorry, it's kind of a done deal," I tell her, desperately trying to claw back the happiness that floated away so easily. "Since when are you going back to Greenville? I thought you hated Greenville."

"I do hate Greenville," she says, deadpan. "But the odds of me finding a job in Charlotte or Richmond between now and graduation are pretty slim, and my parents say they're done paying for my shit. We don't all have trust funds there, princess."

"Fuck off," I laugh. There are people who are allowed to give me shit about it, and people who aren't. Tricia doesn't dislike me for it. That's why she's allowed.

"Oh, boy," she says, looking over my shoulder. There's a mixture of trepidation and glee in her voice that can only mean one thing. Before she can even warn me, Tyler is there.

"Hey Maura," he says, already sounding morose. I grit my teeth and Tricia moves away from us as if we're on fire.

"Hi Tyler." I try to sound friendly and upbeat as I turn around, but my voice is strained. I really don't want to have this talk with him. Again.

He's standing so close that I have to crane my neck up to see his face. I'm 5'9", and there aren't a lot of guys tall enough to demand that of me, but he's one of them.

"I miss you," he says, running his hand over my bare arm. God, when I first met him, that brush over my arm would have brought goose bumps, but now it just makes me wish I hadn't removed my cardigan. He's attractive, but there was something more about him, initially. Something that made me hope he'd be the one who was different. But he wasn't, and now the brush of his hand is about as appealing as a mosquito landing there.

"Tyler," I sigh. I don't want to repeat what I've said before. We barely dated for a month, and he's spent twice as long harassing me about it. I'm continually surprised that, with as many girls as he has salivating over him, he's still mourning me.

"I just don't understand," he says, beginning to show his frustration.

"I'm leaving soon," I say. "You're staying here, and I'll be at Michigan in the fall, so it would have to end anyway. And I really have to spend every free moment between now and then getting my senior project done." This is entirely true, and entirely unrelated to why I don't want to be with Tyler.

I chose him for the wrong reason. I chose him because he reminded me of someone else, and the damage was done by the time I realized it.

"I could visit, Maura," he says earnestly, gripping my elbow, and I feel slightly ill. "I could visit all the time. There's no reason it can't work." I didn't mean to hurt him. I didn't mean to hurt any of them, and yet I can't seem to stop doing it. I can't seem to stop deluding myself with the hope that gray eyes or the flash of an up-to-no-good smile can bring back what is gone.

I shake my head, disengaging myself. "Tyler, I'm so sorry. I don't want to be serious with anyone. I'm still young. I haven't even started law school yet. I've got a long haul ahead of me and I just need to focus on that right now."

It's at that exact moment that I see Ethan's head above the crowd, moving toward us. His timing could not be worse. A lie is necessary. "My brother is here," I say, nodding at Ethan. "I've got to go."

I make a beeline for Ethan and pull him back toward the street without saying goodbye to any of my friends.

"You're early." It's not that I'm not happy to see him, but I did want to spend a little more time at the party.

"We didn't have to run off," he says with a grin. "Are you that ashamed of me?" Ethan has always been good-looking. He doesn't believe for a minute that I'm ashamed.

"No," I sigh. "That was my ex-boyfriend."

"I thought it was Nate, at first."

My stomach twists the way it always does when I hear his name, makes me want to curl in on the wound protectively, as if I can prevent further harm. I can't believe it still has that effect, after all this time.

I shake it off. I have to, around Ethan especially. "No," I reply. "His name is Tyler, and I was just giving him the whole talk about why we broke up and how I don't want to date when you walked in. I told him you were my brother."

"Really?" he asks, pulling me into him. "Would your brother do this?" I scamper away, scared that Tyler will see.

"Don't," I whisper. "Please. I don't want to hurt his feelings."

"Okay," he laughs. "Then let's go someplace where I can do that without hurting his feelings."

We go to a bar down the street, and get a drink. He doesn't kiss me again until a slow dance comes on. I like him and I like kissing him, but our common background hangs over my head like both a blessing and a warning. There is something so pre-ordained about this – he's my brother's best friend, our parents are friends. Shoot, our *grandparents* were friends. This could never unfold naturally. We will either wind up married or the whole thing will go down in flames, an awkward memory I'll relive again and again until I'm old and withered.

We go back to my apartment. We sit on the couch and he picks up my legs and lays them over his lap.

"You know, I always had a crush on you," he says.

I laugh. "No you didn't. You're four years older than me. I was still playing with Barbies when you started driving."

"God you looked hot playing with those Barbies," he jokes.

"Ewww," I laugh. "I think I want you to stay away from my niece from now on."

He grins. "We gave Jordan shit about you for years, calling dibs, that kind of thing. He didn't care. And then out of nowhere you turned gorgeous and he could tell we meant it, and he flipped out. He said no one could lay a finger on you until you graduated college."

"Are you serious?"

He nods. "I'm a few months early, but I had to get a jump on Graham."

"I'm failing to understand why you'd listen to my brother at all."

"First of all, because he's my best friend. More importantly, because he was a defensive lineman in college. I wanted to date you without risking hospitalization."

I grin. "My brother would never beat you up."

He shrugs, and the playfulness leaves his voice. "You were always with Nate anyway." He watches me carefully, assessing my reaction. He wants to know if I'm over it.

I attempt to look detached. "That was a long time ago."

"You guys were so serious, though, for all those years," he says slowly. "What happened?"

Another sick thud in my stomach, the sensation of my lungs caving in, the scraping in my throat that warns of tears. I can't do this now. "He wasn't who I thought he was," I say simply, flatly, unwilling to convey any emotion with the statement.

He appears relieved. "I could have told you that," he smiles, leaning over to kiss me, pulling his own legs on the couch so we are almost laying side by side. He hovers over me, not rushing, kissing me languidly. He runs his mouth over my neck, over my bare shoulders, my collarbone. He pulls the straps of my dress down and reaches inside to cup my breast, before another hand starts sliding up my leg.

"Ethan," I warn.

He smiles ruefully. "Too much?"

"I didn't even know yesterday was a date until you kissed me. Just give me a little time."

He laughs. "What do you mean? Why did you think I called you if it wasn't a date?"

"I don't know. I thought maybe it was one of those broth-
erly 'check on little Maura and make sure she's being fed' kind
of things."

"Maura," he sighs. "I drove up here to see you. *Just* to see you."
I look at him in astonishment. "Seriously?"

"Yes," he says. "I wasn't lying before. Your brother said not
until you graduated. And I wanted to make sure Graham didn't
get to you first. Am I freaking you out?"

"No," I say, sounding a little freaked out. "I'm just surprised."
He smiles. "You'll get over it."

"I'm even more surprised that you thought you had to worry
about Graham."

He grins, and lowers me back down on the couch again. And
it's okay. It's pleasant. But he's not Nate.

CHAPTER 5

My grandfather wasn't born into money, and I think he saw a lot of himself in Nate: in the flash of intellect that crossed his face as he listened, in his sweet nature, in the crooked smile that popped up long before anyone else got the joke. Nate didn't go to private school, he didn't have a tutor or instructor for every subject and every sport. But in spite of that he thrived – he grew smarter and stronger and better each year.

And with every year, Jordan grew more annoyed that it was the housekeeper's son, not even a relative, who was my grandfather's favorite.

When Nate was nine, he beat Jordan in a race. It was a race Jordan had challenged him to in the first place, but losing to Nate was a particularly bitter pill to swallow. And as Jordan endured the ridicule that followed, his dislike of Nate took on a new form. He did his best to exclude him at every turn – if a game was being played, Jordan would say the teams were full. If sides were being drawn, Jordan told Nate that no townies were allowed. Soon it wasn't just Jordan doing it, and it wasn't just Nate singled out, but all the kids from the island. There was never a game or an interaction, after that point, that didn't hold some element of "us" against "them".

Nate and I, however, were fine, too close and too much alike to let the dispute taint our friendship, even when my brother was at its core. That I took Nate's side irritated Jordan even further.

"Don't you have a house to clean somewhere?" he jeered at Nate as we came out of the water.

"Shut up, Jordan," I snapped. I normally steered clear of my brother, because I'd learned the hard way what happened when I pissed him off. But today anger overcame caution. I was sick of him messing with Nate. I was sick of the way Nate seemed to dim a little in response, as if Jordan's words held a thread of truth.

"He's not one of us, Maura," Jordan hissed. "And he never will be. You better watch your mouth or I'll tell Mom who you play with down here."

"So what?" I demanded.

"Let her find out you're friends with the help," he said. "See for yourself how fast she makes you stay home."

I didn't really believe him, but it was the first time I'd ever thought our friendship could be challenged. Little did I know that there were far greater threats to our friendship than Jordan coming down the pike.

* *

I was 12 when it first came up. Too old to be skinny-dipping with the opposite sex, too young and naïve to realize it. I made it all the way to the water before I discovered Nate wasn't with me.

"Slowpoke!" I taunted, exultant that I'd beat him to the water, an event that had never happened before and would certainly never happen again.

He said nothing, but waded in after me, still in his shorts, keeping his distance. I splashed him, and he splashed me back half-heartedly. I dove deep in the water, feeling for his legs so I could pull them out from under him. When I found them, though, he kicked me off.

"What'd you do that for?" I gasped, jumping up. He turned away from me.

"Maura," he said awkwardly. "You need…"

"What?" I prompted, a little annoyed by his weirdness.

"A swimsuit." He sighed deeply, in a way that made me feel very young and freshly annoyed with him, and looked away. "You know. You're, uh, getting older." I'd given the idea so little thought until that moment that I had to look down to see if he was right.

He was. There they were. Barely bigger than a boy's, but definitely not a boy's. I wasn't a late bloomer – I was just late to realize it was happening.

I rolled my eyes. It still didn't seem like a big deal. "So what?"

"Just wear a swimsuit," he said tersely, still refusing to face me.

I wore a swimsuit from then on, and so did he, but it still seemed like he was being weird about it for no good reason.

My friends – Heather, Kendall and Elise — grew boy crazy without me, and Nate was at the center of their fantasies. Most of it was innocent – they argued over who would marry him, who was the most like him. But they also alluded to tongue kissing, even to sex, and I moved quickly from disturbed to disgusted. I could no more imagine doing that with Nate than with my brother.

But when I finally did start liking boys, I arrived at my grandparents' house to discover that Nate was a not just a boy, but a spectacular one. The little boy who'd been my best friend through all those summers was gone, and in his place was the teenager my friends had seen long before me. He had the same challenging gray eyes, the same smile that lifted high on one side, sweet and devious all at once. But the things that were so innocent in him as a boy no longer were. Now they colluded to create something dangerous, something that affected me in ways even I didn't understand.

He was only 15, but he seemed so much older than me, all of a sudden. Not helped by the fact that he came over and mussed my hair like he was my grandfather.

"Well hello there, Maura Leigh," he said with that crooked grin. He was treating me like a little girl, and it made me irrationally angry.

"You're taller," I said, and for some reason it sounded like an insult.

"So are you," he said, and it sounded like a compliment.

In the water, he became the Nate I knew again. Within five minutes he was tossing me over his head into the waves as if nothing had changed. He was the same boy, beneath those devastating looks. The parts of us that had always been there emerged, and the parts of us that had changed fell to the background.

But the one thing that had changed and would not fall to the background was Tina, Nate's beautiful, inane girlfriend. I'd have hated her anyway, but I grew to hate her a little extra for the way she treated me, the way she rolled her eyes when I was with him, clicked her tongue disapprovingly, was always trying to drag him off.

She wouldn't swim, I suppose because she'd mess up her perfect hair and her face full of makeup. Instead, she'd stand at the water's edge, squealing like a girl every time the water ran over her toes, giggling whenever he came near, pouting if he stayed in the water too long instead of paying attention to her.

"Your girlfriend's an idiot," I told him one night when she was blissfully absent.

He shrugged his shoulders. "She's not that bad."

I looked at him scornfully. "She doesn't swim, and she acts like a moron all the time." I mimicked her, jumping up and down squealing "Oooh it's so cold!"

He laughed.

"What do you even see in her?" I asked.

He opened his mouth to speak, then took another glance at me and clammed up. Finally, he shrugged again and said, "It's hard to explain."

She didn't like me either. "Do you always have to bring the little girl with you?" she sniped one night, glaring at me as she said it.

"Yes," he said simply, staring her down. She stomped off,

and he made no move to follow. And soon she was replaced by Ashleigh, even prettier than Tina and a thousand times nicer. She treated me like a little sister, painting my nails and braiding my hair and scolding Nate for teasing me.

Which made me realize that it didn't matter who he dated. Because I hated Ashleigh too.

CHAPTER 6

Within 48 hours of Ethan's departure, my mother calls. I know immediately, just by the way she practically sings her "hello", that she knows I went out with him.

"A little birdy told me you had a date this weekend!" she trills. She sounds more excited than she'd be if *she'd* had the date this weekend.

I pinch my eyes shut, already regretting the whole thing. Ethan is great, but he's not worth this. "Yeah, we went out," I say, trying so hard to sound casual that I almost seem comatose.

"That's so exciting!" she sings again. I swear to God I can almost picture her with a heart over her head and those little cartoon bluebirds flying around.

"It's really not that exciting, Mom," I warn her. "It was just a date. I've had a lot of dates."

"You've had a lot of dates, but not with Ethan!" she cries. "He's practically family."

"If that's the case, then maybe dating him is legally questionable," I suggest dryly.

"Oh, Maura, stop. Let your poor mother be excited for once."

"Mom, you know what's exciting? That I'm going to law school. That I'm graduating with a 3.9 average. That's what's exciting."

"Fine," she sighs. "I'll call Stephanie Mayhew. I know she'll share my enthusiasm."

"Oh my God, Mom! This is freaking crazy. Please tell me you are not seriously planning to call Ethan's mom and tell her!" I cry.

There is silence on the other end.

Crap. "You already told her, didn't you?"

"No," she says defensively. "*She* told *me* at the club this morning."

"Great," I moan. "Did the two of you come to a decision about the flowers and catering for our wedding already, then?"

She giggles. Jesus Christ. She did discuss a wedding. Like I thought last weekend, if I don't marry Ethan now, it will be a disaster of unmitigated proportion.

* *

In spite of my irritation with my mother, it seems unfair to penalize Ethan for it, and the truth is that I *do* want to see him. When he suggests coming up to Chapel Hill, I don't say no.

"I have a paper due on Monday," I warn him beforehand.

"I'll just come up for dinner and be out of your way," he promises.

This time we head out of town, to a vineyard I've never even heard of. This is different than a standard college date, where you meet at a bar, you meet at a party, you go to a game. And I like it. I like how comfortable it is with him, how quiet. I like how easy things are, that he's planned in advance, taken care of the details so things are seamless. Maybe this is what all adult dating is like, but I suspect it's just Ethan.

After dinner we lounge on the restaurant's back deck, where the two of us can just squeeze into an oversized chair with a second bottle of wine and watch the stars come out.

"Who do you stay with when you come up here?" I ask him, realizing it's a question I should have asked the week before.

"I stayed with a buddy from college and his wife last weekend," he says.

"But what about tonight?" I ask. "You can't be planning to drive two hours home."

He grins. "Are you inviting me to stay?"

"To sleep?" I ask sternly. "Just sleep?"

"Of course," he assures me. "But feel free to change your mind about that last part."

And when we wake up the next morning, I'm glad he's there. Unlike with Tyler, and the guys who came before him, there's no part of me that feels like I've made a mistake, chosen him for the wrong reasons. I don't wake up and see all the ways he's not who I thought he was. He's just Ethan. Good-looking, fun Ethan who I've known all my life.

The room is cold and I snuggle up to his back. "Why is your body temperature like 20 degrees warmer than mine?" I laugh.

"I don't know," he smiles. "Maybe you should bring me up north with you so you don't freeze to death."

"That's asking a lot of you when an electric blanket could accomplish the same thing."

"There are still a few things I can do that a blanket can't," he says, and his mouth moves to my neck, to my collarbone, and farther down.

It's the first time since Nate that I've found something better than being alone.

CHAPTER 7

I was 14. Back at the beach after nine months away. Putting on a bikini and makeup and refusing to admit, even to myself, that I was doing it for Nate.

He walked out of the water toward me, and I barely recognized him. I'd grown over the past year, but he had metamorphosed. He was huge, nearly as tall as Jordan, who was the tallest person I knew. And his face. Gah. The easy smile and the gray eyes that stood out against his tan, his dark hair turning light with sun. He was gorgeous, like something straight out of an Abercrombie ad. Everything about him was masculine, from his walk to the way he roughed up his wet hair.

When he saw me, he looked a little surprised, making me wonder if he'd forgotten I was coming. And then he looked torn, as if he wasn't sure whether my presence here were good or bad.

"You want to swim?" he asked with a crooked smile that couldn't disguise how off-balance he seemed to feel.

I agreed, doing my best to feign an ambivalence that would match his.

I headed for the water, and he walked behind me. I'd gotten plenty of attention from boys over the previous year, and I didn't have a lot of experience with self-consciousness, but I made up for lost time in the 30 seconds it took to get to the water. I felt naked, acutely aware of his presence and the fact that I probably looked like a giraffe from his vantage point. I'd grown up, up, up but not out, really – my body a bewildering mix of long, gangly parts. I had a chest but no curves to speak of otherwise. I had never wished more for a curvy figure like my mother's than I did at that moment.

We paddled out into the water silently, his sudden awkwardness coinciding with my inability to speak. I began to panic. Would we never speak again? Why, *why*, couldn't I stop noticing how good-looking he was? Why couldn't I just act normal? It wasn't as if I hadn't been around a cute boy before. Boys even older than Nate had asked me out, though my parents' strict rules about dating had kept me from saying yes.

"That one?" I asked, nodding toward the horizon, as we watched the waves come in.

"Nope. It'll break before it gets here."

He was right.

I saw another one forming. "That one?"

He grinned. "I think you're losing your touch, Pierce."

"Piss off," I replied, made irritable by the situation.

He laughed, and the sound thawed something inside me.

"That one," he said decidedly. We both caught it and rode it in, my body dragging against the rough rocks and shells along the shoreline. It nearly wrenched my bikini top off too, and I struggled to fix it before anyone saw.

"Ouch," I said, looking at the scratches across my stomach and chest.

He shrugged. "That's what you get for dressing like a girl," he smirked. And once the handful of wet sand I'd gathered and aimed at his head made impact, things became – almost – normal.

I saw less of him than in previous summers, now that he had a job, but slowly we fell back into our old ways. When we were preoccupied I could almost forget how different things were, until out of nowhere there'd be that odd tension in the air. I'd sneak a sidelong glance at him and find he was doing the same. Instead of driving us apart, though, that tension made me want to seek him out, as if it had magnetized us somehow.

But it didn't magnetize us enough. There was no one girlfriend that summer for him, but several, rotating in and out of our little group at the beach. At night we no longer played games but instead sat under the pier, quietly if we'd been able to get liquor. Nate stayed by my side until it was late, and then he'd wander off with one of those girls, leaving me behind to pretend I wasn't sick with jealousy.

Only Elise knew. She never said it, but I could tell from the sympathy in her eyes that she thought it was as futile as I did. Nate was everyone's crush — Heather and Kendall could barely function when he was around – so what made me special? Nothing.

Yet Nate was oddly irritable about the boys who came around me. Just Robert and Teddy, two boys from home I'd known my entire life, but Nate's belligerence toward them seemed to grow by the day. "They fucking follow you everywhere," Nate would complain.

"No they don't," I argued, although if I gave it some thought I'd have to admit he had a point.

"Stop encouraging it," he said angrily.

"I don't encourage it."

"Hell yeah, you do," he snarled. "You wear those little tank tops every fucking night. And you do that whole lipgloss thing."

"What lipgloss thing?" I demanded.

"You know what I'm talking about," he said darkly.

I had no idea what he was talking about. But if the tank tops and the lipgloss had made him finally realize I was girl, I knew I wasn't going to stop anytime soon.

"I think he likes you," whispered Elise one night.

"No," I said, shaking my head even as I prayed she could convince me otherwise.

"You should have seen the look on his face when he saw Robert next to you on the beach," she giggled. "The second he saw it he came charging out of the water looking like he was gonna beat someone to death."

"No," I shook my head again, wanting her to be right so badly that I could barely breathe as I argued against it. "It doesn't mean anything."

But it was too late. The tiny seed of hope she'd planted was already growing like an out-of-control weed, and taking over.

* *

As fall approached, Nate stopped bringing other girls around. He stayed with me, always close by but not quite close enough. Everyone was meeting under the pier one night, but our time together was coming to an end and I didn't want to share him. As if he'd had the same thought, he suggested we swim first. Our late night swims were infrequent now, and somewhat uncomfortable, both of us refusing to admit things had changed. I felt strung tight most of the time we were together, but never more so than when we swam alone in the moonlight. But this time the water was calm and we were competing, seeing who could backfloat the longest, and it made us forget somehow, relax.

I laughed as I failed at it, again and again. Eventually I just started splashing him in the face to make him stop floating entirely.

"You must have more body fat," I argued, as I tried it again. "That's why you can float."

He laughed. "Right." Few things were less likely. Nate was the star of his high school baseball team – recruiters had already come to watch him – and he had the body to go with it.

"You're doing it wrong," he said, standing up beside me while

I attempted to float. The moon was like a spotlight across my bare stomach and I suddenly felt exposed, splayed out in front of him. "You've got to push down here," he said, placing a finger in the center of my ribcage, producing goose bumps across the surface of my skin, "and then you've got to lift up here." His hand went under the water, palming my ass, pushing it upward just as he described. The pressure of his hand, the way it forced me to arch upward, made something spasm tight in my stomach and I gave a small gasp of surprise. We looked at each with sudden clarity, and for a single breath our faces were stripped of pretense. We weren't children anymore and we weren't merely friends anymore either. And then he jerked his hands away as if they were on fire, diving under the water, not emerging until he was several feet away.

"We should go find everyone," he said, already walking out of the water, unable to meet my eye.

We dried off, threw clothes on over wet suits, and walked in awkward silence to the pier. As we sat, the proximity of his hand, resting next to mine, tortured me. How many times that summer had I hoped that I'd somehow find our fingers linked? But here it was, my last week at the beach, and we remained painfully separate. I'd spent a whole summer waiting for the accidental brush of our hands, believing I could still feel the warmth of it minutes later. I hated myself for being so pathetic, and yet I knew I'd do the same thing the next summer.

I was so focused on Nate that I didn't realize Jordan and his friends had arrived until my brother began squeezing in between us. Reluctantly I moved my hand back into my lap. He'd clearly had a few drinks too many, and it made him jovial and affectionate, in a Jordan-sort-of-way. He draped an arm around my neck and then rapped on my head with his fist repeatedly.

"Ow," I complained, trying to pull away. "Cut it out, Jordan."

He looked over at Nate, assessingly. Nate looked back.

"Hey yard boy, you know if you touch my sister I'm going to

fuck you up, right?" he asked casually, but there was no laughter accompanying it. He meant every word.

"Jordan!" I hissed in embarrassment.

Nate looked at the ground uncomfortably before he looked back at Jordan. "I've got no interest whatsoever in touching your sister." His words hit me like a blow. I didn't know how much I'd been hoping for until that moment, when it was all taken from me. I looked back on all the weeks that had elapsed with new eyes, and was shocked I could ever have hoped for a different outcome. Of *course* he didn't like me. I was too skinny and too young, too boyish and nothing like the girls he dated. I'd been deluding myself all summer. I sat in silence, pretending to be fine, but there was a roaring in my ears that made it impossible to listen. I was sick, and I was angry. It was the kind of anger I could never admit to. I wasn't even sure why I felt it in the first place, but it seemed very possible that I might explode, whether I knew the source or not.

I stood suddenly. "I'm going home."

Nate shrugged, casually. "I'll go too."

I glared at him. "No."

I stomped off, not waiting, and a moment later Teddy caught up. He walked at my incredibly fast pace, trying to pretend it was normal.

"Are you okay?" he asked.

"I'm fine," I said, sounding so *not* fine it was laughable.

"You seem kind of mad."

"I'm not."

"Okay."

We continued to walk in silence, and finally he said, "Hold up, Maura."

I stopped. "Why?"

He came close, watching me guardedly, and then I knew. I didn't really want to kiss him, but Nate's rejection had left me feeling broken and ugly. Just when I'd decided I was too skinny and gawky to ever have a boy like me in *that* way, a boy was offering to prove me wrong.

But as he approached, there was movement in the darkness and suddenly Nate appeared, coming between us, lightly shoving Teddy backward.

"Go home, Teddy," he muttered.

"Fuck off, Nate," Teddy replied, his hands clenched.

Nate stepped into him, drawing up to his full height. He towered over poor Teddy. "Don't make me tell you twice."

"Asshole," Teddy muttered under his breath. When he walked off I turned toward Nate, livid beyond all comprehension.

"You. Fucking. Asshole," I hissed, pushing him hard in the chest.

"You didn't want to kiss him."

"It's not any of your business who I want to kiss," I said, turning on my heel and heading toward the house.

"Maura," he called. The sound was soft, apologetic. "Stop."

"What do you want?" I snarled. I was sparking with anger. I could feel it buzzing in my hands, in my arm, longing to swing out and strike at him.

"I'm sorry," he said tentatively.

"You should be," I snapped. "I'm sick of you scaring people off. You're not my dad."

"That's not what I'm sorry about."

I looked at him, waiting, and when he said nothing I prepared to walk off again.

"I lied," he finally said. "Before."

"Lied about what?" I asked angrily.

"When I said I wasn't interested," he said, looking at the ground. "I lied."

My anger dissipated, and in its place I felt all of the grief I'd been holding down. "Then why did you say it?" I asked, sounding small and distraught.

He approached me slowly, like I was a wild animal he might

frighten off. He tucked my hair behind my ear, leaving his fingers resting there against my cheekbone. His eyes focused on that point, avoiding mine. "I didn't want you to know. I didn't want things to be weird."

"They're already weird," I whispered.

"I know."

My heart was hammering now, my breath coming quickly. I wanted to make things normal again, and I couldn't do it.

He looked at me for only a second before leaning in to brush his lips against mine. I held my breath, feeling stunned that it was happening even as it happened. He pulled back to look at me.

"Are you okay?" he asked.

I nodded breathlessly.

His mouth tentatively returned to mine, lingering this time. I smelled his soap and the salt on his skin, tasted him in my mouth. And when he finally pulled away I felt it, all the happiness I'd been denied all summer, rolling over me like a wave.

"Was that your first kiss?" he asked.

"Yes," I admitted, wondering if he'd known because I'd been bad at it.

"Good," he smiled, taking my hand as we headed home. "I wouldn't want anyone else to be your first."

CHAPTER 8

My mother calls me three times over the course of the next two weeks. And despite the fact that I haven't said a word about Ethan, she knows every detail. She knows he's come up two more times. She knows he stayed all weekend. I had no idea she was capable of this level of excitement.

"You know, one day he'll inherit the beach house," she coos.

"I think that's sort of crappy. It's a house, not a monarchy. Why shouldn't it be Lily's too?" I barely knew Ethan's younger sister, but I didn't need to know her to see that this was unfair.

"Well honey, it's just that way. And besides, that means one day Jordan will get ours and you and Ethan will have one of your own! It's so perfect."

"Mom," I say sternly. "Stop talking about me and Ethan like we're a done deal. I'm leaving. Moving. That means no spring wedding or whatever other crap you and Mrs. Mayhew have got in your heads. If I have sex with him, that will be the closest our families ever come to merging."

And my mother, who under normal circumstances would be aghast if I referenced anything beyond hand-holding, just giggles. Which tells me that despite my best efforts, this thing is already out of control.

* *

When Ethan comes up the following weekend, I broach the topic.

"Um, are you aware that our mothers are plotting?" I ask.

He grins. "How so?"

I really don't want to bring this up. Even referencing it in terms of "this-is-something-I-don't-want" feels too premature with someone I've only dated for a month. "Like, I think they're picking out baby clothes for our 2.5 children and all that."

He laughs. "I guess I'm not surprised."

"I've been telling my mom to lay off, but she appears to not be hearing me," I tell him. *Hint, hint.*

He shrugs one shoulder. "Let 'em have their fun. This is the most excitement they've had since they won the doubles tournament a decade ago."

"I just don't want them getting carried away," I say quietly. "I thought maybe you could put in a word on your end."

"Maybe I kind of like that they're a little ahead of you," he grins. "I need all the support I can get."

* *

After he leaves on Sunday night, Jackie collapses on the couch dramatically.

"Oh my God, please tell me you finally slept with that poor boy," she begs.

"Not yet."

"That's criminal! He's going to explode. There must be something seriously wrong with you," she says with folded arms and narrowed eyes.

"You just don't understand my family," I tell her, knowing even as I explain she still won't understand. "If I sleep with him, I may as well be wearing an engagement ring. If we're that together, that official, there's no coming back from it."

"And you really find it necessary to announce to your family that you're banging him?" she asks.

"You have such a charming way of phrasing things, Jackie," I laugh. "No, of course I'm not going to tell them but they'll just… know. And Ethan will know. It's as much about Ethan as it is them. He wouldn't be after me if he wasn't serious, so it's kind of a big commitment. I'm moving. I don't want to be making commitments to anyone right now."

"Dude," she groans. "You are so over-thinking this. If you don't fuck him next weekend I may have to."

And knowing Jackie, it isn't entirely an empty threat, but that's not why I give in the next weekend, when my dress is around my waist and Ethan is begging me not to say no again. It still feels like the wrong decision, but I like him, and I want to like him more, the way he likes me. It seems possible that this – sex – is the missing link that will make us feel right together.

"Thank God," he breathes when I concede. Much as with kissing, Ethan is good at everything and it doesn't surprise me. He groans as my nipple tightens in his mouth. I feel it register in him, feel him harden against my leg, and it excites me that I have this effect on him. His mouth trails down my stomach, between my legs.

"Oh God Ethan," I breathe. It's been so long that the words sound almost awed. My orgasm has taken on a life of its own, and is running hard for the finish.

I hear his zipper, hear the slide of his khakis as they fall to the floor. He crawls over me and I reach down to guide him in. I come in seconds, and he's not far behind.

It's good. But it doesn't make me fall in love with him.

And, just as I'd worried, it now feels as if I've agreed to something nameless, something that is much, much more than sex.

CHAPTER 9

When I came back to the beach at 15 I was not the same girl. I'd spent the preceding year dating with a vengeance. I wanted to be as good, as knowledgeable, as the girls Nate was with during the year, older girls who knew what they were doing.

I was ready when he appeared under my window. He caught me when I landed, holding me by my waist, a little tentative. I suppose neither of us knew where things stood.

His hands stayed at my waist. "You look older," he said quietly. I was suddenly insecure. "Is that good?"

"Yes," he whispered. He leaned against me, meeting my mouth. He parted my lips, grazing my teeth with his tongue. It was a single moment better than all the moments I'd spent kissing other boys put together, the first time in my life I had the impulse to progress beyond it. I met his tongue with my own, wrapping my hands around his neck and pressing into him.

He pulled away suddenly, troubled and angry.

"What's the matter?" I asked. Here I'd been thinking it was the best kiss ever, and yet he wasn't happy. I suddenly wondered if all my practice hadn't been enough.

"You didn't kiss like that last summer," he finally said, staring me down.

"Well of course I didn't!" I argued. "I didn't know what I was doing last summer!"

I could tell it was the wrong thing to say the minute it left my mouth.

"That's the problem, Maura," he snapped, folding his arms across his chest. "Because you *do* know what you're doing now. How exactly would you explain that?"

I was momentarily speechless, and he stood there, waiting for an explanation, seething. I'd tried to impress him, and instead I'd ruined everything. "I wanted to practice. I wanted to be good at it when I got back. You're older..." I trailed off as my voice broke.

"I don't like it," he growled.

I pressed my fingers to my temples. "I'm not sure what you want me to say."

He stood, looking at me, still breathing quickly. And finally his shoulders sagged. He stepped toward me, cupping my face in his hands, resting his forehead against mine. I could still feel the tension drawing his muscles tight. "No more practicing, okay?"

I tried to agree, but the sound was muffled by his lips, returning to mine, a little more forcefully than before.

My entire life took place in the hours he was off work. I luxuriated in it, in him, sank myself into those free hours the way you would a soft bed or a deep bath. Saying goodbye to him at night was sharp and bittersweet, happy and yet full of longing, already missing him for the day ahead. He'd walk me home and then press me against the door of my grandparents' kitchen, trying to take in enough to get us through the next 18 hours apart. I timed my entire day around his work schedule, and every afternoon I'd hear his car pull in the driveway just as I got out of the shower, knowing I had just enough time to dry my hair and get dressed before he'd emerge from his house, hair still wet, skin damp from the shower, smelling like soap and fabric softener.

We didn't try to keep it a secret. We thought – naively – that it wouldn't attract attention, and wouldn't matter if it did, until the day we learned otherwise.

I was rushing back from the beach. A whole day spent lounging in the sun, knowing my real day had yet to begin.

I knew something was amiss immediately when I saw my grandfather on the porch. I'd never seen him home before dinner before. I approached warily.

"Have a seat, Maura Leigh," he said, nodding at the rocker beside him. Internally I sighed, already trying to plot what corners I could cut in order to meet Nate in time.

"You've been spending an awful lot of time with Nate," he began, looking at me with an eyebrow raised. His face held a slight smile, as if the fact didn't displease him.

"Yes sir," I said quietly, speculatively.

"He's a good boy," my grandfather said. "I've known him since he was small enough to fit in my hand." I nodded in agreement, unsure what to say in response. "Mayhews ought to be ashamed of themselves. Should have at least provided for the boy instead of pretending he doesn't exist."

I knew only the most basic facts – that Nate's dad had spent his summers at the beach just like I did, had spent one summer after the next glued to Mary's side. Until the summer he got her pregnant and never came back. "Mary and your ma were friends. Did you know that?"

"No," I replied. It explained a lot. My mother was always uncomfortable at the beach house, particularly when Mary was around.

"They were. I've gotten used to it, but it was strange at first, having the little girl who used to play dolls on my living room floor cleaning it instead. Your grandmother never wanted them to play together, but there were so few girls down here Eileen's age." He looked at me again. "Your grandmother has never approved of you spending time with Nate, either. I overrode her. I'd rather you were sneaking out to swim with Nate than playing with those girls you're friends with."

I gasped. "You knew?"

He smiled slyly. "I'm old, Maura, but not that much escapes my attention."

"Did grandma know?"

He shook his head. "Figured I'd best let that one sit. She wouldn't have taken it well."

We rocked in our chairs and I wondered, with growing anxiety, how much more my grandfather knew.

"You and Nate, together," he began. "Seemed pretty inevitable. Even when you were a baby he doted on you. You were two peas in a pod. Always have been."

I smiled. It had been inevitable, hadn't it? I could see our future laid out as clearly as our past. I could see us getting married right here, I could see our kids rocking in these very chairs. As if he had read my mind, my grandfather's tone changed.

"Your grandmother… she doesn't see it that way," he said. He stopped rocking. "Your grandmother didn't even want you two as friends, so she sure doesn't want you dating."

"Does she know?" I asked haltingly.

"Nope, not yet. Cause she'd have already packed you up and sent you back to Charlotte if she did. But I guarantee if the two of you keep carrying on the way you do right there in the backyard she'll know soon enough."

All those times when we thought we were hidden, standing right under the porch light. I writhed in embarrassment.

"I love Nate like a son, Maura," he said. "I don't care where he comes from. He's sharp as a whip, and one day he'll outshine all of these spoiled Charlotte boys down here for the summer. But don't think for a second I'll be able to stop your grandmother if she finds out. Especially after what happened with Mary."

"Yes sir," I whispered, suddenly petrified. I couldn't imagine being sent home. I couldn't imagine the summer without Nate.

"I know you like him, and I know how teenagers are, Maura. But you're a good girl and I expect you to stay that way. You understand what I'm telling you?"

I was mortified. So mortified that my "yes sir" in response was barely audible.

"All right then. You go on and get ready for your date," he grinned at me. "Yes, I know about that too. And when you catch Nate tell him I'd like a word, right here, and make it snappy. Your grandma will be home from bridge within the hour, and I've got to get this done."

I raced to my room, stomach churning with nerves over what he might tell Nate. If it involved a conversation about my virginity – and how could it not? – I didn't envy him. I rushed into the shower and back out, leaving my hair wet to tell Nate, already waiting, about the talk coming his way.

He winced, and gave me a quick kiss before walking with leaden steps toward the front porch. He was ashen when he returned.

"Uh oh," I laughed, looking at his face. "That bad?"

He shrugged. "Come on." We walked to the beach but he refused to take my hand. When I tried to take his he glanced back at the house. "Not here," he said tersely.

When the dunes were at our back he took me by surprise, swinging me into him, his fingers winding through my hair, his breath short as his lips found mine. There was something in him that had never been there before, bewildered and scared. I could feel it in the tight press of his fingers against my skin, in his mouth, in the rapid beating of his heart beneath my hand.

He pulled away abruptly. "We need to be more careful, Maura," he breathed.

"I know. He told me the same thing. About my grandma."

He sank into the sand, burying his face in his hands. "She'll send you home," he said.

I sat next to him, tugging his hand away and grasping it with my own. "It's okay. We'll be more careful."

"There's more."

I felt anxiety winding into a tight knot in my stomach. "What?"

"He said if he finds out we haven't stayed 'chaste' he'll send you home himself, and you won't be allowed back until you're out of college."

I gasped. "He can't do that!"

"I'm pretty sure he can."

I shrugged. "Well, it doesn't matter. We don't do that anyway."

His look was pained, full of need. "No, we don't."

My eyes widened. "Did you want to?"

He laughed, the sound a little bitter. "I'm 17, Maura. Of course I want to."

"Oh," I murmured. I shouldn't have been surprised. "I thought you were happy."

He pulled me to him. "I love you. You know I'm happy. It's fine."

He kissed me then, putting the matter to rest. But once I came back up for air, I felt it there, between us. He might be happy, but how long would he stay that way?

CHAPTER 10

Heather calls one month before graduation, begging me to come back down to the beach. I've avoided it for five years. I'd like to avoid it forever.

"You've got to come back," she urges me. "Everyone misses you. You stopped coming before you were even old enough to drink! You missed the best part."

"I'm pretty sure I managed to drink plenty when I was there, legal or otherwise."

"Come down. It may be the last chance you get before you leave. And you know your grandma is dying to see you."

She has me at the words "grandma" and "dying".

Though the reason I've avoided the beach has nothing to do with her, my grandmother must feel abandoned. She has no idea why I didn't come back, why I spent every summer in Europe or taking summer classes or whatever other bullshit excuse I came up with. But I know, now, that no one lives forever. I owe her one more summer.

It's not the only reason, because I'm just not that altruistic. Staying at the beach means I'm not in Charlotte, subject to every one of Mrs. McDonald's frantic whims in preparation for the wedding. And it puts a nice, safe distance between me and Ethan. Paradise Cove is far enough from Charlotte to provide a graceful transition into something less with Ethan, until I leave for school and it becomes nothing at all.

* *

The next weekend, I go to Ethan. Well, actually, I go to Charlotte for another interminable bridal shower, but he's there too.

"You're so lucky you don't have to go to bridal showers," I tell him on the way to dinner Friday night.

"I thought all women loved that stuff," he says questioningly. "I know my mom does."

"You know what a bridal shower is? It's two hours spent trying to act enthusiastic about towels and Calphalon pans. Do you know how hard it is to feign enthusiasm for such an extended period of time?"

"Why wouldn't you be excited about that stuff? All women love house crap."

"I think you need to revise your ideas about 'all women'," I chide. "I'm not ever going to be excited about a towel or a pan unless it can do something spectacular, like talk or defy gravity."

He grins, and looks at me knowingly. "You'll feel different when it's you."

I shake my head. "I don't think so."

But he keeps on grinning, a secret smile, slightly smug, as if he knows something I don't.

Which makes this a perfect time to break my news to him about the beach. To my surprise, he immediately offers to drive down on weekends.

"It's so far," I tell him, trying to sound as if my worry is for him and not myself.

"I'm sure you'll make it worth my while," he grins lasciviously.

And really, if I'm being honest, I'm not unhappy. I'd have missed him over the summer. It isn't all hearts and butterflies and giddy excitement, but I'm okay with that. In some ways, what I feel seems better, more mature. I enjoy his company, and it's better to have him around than not. And in the long run, once all the silly infatuation stuff dies down, isn't this all that's left anyway? Perhaps I'm just short-circuiting the whole thing, and at least now I'll never have to be the girl wondering where all the excitement has gone.

CHAPTER 11

When I returned to high school that fall, Nate was the invisible presence by my side during every game, every dance. I said the words "I'm sorry but I've got a boyfriend" again and again, until everyone knew. I never once regretted it, because I'd never once met a boy who could begin to compare to him.

During the summer my life didn't begin until he got off work. During the school year my life didn't begin until I was leaving for Paradise Cove. That spring I shopped for the beach thinking only of him – skimpy bikinis and short shorts and make-up – grateful as I looked in the dressing room mirror that I'd finally gotten some curves.

Some of my planning was driven by fear: he was about to enter college. There'd been a divide between us, during those years when he was in high school and I was not. I worried it would return, that I was still young in ways I was unaware of.

We got to my grandparents' on a Saturday. I put on my littlest string bikini and went to the beach. Jordan and his friends had been back from college for a while, and they were all on the beach when I arrived.

"God damn!" shouted Graham when I approached. "Look who turned into a woman!" He walked over with his arms open and hugged me, running his hands over my back. Ethan and Sammy just laughed and raised their beers to me in greeting.

"Get your hands off my sister Edwards or I'll fucking break them off," said Jordan. Then he looked over at me. "Jesus Christ, Maura. Go put on a one-piece."

"Piss off, Jordan," I said, turning away.

"Want a beer?" asked Ethan.

"She's not old enough to drink," snapped Jordan.

"Neither are you, asshole," I said, accepting the offered beer although I didn't much want it.

Nate wasn't there. I stayed at the beach with Jordan and his friends all afternoon, waiting with growing impatience. Finally, disappointed, I went home. He was getting out of his mom's truck just as I reached the yard.

A part of me had worried that he couldn't possibly live up to my memory of him, that after a year of being put up on a pedestal a fall was certain. And he didn't live up to my memory: he was better. So much better that I felt like I couldn't breathe as he approached.

"I thought you'd be at the beach today," I said, mundane words to disguise the things I was actually thinking.

"I had to work," he said, in a subdued voice.

He looked unnerved somehow, and it made me anxious. "Why are you staring at me like that?"

He edged closer. "Because," he said, and stopped, wide-eyed. "Holy shit, Maura. You're... " he pinched the bridge of his nose. "You're all grown up."

My skimpy suit and makeup had worked even better than I planned.

That night we met on the beach, and we didn't even pretend that we were going to the pier. We went straight to the darkest spot we could find. This time his hands went everywhere, and his mouth went to nearly all of those places as well. I was so worked up that when he finally slid a finger under my shorts, I came.

"Oh," I said in awe afterward. For the first time in two summers, I didn't feel like I was going to explode with wanting him.

I felt guilty, suddenly, that the answer to all our frustration had been right there. "Why didn't you tell me?"

He laughed, but the sound was strained and husky. "Did you really not know?"

I shook my head, and reached for the button on his shorts. "Does it, um, work like that for you too?" His laugh died in his throat as I ran my hands over him for the first time.

"You have to show me what to do," I said nervously. "I don't want to hurt you."

"Just keep doing that," he said through clenched teeth.

I was pleased with my newfound power. And frightened by the fact that I'd only just learned that I had it. What else didn't I know that other girls would?

* *

We were finally together. It should have been enough for both of us. But instead, sometimes, it just seemed to emphasize how much we had to lose.

"They're staring at you again," Nate hissed one day as I met him on the beach.

"Who?" I asked, turning to look behind me.

"Your brother's friends."

I laughed at him. "They're just looking out for me."

"Staring at your ass and your rack every time you walk by isn't looking out for you," he sneered.

"Nate, that's crazy. They're in college."

"I'll be in college in two months. Will it seem crazy then?" he asked caustically. "You know your parents and your grandparents would rather you were with one of them."

"Not my grandpa," I countered, surprised that Nate suddenly cared what my family thought. "And his is the only opinion that matters. Come on. I want to windsurf."

"You can go first," he said, as he helped me haul the sail and board into the water.

"You go," I said. "It'll cheer you up." He took one look over his shoulder at my brother's friends and shook his head.

"Not today," he said. Sighing, I gave him a quick kiss and started pulling the board and sail out.

When Graham followed me into the water on his jet ski, my shoulders sank, imagining Nate on the shore watching, growing livid. I knew for a fact that my brother's friends saw me as a little girl, but this sure wasn't helping my cause.

"Windsurfing is too much work!" Graham shouted over the low hum of his motor. He patted his back seat. "Dump that thing and you can ride with me."

Yeah, Nate would love that.

I shook my head, struggling to climb on the board atop the wake he was creating. "Stop coming so close!" I called. "You're making the water choppy!"

I'd known Graham my entire life. I was surprised when he drove off without a fight.

I should have known better.

I got on the board, and in that first dicey moment – trying to get my balance while righting the sail — I saw him. He came at me fast, trying to get enough speed to create a wake that would knock me off my board. I think I knew, before even he did, that he wouldn't be able to turn in time.

I was paralyzed. I didn't look at Graham. I looked at Nate. The panic on his face is the last thing I remember.

When I came to it was Nate's face I saw again. The panic was still there.

"I'm okay," I whispered. We were just getting out of the water, I realized, and he'd been carrying me.

He fell onto the sand, cradling me like a child.

I tried to sit up. "I'm okay, Nate."

"Stay," he demanded gruffly.

I struggled to sit up on my own, trying to clear my head. "Really, I'm fine."

He held me tighter. "I'm not," he said roughly, his face buried in my hair, and it was only then that I felt his heart, hammering between us at twice its normal pace. "Please," he begged. "I just need a minute."

My head was throbbing, and I knew without touching it that I had a major knot up there somewhere, though I couldn't remember how I got it. I gave him his minute and then sat up. "What did I hit?" I asked him. "My head is killing me."

It was then that I saw Graham approaching warily, an apology on his lips that died out when he saw Nate's face. Nate stood then. It took him five seconds and one punch to leave Graham flat on his back.

"Maybe now you'll stop following her around," Nate hissed as he stood above him.

He couldn't stand the sight of Graham after that, so we avoided my brother and his friends as much as possible from then on. We spent a fair amount of time with Brian and Elise, but the truth is we were always happiest alone.

We found a secluded hillside to watch fireworks on the 4th of July, not far from where our family and friends sat, but far enough away that I didn't have to worry about Jordan's friends or – worse – my grandmother.

"Isn't it funny to think we'll bring our kids here to watch this some day?" Nate asked. "I imagined it sometimes when we were little."

I laughed. "You thought about having kids with me when you were little?"

He shrugged. "Sure. In a platonic way – it's not like I was thinking about sex. I just always assumed we'd be together. Didn't you?"

I thought about it for a moment, puzzled by the truth. "Honestly, I guess I always kind of assumed I'd have to marry someone from home? I know it doesn't make any sense – it just seemed like a rule I had to follow."

He stiffened. "So you pictured doing this with Ethan, or Teddy?" he asked, disengaging himself.

"No!" I argued, sitting up to look at him. "I never pictured anything at all. I just didn't understand that I'd have a choice." He remained stiff, refusing to meet my eye.

I climbed into his lap, straddling him and pushing him back to the ground. "I love you, Nate. Not Ethan, not Teddy. You."

Reluctantly he met my eye. "But you still want your big house in Charlotte and your mansion on the beach and all the other shit they have," he said warily.

"You know I don't care about any of that," I chided him.

"You will, though," he replied.

"Never." I rocked against him, knowing it was the quickest way to improve his mood.

"You'd better not do that here," he warned.

"You could stop me if you really wanted to," I teased as I continued.

"Stop," he repeated.

I unzipped his shorts, and reached my hand inside.

"Oh Jesus, Maura, you've got to stop," he pled.

"Are you sure you want me to stop?" I asked, leaning over to whisper in his ear.

"Yes," he groaned, and then changed his mind. "No."

But I'd confused distracting him with consoling him, and they were not the same thing. And I thought his insecurity was something he'd created on his own. I was wrong about that too.

* *

"The two of you are disgusting," Heather said, as we sat on the field at night watching the boys play baseball, him looking over to me before every pitch.

He was the only thing I could see. I loved just being able to stare at him, watching the muscles in his thighs as he ran for base, the fierce concentration on his face as he waited for the pitch. By the time his games ended I no longer heard their ribbing. I was too focused on him, on the look in his eyes as he approached me – it was the same look he had when he pitched. Determined, intense, almost feral, and it made me feel that there was nothing he might want that I could refuse him.

"Nate shouldn't even be allowed to play," carped Kendall. Nate, headed to college on a baseball scholarship, rarely pitched at these games anymore because no one could get a hit off him. But Kendall was right. Even with him on first base, and barely trying, the Charlotte side hadn't won a game all summer.

But I just laughed. "Maybe y'all should get some players that don't suck."

"What do you mean by 'y'all'?" she scolded. "You're one of us, remember? And your brother is playing on *our* side too."

I ignored her. My side was whatever side Nate was on. I watched him, as always, with poorly contained lust, every moment ratcheting up my need until I felt like I'd explode with it by the time he got off the field.

When Ethan stepped up to bat, Nate seemed to tense, taking the game seriously for the first time all night. Ethan wasn't half-way to first before Nate held the ball and had forced him out.

But Ethan didn't head back behind home plate immediately. Instead, he stood a few feet from Nate and said something none of us could hear. I knew, watching Nate's face, that what he said was neither casual nor well-intentioned.

Ethan turned to walk away, while Nate's face morphed quickly from shock to anger. In one long stride Nate had grabbed Ethan by the collar. Ethan seemed to expect it — he twisted out of Nate's grasp, swinging. We heard the shouting but not the words, and watched as the entire infield ran over to pull them apart. By the time they got there Nate had Ethan on the ground.

The game ended then and there. Nate spoke to no one, but came straight to where I stood, grabbed my hand and pulled me away.

"What happened?" I asked.

"Nothing," he muttered.

"Tell me."

He just shook his head.

He led me to the backside of the school where we couldn't be seen. I hated the look on his face — so worried and sad as he turned and placed his palms against the wall on either side of my shoulders, caging me in.

"What's wrong?" I pled.

He started to speak and then stopped himself. Instead his hand curled into my hair as he pulled me into him, and he kissed me hard, as if it were the last time. And my pleasure was tainted by the knowledge that whatever Ethan said had scared him. Scared him enough that he couldn't even tell me what it was.

CHAPTER 12

"Oooh! Towels!" squeals Elise. She's so good. She truly looks freaking overjoyed.

"Pass them around," insists her mother. Fuck. The worst kind of shower. The kind where we're all forced to craft new phrases of excitement for every single item she receives.

"Such a pretty color," says Heather. Damn her. That's what I was going to say.

"Silver-sage," beams Elise. "It's so weird because you'd think it'd be a green but it really looks kind of blue, doesn't it? The bathroom walls are beige. I love blue and beige together."

"They're so soft," purrs the girl beside me, as she places them in my hands.

Expectant, happy faces turn toward me. I draw a complete blank. "Nice," I murmur, but I fail to sound appropriately enthused and the faces fall a little. My mother shoots me a look that tells me to pick up my game.

Elise is opening another gift. It's a pan. I grin, thinking of my conversation with Ethan.

"Oh my gosh! The 3-quart saucepan!" she squeals. Holy. Fucking. Shit. I will never get married if it requires squealing like this over a 3-quart pan. Never. Of course, I don't cook, so I have no clue what you even do with a 3-quart saucepan. Make sauce? How much sauce could you possibly need to make over the course of your life? Especially the women in this room. Have any of them *ever* made sauce? More likely, they've peeked into the kitchen while their staff made sauce.

"Oooh, feel the weight of this thing!" cries Kendall, as it begins to make the circuit. She's good. They all are. All of them but me. I'm not sure what gene I failed to inherit, but I'm missing the one that will make me buzz with excitement about kitchen goods. And it hangs over my head like a dark cloud, one I know every woman in this room can see. It embarrasses my mother. She's embarrassed by the fact that it's not me getting married. She's embarrassed that I don't care. I think she's even embarrassed by the fact that I'm going to law school instead of coming home to pass time in a less intellect-heavy way.

"You should be watching carefully, Maura," teases Mrs. McDonald. "From what I hear, you're next." All the moms titter, my mom and Mrs. Mayhew especially, looking at each other meaningfully. Jesus. We've dated for less than two months and they *all* know.

"Hardly," I mutter sourly, refusing to play along.

When the interminable opening of gifts has finally ended, Elise pulls me aside. "I'm sorry," she says, gesturing back at the room strewn with silver bows and white wrapping paper. "I know you hate this stuff."

"God, Elise, don't apologize! I don't hate it. I'm excited for you," I say. Argh. Was I that obvious? "This was great."

"I have to tell you something," she breathes.

"Okay." Somehow I know, in this moment, that what she's about to tell me will change things. It's a ghost of a premonition, a small curdling in my stomach that warns of danger.

"Brian asked Nate to be one of his groomsmen," she says, watching me with her big worried eyes, holding her breath as if I'm going to explode in response. It's been our rule, all this time: don't mention Nate, under any circumstance. It's the first time in all these years that she's broken it.

I feel my stomach plummeting, my chest tightening. Just the

sound of his name would have had this effect. But God, it's not just that. It's the prospect of seeing him, after five years of silence. It's finally happening, and I really have no choice in the matter.

"Okay," I say, my voice whistling high through a constricted throat.

"I'm so sorry," she pleads. "I hope it's not going to be weird."

Oh, it's going to be so weird that weird isn't even the word for it. "No," I murmur. "It's fine." I feel like I'm replying to her from far away, an international call in another time zone.

She looks relieved. She's the only one of us who is.

I haven't seen Nate in five years. *I have to be over it by now*, I tell myself. *I have to be.*

CHAPTER 13

By February of my junior year in high school, it seemed like it had been winter for at least a year, and possibly two. Nate and I spoke on the phone occasionally, texted constantly, but I needed to see his face. I needed winter to end.

This was what I was thinking when I walked into my parents' house in Charlotte that day.

They were both home. That's how I knew something was wrong.

My parents were never around when I came home from school. At this time of day my father should be at work, my mother at the club. She claimed to divide her day up between tennis and her charities, but on the rare times I saw her, my impression was she was dividing her time between martinis and vodka tonics.

There was no other noise, another unnerving development. Even without them home, there was always the sound of a distant vacuum, the clang of a cookie sheet slapping against a counter.

My mother's eyes were swollen, and she'd cried her makeup off. I couldn't remember ever seeing her without it. She tried to tell me something, but began crying before the words were out.

"Your grandfather died this morning," my father said.

It had to be a mistake. My grandfather played tennis every Saturday at the club, and golf every Sunday. He hadn't even retired yet. "He's healthy!" I argued, as if I might somehow make them recognize their error. My mother cried harder.

"He had a heart attack, Maura," my father said quietly. "It happens."

We left for the beach, stopping by USC to pick up Jordan on the way. For once even he didn't try to lighten the silence.

The town was so different in the winter. Not cold, really, by anyone's standards, but grayer and wetter. Without the sun to burn off the moisture, the air hung like netting around us, settling on our shoulders and refusing to push away. And it was quiet. The stores were closed, the beaches were empty, the tourists had disappeared. It felt like the island had died too. As if it had been my grandfather who brought all the people and the weather to life, and without him nothing could flourish.

Nate wasn't there. I'd known he wouldn't be. UVA was too far away and he'd have had no way to get home anyhow. But it only made the emptiness, the lack of reality, more intense. Even after I saw my grandfather lying there at the wake it remained unreal. He didn't look like himself, with his face waxen and his hair flat to his head. I was still unconvinced that I wouldn't find him the next summer swinging golf clubs into the trunk of his car or sitting on the porch. I felt, from the time we arrived until the time we left, that I was merely caught up in the gray fog of a dream that I couldn't seem to scratch away. That I would wake. But of course, I did not.

There had only ever been two people in the world who could comfort me, and now one of them was gone. I stayed back at the house while my family went to hear the will read, realizing for the first time how safe I'd felt with my grandfather. How, at times, he and Nate felt like the only normal things in my life, the only people whose love wasn't offered as a bargaining chip for good grades or good behavior. Without either of them there, the world felt like a precarious place.

**

I kept it bottled up through the spring, waiting for the one thing I knew that could fix me. The beach was crowded on my first day back that next summer, but I saw nothing but him as he approached. He pulled me to him tightly and neither of us cared who saw. I knew, suddenly, that my home wasn't Charlotte or the beach house. It was him, here, and as I sank into him I couldn't imagine how I would ever leave it again. I wasn't able to wait for it to get dark until I had him to myself. "Let's get the canoe," I whispered. He knew what I meant.

We paddled quickly toward our old fort. He jumped out the minute it ran aground and tugged the canoe onto the sand. And the moment it was there, he was pulling me out of it, our movements made frenzied and desperate by the long separation, by the way the earth had shifted during it. I stripped his shirt off of him and then my own. He loosened the strings of my bikini and it fell to the ground.

"Maura," he breathed. It was the first time we'd been together in daylight. "God you're beautiful," he said quietly, regarding me. I stood before him in nothing but my bikini bottoms, and then I removed them as well. He stepped back into me, his kisses almost reverent, and I sank to the ground, pulling him with me.

"Nate," I said, as he hovered over me. "I'm ready. I want to."

"Are you sure?" he asked. I nodded.

He grabbed his wallet and pulled out a condom. I was both surprised and relieved he'd thought to bring one — it hadn't even occurred to me. I watched him put it on, feeling torn between need and outright fear.

"Are you ready?" he asked. I nodded, and he began to slide into me.

"Stop!" I cried.

His face looked strained. "I'm barely in, Maura. Does it hurt?"

I tried not to wince. "Just give me a minute. Let me get used to it."

He pressed in farther and I began to think that maybe I didn't need this after all. I gripped his arms. "Just do it," I gasped, bracing myself. He did, and I proceeded to inhale sharply and curse on the exhale, in too much pain to worry about how absolutely-not-hot I was making this.

"I'm sorry, baby," he groaned.

"It's okay," I whispered. "It's over."

"Um, not exactly, Maura," he replied.

Just as it stopped hurting, just as it began to feel unbelievably good, he came. And it was worth every ounce of lingering frustration I felt afterward to be able to watch it happen, and to know I'd made him happy.

* *

We went to the pier that night. He held my hand carefully, as if it could be crushed under the pressure of his if he wasn't diligent. We sat with everyone but his fingers constantly returned to me, entwining with mine, running along my cheekbone, combing through my hair.

After an hour of sitting next to him, feeling his thigh brushing against mine, sharing a bottle of beer, touching his hand every time we passed it back and forth, my desire for him was overwhelming me. Just the memory of watching him come made me weak.

"Can we leave?" I whispered in his ear. He silently took my hand and pulled me behind him. The second we found darkness I grabbed him, tugging at him with a desperation even I didn't understand.

"I don't want to hurt you again," he said, his voice hoarse.

"Please, Nate," I breathed, placing my palms on either side of his face and kissing him. "Please."

As soon as the words were out of my mouth, his hands went to my hair and he was pulling me into him. He laid me down in the sand and pulled my dress around my waist, unable to move quickly enough.

I braced as he slid inside of me, and was amazed to discover it didn't hurt. I gasped when he was all the way in.

"Am I hurting you?" he asked anxiously.

"No," I moaned.

He hovered over me, moving slowly. I felt desperate and greedy for more, arching against him, without entirely knowing what I wanted more of.

He was saying my name, fervently, like a prayer, against my ear. The ache grew unbearable, and my hips rose to meet his. I wrapped my legs tight around him, like a vise, wanting more.

"Maura," he gasped, a warning in his voice, and I didn't listen, I couldn't listen, just pushed harder and harder until finally I was shattering in a million pieces, crying out, and not a moment too soon. There was one long, guttural noise from his throat and then he clutched me to him, moaning, exploding inside of me.

"Do you know how much I love you?" he whispered against my neck.

"Not half as much as I love you," I answered with a smile.

He grinned, brushing my mouth with his. "That's impossible."

For as close as we'd always been, we'd never been as close as we were right then.

"You're going to be sore tomorrow," he warned, kissing the top of my head.

Something thudded in my stomach uncomfortably. I paused, wanting to ignore the unnerving thought that danced at the edge of my mind, wanting to return to the satisfaction I'd felt only seconds before. I couldn't do it. "How do you know?" I asked.

"How do I know what?" he said, still trying to catch his breath.

"How do you so much about it? How do you know I'll be sore?" I said, sitting up, my voice rising.

It wasn't his words that made my heart constrict, that made my stomach rise and threaten to empty. It was his face, the deer-in-the-headlights look to his eyes while guilt swam across his features and engulfed them.

Suddenly I knew. I knew why he had condoms. I knew why he'd been so patient with me for so long. I'd worried that my youth and my inexperience would be a problem for him, and I was right. All along I was right. "You cheated," I gasped.

That guilt, it only grew, even while he shook his head to deny it. "It wasn't like that..." he began.

I didn't let him finish. I clutched at my stomach as I jumped to my feet. "Oh my God. Don't make it worse. Don't lie. It's written all over your face."

He pressed his head into his hands. "Maura, please just let me explain. It's not what you think and I was going to tell you... "

"No," I cried. "I don't want to hear a word out of your mouth."

"I never even wanted to date anyone else... " he began.

I ran. I couldn't listen to him. I couldn't stand to hear whatever he was going to share, whether it was the awful truth or his rationalizations. I got to my room, and within seconds I heard gravel at my window. I ignored it. I had to. I knew the time would come when I could hear what he had to say but right now I felt like I would explode if offered a single detail.

I lay there, sick to my stomach, my anger at him slowly morphing into anger at us both. I hated that he'd slept with someone else, but I hated even more that I hadn't been better at these things, that I'd been too young and stupid to understand the things he wanted. Because maybe he had an explanation that wouldn't hurt quite so much, and maybe I'd forgive him. But we could never get back what we had. If he'd slept with someone else, I knew I'd never entirely recover.

CHAPTER 14

Ethan drives up the night before graduation.

"You're tense," he comments that night, laying on my bed and watching me pack.

I shrug. "Maybe a little. A lot is happening at once. I'm graduating, moving, saying goodbye to my friends… "

"So you're not nervous about your parents seeing us together?" he asks, grinning.

I laugh. "Yes, although I don't know why. They've met other guys I've dated, and anyway, they already know you and they're totally thrilled."

"I'm not just 'other guys', Maura," he replied. "So this *is* kind of a big deal."

I sigh, because that's precisely the problem: I don't want this to be a big deal, and it is. Tomorrow, being together with my family, makes it official.

* *

My parents arrive at almost the same moment as Jordan, Mia and the baby. It's a relief to have my niece to focus on instead of the portentous looks my parents throw back and forth watching me and Ethan.

"Come here, Catherine," I say, plucking my little niece out of her carseat. "Look at how big you are!" I coo. "Mia, she's so cute I could just eat her up!"

Mia offers me a tired half-smile. She's been wan since she had Catherine last September, as if something vital departed with the baby's birth. I keep waiting for the Mia I knew to return, with her little-girl giggle and her happy innocence but every time I see her she looks a little worse, a little quieter, a little more... resigned.

I tuck the thought away and return to my niece, extending a pinkie for her to grab. She immediately pulls herself to standing with that one small grip, and I laugh. "Look at her! She's like a superhero baby!"

"Babies do stand, moron," says Jordan.

"But she pulled herself to standing only holding one of my pinkies, asshole. Let's see you do that," I argue.

"Looks like you're next, dude," Jordan tells Ethan. I focus on Catherine, my stomach clenching as I wait for Ethan to rebut it. But of course he doesn't. I'm making a big deal out of nothing, I know. Jordan was just joking and Ethan was in an awkward position – he can hardly act dismissive about our relationship in front of my family.

But all through the afternoon and evening the comments continue to flow, both subtle and not at all subtle, and Ethan seems to welcome them. He doesn't act like someone who's just being polite.

Over dinner Jordan glares at Ethan. "So we haven't discussed this, but I'm pretty sure I forbid you to ask my sister out until after graduation."

"What's this, now?" my mother asks, looking frantic. Probably petrified something will get in the way of the Maura-Ethan Wedding Express.

"Jordan told Ethan and Graham they couldn't ask me out until I'd graduated," I explain.

Ethan smiles happily at Jordan and puts his arm around my shoulders. "Come on, man. Who'd you rather have for a brother-in-law, me or Graham?"

I stiffen. He says it so casually, as if we've discussed it, as if it's a foregone conclusion. He doesn't notice my shock. Neither does Jordan. My mother casts a knowing glance at me, and I'm just relieved she doesn't give me a thumbs-up.

Jordan relents. "God, it would suck to have Graham in the family. You know I hate Clemson. Fine, you're forgiven."

The conversation moves on, but I do not. I can only think about Ethan, about what he is expecting and what my parents are expecting. I find it somewhat annoying that they are so thrilled by my relationship with Ethan, that for them it completely eclipses graduation and law school. I know my mother, and I know she is already imagining me buying a house on their street, spitting out a baby within a year of marriage and leaving him or her with a nanny so I can don my tennis whites and spend my days at the club. I can't really fathom her sudden desire to have me living in her world, seeing her often — she'd certainly never been interested in it when I was a kid. But with or without Ethan, it isn't a future I want, and the need to explain that to everyone at this table weighs on me.

"Maybe Maura could help," Ethan is saying. Every face is turned toward me expectantly.

"Help with what?" I ask.

"Nice attention span," my brother gripes. "You're gonna make one hell of a lawyer."

"With the lawsuit," Ethan replies.

"What lawsuit?" I ask.

"Maura," my mother chides. "Were you not listening at all?"

"Sorry," I say sheepishly. "It's been a long day. What lawsuit?"

"At Old Cove. We're trying to block off the beach road and get rid of the public access points," my father tells me.

"What?" I stammer. "Why?" The beach road in front of my grandparents' house is the main thoroughfare – limiting use of the road and access ways would make it virtually impossible for most of the residents on the island to get to the only decent beach.

"Because we're sick of having the entire beach full of riff-raff all summer," he says.

"But the beach is public land," I argue. "And what about the people who live a block or two behind us?"

"They can use the beach farther down," my father says.

"But that's at least a mile away," I gasp. "You can't expect people who live one block from the beach to walk a mile to get there?"

"They don't have to walk," my mother chirps. "They can drive."

"That's so crappy," I exclaim, looking at them, aghast. "The beach is public property."

"Actually," says Ethan, surprising me. "The state's ownership ends at the high water line."

"You *agree* with this?" I ask.

He shrugs. "It would be nice to have the beaches less crowded."

"So what exactly is being proposed?"

"We're petitioning the state to make the frontal road local access only, and to remove all the public access boardwalks along the mile of Old Cove," my father tells me. "I was suggesting you might want to help with things on the legal side, but given your attitude, I guess not."

"You're goddamn right," I mutter. "I'm completely appalled by all of you."

And they just laugh, as if I'm a silly little girl who doesn't understand the bigger picture.

"You'll change your mind when you've got the whole beach to yourself without some redneck's speakers next to your ear," says Jordan, and they all nod in agreement.

I say nothing, but inside, I fervently hope that I never become the person he described. I hope I never become one of the people who think they deserve so much more than everyone else. People who already have so much, but insist on taking more. And the fact that Ethan clearly is one of them makes me doubly sure that I don't want to be committed to him in any way.

It's not until my parents leave that night, taking Mia and Catherine with them, that I relax. We go to a bar with my roommates, and once I've had enough beer I feel the strain rising off of me and floating away. People can say what they want, they can expect what they want, but I'm still leaving in three months no matter what.

"All right, boys," shouts Jackie, who was a little drunk when graduation began and is now far beyond that. "Which of you is gonna convince this girl to stay in the south?"

Jordan smirks. "Don't worry. She'll spend one month in that cold weather and come crying home." Everyone laughs, but I look at him in surprise. There is a bitter note in his voice. He almost sounds jealous, which is impossible. Jordan has always been the golden boy. He's my parents' favorite. He's always been popular, he's always been good looking. He's got every single thing he ever wanted. What could he possibly be jealous of?

By midnight I am yawning, so tired I can barely imagine summoning the energy to walk to Ethan's car. "You're gonna have to carry me home," I smile at him.

"Gladly," he says, pulling me from my seat. Jordan doesn't take the hint, perhaps a little preoccupied with Jackie, who now sits in his lap – a situation I can't imagine Jordan's wife appreciating.

"Time to go Jordan," I say, attempting to shove him off the chair. It's like trying to push a mountain.

"Come on!" he shouts in dismay, wrapping his arm around Jackie's waist to keep her in place. "It's your freaking graduation! You've got to stay out!"

"Jordan, it's late, and I've got a whole day of packing ahead of me," I lament.

"What's your excuse?" he asks Ethan.

"I want to sleep with your sister," replies Ethan. "That's my excuse."

"Ugh," Jordan groans. "Then I'm definitely staying out. Make sure you're done before I get back."

But when we wake the next day, he still isn't home. Jackie isn't there either, but that's hardly unusual for her. I call his cell twice and he doesn't answer, and that's when I begin to panic. Jordan has many gifts – an ability to know when it's time to stop drinking isn't one of them. I stare at the phone in my hand, and then Ethan, eyes wide. "I don't know what to do. Should I call the police? Am I being paranoid?"

Ethan looks a little guarded as he replies. "He probably just slept somewhere else," he suggests. "I bet he's here within an hour."

"Where else would he sleep?" I argue. "He doesn't know anyone here but me."

Ethan is quiet for a moment, and then shrugs. "You know Jordan. He makes friends everywhere he goes."

Jordan strolls in only a few minutes later, so cheerful and unworried that my temper flares.

"What the hell?" I cry. "You scared the crap out of me, Jordan! Where were you?"

"I went to an after-party somewhere and passed out on the couch," he says. He shoots a glance at Ethan. It kind of looks like a warning.

CHAPTER 15

I woke the morning after my fight with Nate feeling ill-at-ease and unsure. I was still upset, but at the same time I was ashamed of how harsh I'd been, how I hadn't given him a chance to explain. And all the words I hadn't been able to hear the night before were words I had to know now. I had to know the extent of it. I had to know if I'd be able to forgive him. I got up early, hoping to catch him before he left for work.

I ran downstairs toward the back door, surprised by the silence. The kitchen was empty, and there was no food out. Mary hadn't come in yet, and in all the summers I'd been here, that was a first.

From the back stairs I could see that her truck was gone. I texted Nate and he didn't reply, so I biked to the northern beach where he was lifeguarding, though it was too early for him to be there. The beach was empty.

As I returned home, foreboding stole over me. We'd never had a real conversation about our relationship. Sure, it had seemed serious and we'd talked about being married as if it were an established fact, but we'd never really discussed what should happen each year while we were apart. Perhaps it was unrealistic for me to think he'd be alone nine months out of the year. Perhaps I'd been unfair the night before. I should at least have heard him out.

When I got inside I found the house was still curiously silent. Not that it was ever particularly loud – my grandmother had let a lot of the staff go after my grandfather died — but this was a new kind of silence, like the absence of a whirring fan you'd come to expect. The kitchen was empty, clean, no signs of life.

I found my grandmother in her room.

"Where is everyone?" I asked. "There's no food out."

"Sorry, my dear," she said a little frostily. "You'll need to make your own breakfast today. Mary's gone."

"Where'd she go?"

My grandmother arched an eyebrow. She had very rigid ideas about any kind of presumed interference with the staff. She'd done the same to my grandfather, though he had paid the bills. "She had to take Nate back to UVA." She picked up her paper.

I felt like I'd been punched. "What?"

"Close your mouth dear. That's so unattractive, the way you gape."

I ignored her. "Grandma, why did Nate go back?"

She lowered the paper again and looked at me with irritation. "Some nonsense with his girlfriend at school. He's decided he can't spend the summer away from her, apparently. Poor Mary must be devastated, so please don't bring it up."

I sank into a chair across from her, scared I might fall. She didn't look up from her paper.

"Did he leave me anything?" I asked, though even I could barely hear the words.

"Like what, dear?" she asked peevishly, clearly wanting to return to her paper.

"A note?" The words were mere scratches against the air.

"A note? Why would he leave you a note?" she asked, now sounding truly annoyed. "Run off to the beach, Maura."

Somehow I made my way to my own room, crumpling to the floor the moment I got there. My grief, my desperation, seemed boundless. It clawed at my brain and at the lining of my stomach. That Nate loved me and would never do this were facts, as solid and unshakeable as the fact that he was no longer here, and they were facts that couldn't coexist.

I texted him, again and again. Half of them angry, half of them grief-stricken and begging. He answered none. I called him and only got his voicemail, the sound of his voice like a knife in my chest.

I could do nothing but remember, think, go over the whole thing again and again looking for the clue I had missed. He couldn't have a girlfriend. Only last night he'd said he hadn't even wanted to date anyone else. A small voice in my head pointed out that he'd never actually said that he hadn't dated, merely that he hadn't *wanted* to.

The next night my grandmother came to my room. "Mary's back. Nate did send you a note," she said, handing me an envelope. She didn't meet my eye, as if she knew, like I did, that it couldn't possibly contain good news. My hands shook as I pulled out a single, typed sheet of paper.

Maura,

I should have done this a long time ago. I haven't been telling you the truth. I've had a girlfriend at school most of the past year, and though I care about you as a friend, it's just not the same. You're too young, and I need to be with people my own age. I'm sure you don't understand this now, but maybe you will when you're in college. It would never have worked with us anyway.

I'm not coming back to Paradise Cove, and I hope you will respect my decision and leave me alone. Please stop texting and calling. You're just embarrassing yourself.

You'll be better off with someone your own age and from your own background, and so will I.

Nate

Disbelief and anger were two emotions that visited sporadically, but beyond that was simply a pain so great that I would have done anything to end it. How could he have lied to me like that, and for so long? Had he really never loved me? I couldn't reconcile the boy I'd known for my entire life with the one who'd left with me with this hateful, impersonal note.

His letter broke me. I staggered through that day, and the ones that came after it, unable to eat, unwilling to leave my room. I held the letter against my chest at night. Each time I woke, for just a second, I thought "this couldn't really have happened", only to find the evidence still clutched in my hands.

I reread it a hundred times, stunned that something so insubstantial could have the power it did over me. The power to change the way I saw the world, the power to take away everything I loved and reveal it for the illusion it was.

Mary, when I saw her, looked as sick and staggered as I felt. Once upon a time she had doted on me, but now her eyes – so much like his – looked at me with barely civil disdain. She blamed me for him leaving. I knew that. In a way, I blamed me too.

I wanted to go back to Charlotte, to be in places that weren't permeated with him, but I didn't. I waited, because I was hoping he'd come back. In spite of what he'd said. Every minute of every day, from the moment my eyes opened in the morning until the minute I dropped off to sleep, I waited for him. Even at night I'd lie awake, imagining I heard gravel against the window, but there was no one there when I ran across the room.

I continued to call, and text, until one day there was a message that the phone was not in service. My emails got bounced back. I was humiliated by my own desperation, by the way he must see me now, but I had to hear his voice. I needed to hear him say it.

I searched the Internet under each of his roommates' names until I found the phone for the house they all shared. A girl answered, and my stomach sank. There really was a girlfriend, one of so many parts of this I'd prayed weren't true. It made me so sick I could barely speak.

"Who's this?" she demanded with suspicion.

"Maura Pierce," I choked out.

She laughed without humor. "The girl from the beach?" she asked. "He doesn't want to talk to you."

I began crying. Somehow, her knowing, and confirming it, made it real. "Can you just tell him I called?" I asked.

"Don't hold your breath waiting for a call back," she said as she hung up.

I stood there crying, holding the phone, knowing it was really over. I finally accepted the truth. He'd gotten what he wanted, and it hadn't been enough.

* *

I went through the motions of being a senior in high school. I dated, I went to the dances. And every night all I wanted was the comfort of my own bed, where I could remember the way it felt to lie on his chest, to float beside him, to see him from my bedroom window and know he was mine. He was not the person I thought he was, but it didn't stop me from loving the person he was not.

Over time, my anguish turned into hatred. I hated him for what he did. I hated him for making me fall in love with a person who did not exist.

Mary died of an aneurysm the next year. She drew her last breaths standing in my grandmother's kitchen before crumpling to the floor. I didn't hear about it until almost a month after it happened. I wept for her, wishing someone had told me sooner, wishing I'd found a way to explain to her that I hadn't wanted Nate to leave either. And I wished I'd gone to the funeral. Because I loved her, and because I would have seen him. Even through the gray screen of his grief and mine, I would have seen him.

PARADISE COVE

CHAPTER 16

Seven days after graduation, I am headed to the beach, and not a moment too soon. If I have to endure one more endless tea at the club, or one more ribbing about Ethan from my mother's friends, I am going to explode.

"You and Ethan were sooooo cute together last weekend," my mother giggles as we drive.

"Mom, stop," I warn.

She frowns at me. "You've been dating him for three months! Your father and I were married in that length of time."

"Times have changed, Mom. I'm not a war bride."

She bristles. "I was not a war bride! Vietnam ended 15 years before I met your father."

"Just ease up," I say. "I don't know that I even want to get married. I've got to get through law school first anyway."

"I don't get the sense that Ethan wants to wait that long," she says.

"Well, it's not his decision."

"You might get pregnant."

"Jesus, Mom. You actually sound *hopeful*."

"I want grandkids!" she cries. "So sue me!"

I look out the window and ignore her. As annoying as the whole conversation has been, it's a distraction. Because it's been five years, and I should really not be thinking about Nate anymore.

But I can't seem to think about anything else.

* *

It's dusk when I arrive at the beach house. We enter the back door and I smile tentatively at the staff. I'm used to Mary. It's odd seeing strangers in the kitchen, although it's me who's been gone, so I guess I'm the stranger.

My grandmother enfolds me in her arms, smelling of soap and Chanel #5 and some kind of odd baby powder that only old people seem to use, and for a moment it's as if I never left.

She's smaller, shrinking, I realize as she hugs me. I feel a pang of guilt. The shrinking is a sign, a way she is beginning to tell me goodbye. And I've spent five years not saying goodbye back to her.

"My God, look at you Maura! What a beauty you became!"

She talks about me in the past tense, like she is narrating a story.

"And you and Ethan finally got together. I knew it would happen eventually." I wonder how she knew this. I never showed a moment's interest in Ethan, aside from trying to dodge the bra snaps and wedgies and general abuse you endure at the hands of your older brother's friends.

It's strange here, without Mary. She was unobtrusive, and yet without her the house is empty. Like my grandmother, it seems to be withering, shrinking. Saying goodbye.

With his mother gone, there's no reason for Nate to come back. He must have finished school by now. Why would he ever come back to Paradise Cove, where, no matter who he becomes or what he does he'll always be a second-class citizen?

I wonder what they did with Mary's belongings, and who took over the carriage house. Did he have to come here and box up his mother's stuff? As much as I hate him, there's an odd ache, a fissure in my chest, as I imagine him doing it. I can hate him but still love who he once was, the little boy who waited outside my window. I'm sad for that version of Nate.

My mother stays with us for only one night, and for the first time I begin to see why it's always been that way. Dinner, only the three of us, is so tense it's painful. The only thing my mother and grandmother seem to agree on is that Ethan is wonderful and that me ending up with him is the inevitable conclusion to this story. There is no other topic – not politics, not family friends, not even shopping, that they don't find a reason to snipe at each other over.

At some impasse in their bickering, I ask the question that's been lodged in my throat since we arrived. "Is Stacy in the carriage house now?"

My grandmother looks surprised and then, quickly, guarded. "Well, no," she says mildly. I look at her expectantly, and she offers no further explanation.

"So what did you do with it?" I ask. I've come this far, so I may as well press my point. She and my mother exchange a look.

"Her son lives there now," she replies flatly, with distaste.

"Stacy's son?" I stammer, knowing even as I say it that Stacy can't possibly have a son old enough to live on his own.

"No," says my grandmother with a weary sigh, focusing intently on her plate with lips pursed. "Nate."

I press my feet to the floor as if I can root myself there to contain the fountain of excitement, of panic, that flows through me. I want him to be here and I so don't want him to be here that every nerve in my body is firing, screaming, celebrating, mourning. I hate my reaction, and yet I can't stop myself.

"Oh," I say quietly, biting down on every thought exploding in my head.

It's been five years. The last time I saw him I was a girl. I was young and naïve and inexperienced. Now I'm a grown woman with a boyfriend and a degree and an apartment in my name waiting in Ann Arbor, and this – whatever it is – this joy, this panic, this need – it should have changed, it should be gone. I've grown, but this thing in me is still 17. It hasn't aged a day.

CHAPTER 17

I spend the next two days going to the beach and pretending to read while I think about Nate. And then I go home and I wait and I listen for him, even as I tell myself I'm not. I justify my stalking by saying I just need closure, but I know it's more than that. The sound of his truck rumbling over the gravel goes off like a gunshot in my head, but the huge pines my grandmother has installed screen the carriage house now so I can no longer see him walk in or out from my window. It wears me down a little more each day, until I would give anything to stop thinking about him. If only there were something to give.

I'm relieved that Ethan is coming down for the weekend. I need the distraction.

He calls from his car on Friday. "Where's my girl?" he shouts into the phone.

I smile. "Sitting on the beach. Where else?"

"Oh God. Tell me you're wearing that little black bikini you wore in high school."

"Actually, I'm wearing a red bikini that's even tinier."

"Shit. Stay there."

Five minutes later, he walks on the beach, still dressed in his suit. His shadow falls over me and I burst out laughing. "Why didn't you change?" I ask.

"I haven't even gotten to the house yet. I was crossing the bridge when you lured me here with talk of a red bikini."

"You could have waited. The bikini doesn't turn into a parka at five."

"You might have been able to wait, but I couldn't," he says, offering a hand to pull me up. "The bikini is fantastic. Too fantastic. Let's go take it off."

"And where exactly do you plan to do that?" I smile. "I'm pretty sure public nudity is still frowned upon here."

"I think I need a really thorough tour of your room. One part of it specifically."

"My grandma will love that," I say dryly. "Maybe she can bring up a plate of cookies for us once we're done."

He pulls me in for a particularly lingering, public kiss, his fingers "accidentally" grazing my breast as I push away. "I can't go through a whole summer of this," he says. "I will literally combust if I have to spend an entire summer at second base with you dressed like that."

"I think second base is optimistic," I giggle.

"I don't care if grandma is sitting a foot away and we're in church, I'm at least hitting second base," he groans.

He walks me back to the house, refusing to let me carry my towel and backpack though it gets sand all over his suit.

I turn on the faucet to rinse off and he grabs the hose from me. "What are you doing?" I ask warily.

"Just being a gentleman, helping you hose off," he says, all too innocently. He gently sprays my feet. "See?"

But then the hose rises. "Your ankles are sandy, too," he says.

"Ethan," I warn.

"And your calves." The hose goes higher, and his smile grows devious.

"Enough."

"And your thighs."

"Okay, seriously, if my grandma's watching you are never going to be welcome here again."

"Your grandma loves me. Turn around."

It seems safer, so I turn.

"God you've got a great ass, Maura."

Before I can even yell at him, I hear it. The low thump of a truck pulling into the driveway behind the house. I turn, too quickly, and Ethan hits my stomach with the water. I can't even feel it, because I'm looking at Nate Sullivan for the first time in five years.

He has been the principal figure in every single fantasy I've had for my entire life, no matter how often I've tried to replace his face with someone else's. I thought when I saw him in person he'd finally lose some of that searing perfection he held in my mind. But he doesn't. He is everything I remember, and more. I'm frozen in place, taking him in. Our eyes meet, and for just a second he's frozen too.

He looks the same in some ways, radically different in others. He has those same cloudy gray eyes, that same smudge of dark lashes, that same mouth – his upper lip just full enough that it draws your eye.

And yet he's so different. The last time I saw him, he was a lanky 19-year-old, with a sweet smile that crept over his face without hesitation, with adoring eyes that looked into mine like he knew things about us that no one else knew. Which I guess he did.

He's an adult now, broader, his body a solid wall of muscle, but the most important difference is difficult to pinpoint. The sweetness of his eyes, his smile – it's gone, replaced with something that falls between anger and calculation. What was once mischievous is now deadly serious, perhaps even a little dangerous.

I know what kind of person he is, and all the things I loved about him are gone, so I can't account for the fact that I feel my chest dropping into my stomach at the sight of him, that my legs are rubbery. That the things I always felt for him haven't just lingered – they've doubled down. Seeing him should fill me with rage, but instead it leaves me weak with thirst. He says nothing to either of us. Ethan never even looks over at him. And then he turns and walks away.

He is not the person I remember at all, so why am I leaning against the wall for support, letting Ethan spray my breasts without murmuring the slightest objection?

* *

I've seen everyone at home for holidays, but they still jump up from the table and encircle me like I'm a returning war hero when we arrive at the bar.

It's funny how different everyone looks, without really having changed at all. I can't quite put my finger on it, but when I left they were kids and now they are not. Perhaps it's just that we're all legal, sitting in an outdoor bar called Oak and drinking gin and tonics instead of warm, pilfered six-packs beneath the pier.

"So you've stolen Ethan," says Kendall, "which means we get Jordan and Graham."

"Uh, I was hardly going to fight you for Jordan," I laugh. "But given that he's married and has a kid, his wife might."

"All right, Heather," says Kendall. "I'll arm wrestle you for Graham."

After a few drinks, Nate merely hovers somewhere in the back of my mind, in a place I can ignore. I rest my head against Ethan's arm, and feel, for a moment, that maybe I could keep doing this. It's nice being with Ethan. Maybe, once I'm done with school, this could work.

Everyone is talking about the lawsuit, and everyone but me fully supports the idea.

"How can you?" I ask, looking particularly at Kendall and Teddy, who are among the people that will have to drive a mile instead of walking a block. "The beach is public property!"

Kendall shrugs. "I can still use your walkway."

"But think about what that will do to property values! All

those houses that are a block from the beach become, for all practical purposes, a mile away."

"It's not like my parents plan to sell it anyway, so who cares?" she argues.

I'm stunned by their ambivalence and self-interest. Not a single person here cares to consider how this will impact anyone but them.

"Let it go, Maura," booms Graham. "There's no way they can win."

"They could bring a lawsuit against Old Cove," I suggest.

Graham snorts. "Sure, until they run out of money." His point being that they can only sue as long as they can afford to sue, and the families of Old Cove can afford it for a hell of a lot longer than anyone else.

Ethan tickles me and leans down to kiss my ear. "What a little do-gooder you are, Maura. Your grandpa would be proud." I let the discussion go, wondering vaguely what my grandfather would think of me with Ethan. I'm kind of glad I'll never know.

Ethan and I leave shortly thereafter – me, because I'm tired. Ethan, for different reasons entirely. We haven't even reached his car before he starts groping me.

"Ethan," I laugh, disengaging myself. "I think this is going to be a very hard summer for you."

"Literally," he jokes, pressing his crotch briefly against my thigh. "Come on. We'll just walk on the beach."

"I'm not having sex with you out there," I warn.

I see a flash of anger on his face, a desire to argue that he overcomes. "What a dirty mind you have," he says. "I just want to walk."

The second we're on the beach he's got his hand up my dress, his tongue in my mouth. I've been sleeping with him for nearly two months, but my unwillingness to do this with him here, now, is so overwhelming I can barely put words to it. I guess I can't stop thinking of the last time I slept with someone out here. How good it was. How wrong it ended up being.

"This isn't like any walking I've done before," I complain, pushing him away.

"Maura, you're killing me," he says, reaching for me again.

"Please, Ethan."

He throws his hands up. "Okay, okay! If this is just a ploy to get a ring on your finger by the end of summer it's working," he laughs.

The joke falls with a sick thud in my stomach. There is so much implied there, but mostly I don't laugh because I don't think he was joking.

He walks me to the back door. I stand on the steps where I once kissed Nate, on a night just like this. Ethan cups my jaw with his hand. "My parents want you to come for dinner tomorrow," he says.

My heart beats rapidly, and it's not from excitement. "I'm going to Heather's," I lie, so quickly and so poorly that I have to assume he knows, but he shows no sign of it.

He pouts. "I drove all the way down here to see you and you're ditching me for Heather?"

"I'm sorry," I say, and I mean it. I feel bad that I am freaked out by this. Ethan Mayhew is the guy that every girl I know wants, the guy that my whole family wants me to marry, but here I am reluctant to go meet his parents, suddenly so unnerved by physical contact that I can barely function.

"I'll forgive you," he murmurs, tugging at my waist and bringing his mouth next to mine, "if you promise to make it up to me."

I am spared making a promise that I'm not sure I can keep by Nate, who seems to materialize out of thin air. The look he fixes on me, for just a moment, is so full of hate that it chills me. He turns to Ethan. "Long time no see," he says, as if they've just run into each other at the diner. As if he and Ethan are friends and not two people who've barely exchanged a word in over a decade. "Maura." He says my name with decidedly less civility.

Ethan steps back in surprise, releasing my waist with clear reluctance, greeting Nate with an audible strain in his voice. I wonder which element of this is troubling him – that Nate is his cousin? That Nate is my ex? "How's it going?"

This should be Nate's cue to go, to give us a meaningful look that tells us he knows he's interrupted something. Nate has never been clueless, but he makes no move to leave. "Going well," he answers, never looking at me. "Are you down for the summer?" He's speaking loudly. He *knows* not to do this. He knows that at any minute the kitchen light will flip on and my grandmother will be standing there with her arms crossed, sour and disapproving.

"No," says Ethan. "Just here for the weekend." He reaches out to grab my hand. Nate's eyes follow the movement, observe our entwined fingers, and his nostrils flare for a fraction of a second. He glances at me again, and the hate I see on his face is deadly. Never once, in my entire life, have I seen his rage directed at me.

"So who else is in town?" he asks, his voice still loud in the quiet evening.

I don't hear Ethan groan, but I feel it, as if it's a weight that ties his feet to the ground. A second floor light goes on inside, like the sound of thunder in the distance. I watch as Nate's eyes flicker to the light, and then to me. He barely conceals his smirk.

He did it on purpose.

It wasn't enough that he broke my heart in the worst way possible. He's going to find little ways to keep hurting me. And none of those little ways are nearly as painful as the fact that he wants to hurt me at all.

"I'd better go," I say. "I think we woke her up." And just because I'm so pissed at Nate, I place both hands on Ethan's face and pull him in for a lingering kiss goodnight. When I step back, Ethan looks a little dazed, and Nate is turning away, his back rigid. And now it's my turn to smirk.

* *

To my chagrin, Heather's unwilling to fully cover for me the next night. "You can come over for dinner, but I'm not staying in on a Saturday!"

"It'll be fun!" I wheedle. "Like old times. I'll paint your nails and you can tell me all about how Teddy's cousin grabbed your ass during that assembly and tried to make it look like he was swatting something off of you."

"Maura, that was barely interesting five years ago. And I don't want anyone touching my nails. These are acrylics and they cost a fortune. What's wrong with you anyway? Ethan's your boyfriend, and you already know his parents. What's the big deal?"

I know I can't possibly make sense of it for her. "I just feel overwhelmed."

So I end up with the worst of all possible worlds: I have to make polite, strained conversation at dinner with Heather's parents, and then I still am out with Ethan, wishing I could make myself want the things that want me back.

CHAPTER 18

Signs go up around town, seemingly overnight, against the proposition to close off public access to the beach. I check out the website when I get home. The opposition is being led by Peter Folz, my grandfather's attorney, which I find reassuring. Anyone my grandfather would trust is good enough for me. Aside from Nate, that is.

The movement appears well-organized, also reassuring. My family and the others are under the impression that no one would dare fight them, that no one can afford to fight them, and they are wrong. At least for now.

* *

Nate walks into Oak that night. Our eyes lock, for just a moment, and I watch as his fill with contempt. I still can't believe he has *nothing* to say to me – no explanation, no heartfelt apology. He broke my heart but acts as if I'm the villain.

It makes no sense.

I focus my eyes straight ahead, but I can feel him, even when he's not looking at me, like a heater blowing too hard from a vent. When I go to the dance floor with Heather or Kendall or one of the boys, I dance with my back to him, refusing to meet his eye, but he is everywhere regardless of where I look. My seat at the table is facing the dance floor, so I can't avoid seeing him dancing, first with a slutty brunette, followed by an even sluttier blonde.

Good, I think bitterly, my hostility so sour that I can taste it. *Go saddle yourself with a nice townie girl, Nate. More your speed than I ever was.*

I'm appalled by the ugliness of my thoughts even as they appear, but of course what really underlies them isn't contempt but pain. Because every one of those girls is someone he has chosen instead of me.

He leaves with the second girl, his hand on her ass, and I spend the next hour gripped by emptiness before I call it a night. His car is there when I get home. I feel a rush of ease, relief. And then, overhead, a girl laughs in the carriage house, and it's gone, replaced with a fury so severe I have a hard time getting my key out of my purse.

* *

It suddenly seems as if I can't escape him.

On Wednesday we are out, and Kendall is telling us how she got caught giving someone a blowjob in the church stairwell back home. Teddy is laughing a little too hard, blushing at the same time, making me fairly sure that he was the unmentioned recipient in this story.

"Jesus, Kendall, what could they possibly have been talking about in church that would get y'all *that* worked up?" Robert laughs.

"There's a lot of kinky stuff in the Bible!" she insists. "Tell me you don't think there's kind of a whole hot submissive thing about Mary Magdalene washing Jesus's feet."

My head is thrown back laughing, and before I've even brought it up I sense a shift in the air. The laughter at our table hasn't changed, hasn't decreased, and yet the air has a different tang, less sweet, more salty, and my head comes off the chair.

Nate is passing our table. He's with a girl. She's a pretty girl, tiny aside from her disproportionately large chest. I deflate at the sight, and for the next hour, my only goal is to pretend I am not deflated, not affected at all, really. Everyone at the table is watching me. They all remember how we were. I am with Ethan, but not a single person here doesn't wonder if a part of me isn't still with Nate. In my desperation to prove them wrong, I only manage to prove to myself that they are right.

I listen for the sound of his car. I sleep fitfully, jolting awake at the smallest sound, but he never comes home.

* *

Ethan calls me every night. He tells me about work, he asks how my day was. I feel ridiculously idle, and young, in describing it. What did I do? I ran, I swam, I laid out, I took a book to the beach and fell asleep after one page, and then I met Heather and Kendall and they snuck vodka out in a flask and we were so good and liquored up by the time we got to the bar that it's all kind of a blur.

I don't feel guilty about it – the next year will be hard and it's the last summer I'll have free. But there's an odd disconnect when I discuss it with Ethan. He is talking to me like we are adults, like we are a married couple — "How was your day, honey?" — and I answer like a child who is telling her dad way, way more than he wants to hear. We are in different places, but I'm the only one of us who seems to notice.

And yet I'm not unhappy that we're dating. Our relationship might not offer the breathless excitement I felt when I was a teenager, but it's a comfort. I like seeing him beside me when we're on the beach, the pressure of his hand as we walk out of my house at night. His presence saves me from Graham too, who suddenly thinks he's my brother in Jordan's absence, and insists on walking me home every night. And Ethan is a buffer, a reminder as I watch Nate that I have something better, and that I'm no longer supposed to care.

* *

Nate's with that same girl on Friday. I struggle not to wince as Ethan and I pass them on the way to dinner, not to reveal that seeing him with her makes my stomach curl. In my head I've nicknamed her "Bitsy" because she's so little and cute and simpering and pointless. Nate and Bitsy walk beside each other, and she looks up him as doltishly as you'd expect of someone named Bitsy. They are there again, later, at Oak. I wish to God he'd find a new place to hang out. With every drink I'm increasingly compelled to ask him if there's not a townie bar he could hang out at instead, but of course, this *is* a townie bar. I hate my thoughts, how arrogant and ugly they are. I'm becoming the exact kind of person I once loathed.

Later, we attempt to have sex in Ethan's tiny BMW. I want it desperately, in a way I haven't ever wanted it with him before, and that makes it so much more frustrating that his car is too small to manage a single position.

I groan my frustration as I climb back into the passenger's seat. "Maybe you should trade this in for a van."

He grins. "Don't suggest it unless you plan to follow through."

I laugh. "I swear on my grandma's life that if you show up in a van I will follow through."

At the back door he runs his hands through my hair and pulls me toward him. His lips glance off mine, softly, before he presses against me and deepens the kiss. He's good at this, and, in the safety of my grandma's porch light, I'd probably enjoy it, were it not for the pulsing expectation that Nate is somewhere here, watching.

Ethan spends most of Sunday with me, his hands always on me in some way – running along my leg, grazing my back.

"I'm going to try to get back down here by Thursday," he says as he kisses me goodbye. "My mom wants you to come over for dinner."

This time, this far in advance, there's really no excuse I can make.

As soon as he leaves, Kendall collapses back into the sand. "Oh my God I'm so freaking jealous!" she screams. "He is so into you! And he's so affectionate. I've never, ever seen him like this with someone."

I haven't either. I wish it was still true.

Late that afternoon, when the beach has cleared and I'm finally alone, it feels like a weight's been lifted. I swim out, past the breakers, to the sand bar and back, and collapse on my towel in the waning sunlight. I wonder, as I lay there, if this is the last time I'll feel free until my plane lands in Michigan in August.

I am half asleep when I realize that something is blocking the dim light that remains. I open my eyes. Nate stands in front of me, shirtless, in a swimsuit. He is not the boy I knew. His shoulders are broad now, and his entire body ripples with muscle. I feel a shot of lust fire through me before I can stop it, before I can remember how much I hate him.

"Hello Maura," he says, his mouth twisting. There's nothing friendly about the words. He's not extending an olive branch. He's throwing down a challenge. His eyes are flat and angry as he observes me, his mouth grim.

I could ask him right now why he did it. How he could possibly have done it, at what point he became capable of inflicting so much damage on another human being and how he'd hidden it so well. But I won't. I refuse to give him the pleasure of knowing it still hurts. Let him think it meant as little to me as it clearly did to him.

I don't even bother to sit up. "Nate," I say, as coolly as possible. I look up at him but I am trying not to look *at* him, trying not to allow his looks to register. Despite my efforts, his effect on me is palpable. "You're blocking my sun."

He doesn't move.

"Where's your boyfriend?" he asks with a sneer.

"He went back to *work*," I say pointedly, though I don't make much of a point. Nate clearly has a job now too. "Why do you care?"

There's just a hint of confusion in his eyes before it turns back to anger. "Good point," he says. "I don't."

I flip over onto my stomach and close my eyes, just to make sure this conversation is done. Just to make sure I don't have to spend one more second watching the boy I loved for almost all of my life looking at me with disgust.

CHAPTER 19

I remember the way it seemed there weren't enough hours in the day here when I was younger. The way I'd burst out of bed the moment the sun crept into my room, and fight sleep at night until I couldn't fight anymore.

I've only been at the beach for a few weeks, and it's already grown tiresome. There is never any variation. If I'm not at the beach, I'm sleeping or drinking. It's not enough. Perhaps it is boredom, more than anything else, that leads me to Peter Folz's office.

"Little Maura!" he proclaims happily. "And not so little anymore! What can I do for you?"

"Well," I begin, suddenly nervous, "I wanted to find out what's going on with the defense against Old Cove's proposition."

His face clouds, slightly. "Well Maura, I don't know that I really can talk to you about that. You're kind of the opposition."

"I want to help," I explain, wondering if he'll believe me. "I just don't know how. I'm going to law school in the fall, so I'd love to get the experience, but it doesn't have to be legal stuff."

He pauses. "Does your grandmother know you're here?"

I sigh. "I'd rather she not know," I tell him. "It'd avoid a lot of arguments all summer. But I am 22, sir. I don't exactly need her permission anymore."

He says he'll let me know if anything comes up, but his smile is merely polite and his tone is distant. This is what it says: you're one of *them* now, and you can't be trusted.

He doesn't want my help and he never will.

* *

When Ethan knocks on my door Thursday night, I know by his smile that something is up, before I ever look out to the street. It's a van. A big, new, shiny Honda Odyssey.

"You didn't," I gasp.

His laughter echoes off the porch roof.

"I did."

I'm at a loss for words.

"Don't worry, I just borrowed it."

I say a silent prayer of thanks. As flattering as it'd be to have him give up his BMW just to have sex with me, I really don't want to ride around in a van all summer, and I really don't want him making permanent changes on my behalf.

"Not ready for the minivan with carseats in the back? It even has a DVD player."

"That's at least a decade away for me," I say firmly, just in case he was really asking. "Who the hell loaned you a van so you could have sex in it?"

"I may have borrowed it under false pretenses," he grins.

I laugh. "You told someone you were moving, didn't you?"

"What can I say?" he asks. "I'm getting desperate here."

Later that night, after we've left the chaos of Oak, he drives us to the back of the parking lot at Kroger.

"Oh God," I say, looking around. "*Really?*"

"You promised," he reminds me.

"Getting caught in a van behind Kroger is so much worse than getting caught on the beach."

"Come on," he kids. "It'll be fun. All the locals do it." I laugh, but his words make me think of Nate and the girls he's been bringing home. Somehow the thought makes me far more willing to follow Ethan to the back of the van than I was moments before.

* *

"You're having dinner at the Mayhews tonight," my grandmother says over breakfast.

"Good news travels fast," I sigh.

"His grandmother told me," she says.

I find it unnerving that even our grandmothers are in on this.

"It's just dinner," I say, a touch sourly.

"Of course, hon," my grandma soothes. "I'll have Rebecca get some wine for you to take over."

I make the long walk to his house that night, feeling jittery. I've known his parents my entire life, but this is different. It feels portentous, somehow, like the first scene of a movie that tells you how the rest of it will go down. This is how it starts, with me at their big formal table, being brought into the family. I haven't entered the door, and they already fully expect that this is one of a thousand dinners, that this is the prequel to the story of me and Ethan and the two perfect grandchildren we'll provide them. His mother probably made this walk, once. His grandmother too. I walk slowly and my legs feel heavy.

There is the squeal of brakes of an old car slowing beside me. For some reason I expect it to be Ethan, in the van, but it's not. It's Nate, in the truck that belonged to his mom.

He idles beside me, so I stop walking and look toward him. I remember the old Nate in the same moment I'm protecting myself against the new. He was so sweet. God he was sweet. When did that change? How did it change without me noticing?

"Going to Ethan's?" he sneers.

I narrow my eyes and face him defiantly. "Yes."

He takes a look at the bottle of wine in my hand with disgust. "Of course. The big 'welcome to the family' dinner."

"No," I say stonily. "It's just dinner." His anger makes absolutely no sense. He's acting like I'm the one who used and abandoned *him*.

"I'd offer you a ride," he says between gritted teeth. "But I guess it'd be bad form to show up with your first... everything, wouldn't it?"

My jaw drops and anger surges from somewhere deep in my stomach, so forceful I can feel it rocketing out. After what he did, he has the gall to bait me about it? My head whips toward him. "You'd know all about bad form, wouldn't you Nate?" I hiss.

"What the fuck is that supposed to mean?" he snarls.

"Think about it, asshole. And stop following me."

He hits the accelerator so hard that the tires spin before he peels away.

I take deep breaths all the way to Ethan's to compose myself, until only a slight heat on my cheeks is left to remind me of my anger. And really, Nate has done me a favor, because I'm suddenly glad that the Mayhews are here, that they want me. That I'm with Ethan, who would never dream of treating me the way that Nate just did.

I ring the bell, and Ethan pulls me in for a quick kiss before we hear his mother's feet tapping across the floor. I want to linger in the comfort of him, and he laughs at my reluctance to pull away. "Nervous?" he asks.

I shake my head.

"Maura Pierce!" she cries, enfolding me in a hug and then backing away. "Let's look at you!" And she really does. She even has me turn, as if I'm modeling a dress she may purchase. It's ridiculous on many levels, particularly because she just saw me in Charlotte a month ago, and I doubt I've changed much.

"I always knew you'd be a beauty," she says, linking arms with me as we walk toward the formal living room. "Even when you were a baby we knew it. But really, you're even more stunning than I ever imagined. Lord, what a figure you've got." She grins over her shoulder at Ethan. I feel desperately uncomfortable now. I half-expect her to ask me my bra size next. Ethan's dad is in the parlor. He stands and, to my vast relief, is much more restrained in his greeting.

"Maura," he says genially, kissing my cheek. "It's lovely to see you again. How are your parents?"

"They're doing well, sir. I think they're traveling at the moment."

He nods. "And Jordan is a father. You must all be very excited. They had a boy?" There's something about him that I find both comfortable and yet unsettling at the same time, but I can't pinpoint what it is.

His mother chides him. "You never listen, Stephen! They had a girl. Catherine, right?" she asks me.

I smile. "Yes. She'll be 10 months old next month."

"Your mother is so lucky," sighs Mrs. Mayhew, winking at Ethan. "I can't wait to have grandchildren."

A server in uniform sets a tray of canapés on the table – carpaccio on thinly sliced crackers, watermelon and feta on skewers, tiny miniature quiches and crabcakes. It seems like a lot of trouble to go to when your guest is only 22.

The uniform troubles me too. Perhaps it's standard here, but we only do that in my house on special occasions, and I really don't want them to consider this dinner special.

"So Ethan tells me you're headed to law school?" Mr. Mayhew asks.

"Yes sir," I answer. "I start at Michigan in the fall."

"Well, if you want to get your feet wet, you can help with the proposition to privatize the beach," he suggests.

Ethan laughs uncomfortably. "I don't think so, Dad. Maura kind of falls on the other side of the equation." He turns to me sheepishly. "My dad is the one heading up the proposition."

I'm a little stunned to be learning this now, with the number of times the proposition has come up around Ethan over the past month. I manage to squelch my surprise, but not the tiny feeling of revulsion I suddenly feel for Ethan's father, and a bit for Ethan himself.

More than a thousand people will be impacted by this, the greed of 15 families. And all of their efforts can't possibly combat Stephen Mayhew, with his power and his bottomless checking account.

I'm not normally a deceitful person. I can't really explain what I do next. I just feel an unpalatable combination of revulsion and anger and indignation, and it occurs to me that even if Peter Folz won't accept my help, knowing what the opposition has planned may be of use to him at some point.

"I've changed my mind about that," I say, my heart hammering hard as I begin telling a lie I'd never planned to tell. "Now that I'm back and I see what a nightmare the beach is becoming with all the crowds, I've got to say I'd welcome a little privacy."

I'm shocked as the words leave my mouth. But I don't regret them, either.

Ethan looks at me questioningly, but his dad just nods his head. "They get worse every year. I can barely get a spot on the beach anymore."

Over dinner they recall stories about Ethan, Graham and Jordan as boys, stories I've never heard. I hadn't realized, until tonight, that my brother was considered the ringleader, which is really just a euphemism for being the one with all the worst, most dangerous, ideas. The Mayhews don't seem troubled by it, but I wouldn't want my son around the kid they describe. Jordan sounds malevolent, not mischievous, in their stories. I can't help but think my parents' money is what earned him a pass, a pass no one would ever have given Nate under the circumstances.

I wish I could say I'm surprised to discover how repugnant Jordan's behavior is as described, but I'm not. He was always awful to Nate, and to me. The way Ethan treats his sister is a world apart from my best moments with Jordan. I can guarantee that Lily has never been scared of her brother, has never taken the back stairs or hidden in the shed to avoid him. Ethan teases her, but in an affectionate way, not a mean one. I don't want to think it, or admit it, but he'll be a good father some day.

When dinner is cleared, his mother gives a start of surprise that feels slightly premeditated. "Maura, I just realized, you've probably never had a tour of the house."

"She's been up there," Ethan laughs, looking a little ashamed. "Jordan told her we had candy, and then he locked her in the closet and said there was a ghost inside."

"God," I laugh. "I'd totally forgotten. You guys scared me to death."

"Ethan Mayhew!" his mother scolds, though it was over a decade ago.

He throws up his hands. "I know! I'm not bragging about it, Mom!" He grins at me. "I think, technically, that makes you the first girl I ever had in my room."

"Lily, take Maura around and show her the house," Mrs. Mayhew says with a smile. "I'd send *you*," she says to Ethan, "but I don't want you locking her in any closets." Ethan gives me such a lascivious look that I kind of wish he *was* giving me the tour.

The house is a lot like my grandma's, not surprising as they were built around the same time — the same creaky old pine floors and high ceilings and elaborate wainscoting at every turn.

The rooms here have been decorated in this century, however, which is a radical departure from ours. Lily proudly shows me hers – black and neon and purple, covered with tacky slogans and posters, the exact kind of disgusting room I'd have wanted when I was 14. I guess there's something to be said for a grandmother who doesn't embrace change. I'd hate to be sleeping in a room decorated by my teenage self.

Before we head downstairs she places a hand on my forearm to stop me. "Mom told me not to ask," she whispers, casting a furtive glance over the banister. "But can I be a bridesmaid? Not a junior bridesmaid. A real bridesmaid."

I feel like I'm listening to a conversation occurring in a parallel universe. "Um, where?"

"At your wedding," she laughs. "Duh."

"I'm not engaged," I say. I feel a small swell of panic.

"Well you know, after he asks," she says, conspiratorially.

"We aren't even talking about marriage, Lily," I breathe.

She giggles. "Maybe *you're* not."

I start down the stairs with a knot in my stomach. I don't want to hear anymore. I don't want to commit to anything more. I've clearly already committed to too much, it seems, without saying yes to anything at all.

I practically launch myself in the van as we head out to meet everyone after dinner.

"So that went well, I thought," says Ethan.

"Yes," I murmur.

He looks over at me skeptically. "What?"

"Nothing."

"Oh, there's definitely something."

I sigh. "No offense, but your family is kind of getting all 1800s on me. Your mom and your sister are acting like we're getting married next week."

He shrugs. "They're just happy for us. They're excited."

About *what*? I long to ask.

"But they know I'm leaving," I persist.

He shrugs again. "Plans change."

"Mine don't," I warn him.

"We'll see," he smiles, and his smile suddenly strikes me as unbelievably smug, as if he knows more about my future than I do. His family members, apparently, are not the only ones stuck in the wrong century.

It takes me three drinks at Oak, and the pleasant numbness that comes with them, to relax. Ethan's family is just another funny anecdote I'll tell at school next year. I look over at him and he catches my eye and smiles. I love his smile – crooked and cocky and sweet all at once. It's his best feature, and he has a lot of good features.

And then, just past Ethan's shoulder and ruining everything, is Nate, looking directly at me as he walks into the bar. I realize, with a sickening thud, why I love Ethan's smile. Because it's Nate's. They look so different that I'd never put it together before, but as I look back and forth between the two of them the truth is undeniable. It makes me question things with Ethan even more: I thought I'd finally found someone I liked for who he is, not who he reminds me of, and now I'm not entirely sure.

But I may not be the only one with a type, because the girl Nate's with looks an awful lot like me. From the back she could almost *be* me, with her height and her dark hair, were it not for the fact that she's wearing four-inch heels and her shorts are cut so high I can see the bottom of her ass.

Ethan and Graham exchange a look as they pass us.

"What's all the grinning about?" I ask suspiciously.

Ethan leans over. "We call her Maura Lite," he laughs. "All the body but only half the brains."

"You're just pissed she didn't sleep with you," scoffs Kendall.

"Au contraire," Ethan says. "The one she wouldn't sleep with is Graham."

Something sinks in my stomach. "Are you saying you *did* sleep with her?"

His face changes from snide to apologetic in a heartbeat. "Maura," he pleads. "Your brother said hands-off for six years. At least I went after girls who looked like you, right?" She's hardly the only girl he was with — I know way more about his past than he thinks — but I don't argue it.

"I guess," I say quietly. I feel sickened by this, and I'm not sure why.

"Baby," he pleads, now looking truly concerned. He comes around the table and pulls me from my chair. "Let's go dance."

"I don't want to dance," I say sullenly, allowing myself to be pulled to my feet.

It's a slow song so at least I can fake it. He pulls me into his arms, far too close to even be considered dancing.

"I'm sorry, Maura, I shouldn't have said anything."

I shake my head. "You didn't do anything wrong," I sigh.

His lips brush my forehead, his hands rub my back. He's still apologizing because, despite my words, I'm clearly not okay.

"I never thought you'd be the jealous type," he says, nipping my earlobe with his teeth. "I like it."

I smile, trying hard to will away my unreasonable sulkiness. It doesn't bother me at all to imagine Ethan with her, so I'm not sure why I feel so upset. A faster song comes on, and we stay on the floor. He rocks my hips against his. He's a good dancer, and if I wasn't in such a pissy mood, I'd enjoy it.

Suddenly I am jostled from behind hard enough that I fall forward into Ethan.

"Sorry," sings an unfamiliar voice, sounding entirely unapologetic. It's Maura Lite – whose actual name is Jenna, apparently – making her way onto the dance floor with Nate, and shoving me so hard that there's no way it could have been an accident. Nate glances back at her, surprised, a flash of anger across his face that for once is not directed at me.

We continue to dance, but no matter where we are on the floor, I can still see Nate, with his hand on that girl's ass, dancing with her in a way that makes Ethan and I look like we're at a church social.

"Someone should tell her it's a dance floor, not a stripper pole," I spit out as I watch.

Ethan looks at me in surprise, and then smiles. "You *are* jealous! I am loving this side of you, Maura Pierce."

There is something building in me, some combination of recklessness and anger and lust that makes me feel unstable here in this room. I press up against Ethan.

"Why don't we go out to your van and you can see what the jealous side of me acts like there?" I whisper in his ear.

"Holy shit. I'm bringing Maura Lite everywhere from now on," he says, pulling me out of the bar.

We don't even say goodbye to everyone. I don't climb into the passenger seat, I climb directly into the back of the van, and he follows.

"What happened to worrying about being caught?" he asks.

I don't even answer, because I'm too busy unbuttoning his shorts, pushing him on the floor, falling on top of him.

CHAPTER 20

On Sunday night, the ten public walkways to Old Cove beach are destroyed simultaneously.

"Damn," laughs Heather, as we survey the damage to the one nearest my grandmother. "How do you think they did it?"

I don't know about the other ones, but here it looks like someone came through and ripped out the entire center of the boardwalk. 2x4s litter the dune beneath or hang precariously from a single tress left standing. The dunes are high here, nearly impossible to climb and maintain enough traction in the sand to get all the way to the top. I imagine trying to climb it, carrying a cooler or holding a child's hand. Impossible. And even if it weren't, water tends to pool in the valley at each dune's base, creating a muddy and miserable obstacle to anyone who tries to brave it. Until they are repaired, only the 15 families with private walkways can get to the beach.

I go see Peter Folz as soon as Heather leaves.

"You're not going to let them get away with it?" I ask.

He sighs wearily. "What do you want me to do?"

"Someone destroyed public property! They should be brought up on charges," I insist.

"Yes," he says. "But who, Maura? We have no idea who did it."

I deflate as what he's saying sinks in. As I realize that Old Cove can and will do whatever they want regardless of how the proposition turns out.

He's quiet for a moment. "Look, if you really want to help, I could probably use it."

He sets me at a spare desk in the back room and has me begin culling through similar cases, looking for a legal precedent. The cases are interesting, which is fortunate because I'm not optimistic about finding anything useful. And the truth is that I'd be far more helpful to the cause if I could just prove who destroyed those walkways. I don't dwell on the fact that that person may be Ethan's dad.

* *

There is one thing that remains consistent over the course of the week: Nate is never at home, unless he's with a girl. I see him at Oak nearly every night, and it's ridiculous to feel like he's throwing these girls in my face, but I feel it anyway. When I'm on the dance floor with my friends, he ends up a few feet away. No matter which way I face, I end up watching him dance, always well, always suggestively. His dancing is like foreplay, and the girls eat out of his hand, grinding against him. I turn my back and a minute later, I find him in my line of sight again.

When slow dances come on I sit. I have a boyfriend, and while these guys are like brothers to me, they are not brothers, and slow dancing seems to be blurring the line. Not that I'd slow dance with my own brother in the first place.

But he keeps dancing, and it's always some version of the same move – his hand pressing into her lower back, pulling her closer, her hips swaying against his. The knowing little look he gives her, the way he manhandles her and the way she appears to love everything he does. It is always the same, even though the girls change.

There is a particular progression of noises, on the nights he comes home at all: his car pulling into the driveway, the slam of two doors, the sound of feet skittering over gravel, odd thumps I can't place, and always, always a high, girlish giggle. And half the time I already know who she is, because I've seen them earlier at

Oak. Two blondes, two brunettes. One of the brunettes is Maura Lite, whose continuing dislike puzzles me, since we've never even met. I walk out of the bathroom on the night he's there with her, just as she's walking in. She knocks into me so hard that my shoulder slams against the frame of the door.

"Oops," she giggles, "My bad."

"Knock into me again and the only 'bad' will be your severe blood loss," I threaten.

"Oooh," she taunts. "How terrifying."

I walk away, but instead of returning to my table, I walk directly to Nate, who's been watching us from the bar. For once he doesn't look pleased to see me hurt.

"That's a nice girl you've found yourself there, Nate," I seethe. "Kind of scraping the bottom of the barrel, aren't you?"

His eyes turn the color of steel. "I hit bottom about five years ago, Maura. I'm definitely working my way back up." His words are like a physical blow. I keep expecting an apology, an explanation, and everything I get instead is so much worse, so much uglier.

"The next time your townie girlfriend touches me, she's leaving in an ambulance," I hiss. And though I have no reason to believe I could kick anyone's ass, I mean every word.

"What are you going to do?" he smirks. "Call your grandmother in?"

"Watch carefully the next time she messes with me and you'll see for yourself."

My breathing is so shallow, my body hovering on such a fine line between rage and tears that I don't dare say another word.

That night I hear them come in. And then I hear other sounds. She is moaning — so loudly that they might as well be in the room with me. I slam my window shut, and I can still hear her, their groans taking on a rhythm that grows more urgent. I plug my ears, and finally, in frustration, I slam my hand flat against the window pane, and the glass shatters.

CHAPTER 21

Elise calls to tell me she and Brian are coming down for the weekend. I should be excited, but instead, I am horrified. Nate is one of Brian's best friends. Are we going to be expected to play nice all weekend? I can't imagine either of us being able to pull it off.

"It'll be just like old times!" she cries. "They're even going to get a game together on Friday night!"

A game. It just gets worse and worse. But I sense something anxious behind her excitement, so I don't complain.

"Elise," I ask quietly. "Is everything okay?"

"I just need a break from my mom," she says, but she doesn't sound tired – she sounds hopeless.

"Maybe you should just elope," I suggest.

"Please," she says. "My life will end if my mom doesn't get her big wedding."

"Elise McDonald, don't put this off on your mother. You've been planning a big-ass wedding since you were five."

She laughs. "I guess, but it's getting to be a bit much even for me."

"Are you interviewing at all or is she keeping you too busy even for that?"

She hesitates. "She and Brian don't want me interviewing right now. I guess it makes sense. I'm too busy with the wedding to really start work anyway, and then we go on our honeymoon. I suppose I'll just wait 'til fall."

"You don't sound happy about it," I venture, troubled by the hint of despair in her voice.

"Sometimes I wish I was doing things the way you are. Getting out of the south for a while. Doing my own thing first," she answers. "Brian would prefer I not work – *everyone* would prefer it –and it's not like we need the money. I get the feeling that once we're married, I'm going to turn into my mom whether I want to or not."

"That's not going to happen," I murmur. But inside I worry she's right. That my brilliant friend Elise with her amazing GPA and her degree in finance from Duke is going to discover it's just not possible to move up on the tennis circuit and work full time. And she's going to make the wrong choice.

* *

I wanted to avoid the Friday baseball game like I've wanted to avoid nothing in my life, but I can't do it to Elise, or Ethan, who's playing, so here I sit.

Kendall plops down on the picnic blanket beside me with an exhausted sigh. "Gah. We're gonna get eaten alive out here watching this stupid shit when we could be sitting at Oak right now," she grouses.

"Well, I love it," counters Elise. "I feel like I'm 16 again."

I feel 16 again too and that's exactly the problem. The humid air is thick, plump with the smell of grass and salt, the way it always was. I am leaning back on my arms, waiting, just like I once did. And it's the contrast that tears me up. Because leaning back on a blanket like this, feeling the sweat bead up between my shoulder blades – this I associate with Nate. With waiting for him, with watching him, with the secret shot of joy I felt every time he looked over and caught my eye, the slight upward quirk of his mouth. He could look at me from 40 yards away and I knew what he was thinking. And I would watch him, all lean muscle and propulsive speed, with a slow burn of desire. It would start small, and I would allow it to grow, as the game neared completion. And when the game ended all that need rushed in, overwhelming me as I stood on the sidelines waiting for him. It did for him too – I could see it in his face, in the way he plowed toward me like he'd run down anything that got in our way. He would grab me, lifting my legs around his waist, not even slowing his pace as he moved us into the darkness. We never made it off the school grounds before I was tasting the dust and sweat on his neck and pushing against him, wanting more.

This is what I think as I sit here. That I want that back, the experience of wanting something desperately that is actually yours. Of wanting what you already have, instead of wanting what will never be yours again.

And then Nate walks around the corner of the school, and the first thing he seeks, the first thing he finds, is me, as if seeking and finding each other on this field is so engrained we can't help but continue to do so even now. What I see when I look at him is, inexplicably, pain. A mirror of my own. He jerks his head away with a scowl.

I try to watch Ethan, but the truth is that I can't stop watching Nate, can't stop watching the flex of his calves, the way he moves as he stands by first base, the lean line of him as he whips the ball to the pitcher.

During the second inning, when Ethan steps up to bat, there's a sudden change in the infield.

"What the hell?" breathes Elise.

Brian, who's been pitching all night, changes places with Nate. I watch as Ethan narrows his eyes, visibly angered by the change, and steps up to bat. Nate's pitches are fast, hard, unpredictable. Ethan hits nothing, gets an out. And Nate goes back to first base as if there was nothing unusual about it.

It can't be about me. He left *me*. I say it to myself again and again. Maybe he's just come to resent the way the Mayhews treated him, to recognize that all the things Ethan has should have been his as well. But it can't be about me.

The game ends and our eyes meet once more. For a moment, I can't look away, can't pretend that I hate him. And for once, he doesn't either. But when Ethan enters our line of sight he changes visibly, steels himself. He turns on his heel and walks in the other direction, and I only want to follow him. I want to run and jump on his back, the way I once would have if he were walking away from me, to have him spin me to face him, wrapping my legs around his waist, pressing against me, his mouth on my collarbone, his hands firm beneath me…

"So what'd you think?" asks Ethan, placing a gentle kiss on my forehead.

"You were good out there," I grin, forcing myself back into this moment instead of the one I was in.

"No I wasn't," he says, grabbing my hand. "Although it doesn't help that your ex-boyfriend seems to have a vendetta against me."

I shrug. "I guess he's got a bigger grudge against your family than he let on."

Ethan scoffs. "This has nothing to do with my family," he says acidly. "It's not *my family* he stares at every time we're out. He spent so much time watching you tonight I'm surprised he ever caught the ball."

"No," I shake my head in disagreement. "That doesn't make any sense."

"All I know is that it better stop," he says as we reach the parking lot. "I gotta go take a shower. You want to wait for me at Oak?"

"Sure," I reply. "I'll ride over with Heather."

I never wanted Nate to shower after one of his games. There was something about it, something raw in his playing that I wanted on me. If he'd ever suggested showering first – and I don't remember him ever being able to restrain himself that long – I'd have balked. But I'm happy Ethan is leaving, and I wish that wasn't the case.

* *

"You want to know something?" Elise giggles drunkenly later that night, pulling me away from the table into the corner of the bar.

"What?" I laugh. Elise is like a 12-year-old when she drinks.

"I think Nate still likes you," she whispers.

Unexpectedly, my eyes well up. I shake my head. "No, he doesn't."

"Didn't you see him tonight?"

"Elise, are you forgetting the way he left in the middle of the night to go back to his girlfriend at UVA and never spoke to me again?" I ask angrily. "He didn't even care about me enough to stay with me when he was sleeping with me, so he sure as shit doesn't now. I wouldn't take him back anyway." The last is a lie, but I keep hoping if I say it often enough it'll be true.

A shadow passes over her face. "Brian asked him about that once."

"About the girlfriend?" I ask, feeling my chest cave in. Still, after all these years, I can't stand to hear it.

She nods. "He said you were lying. He said that's not what happened."

I look over at Brian and Nate at the bar, and now I am seething. They are watching us, and I glare at Nate with as much hatred as I've ever summoned for anyone. "Then he's a lying piece of shit, Elise. Who are you going to believe, me or him?"

"Don't get mad, Maura," she pleads. "Of course I believe you, it's just… Nate's a really good guy. I don't know what happened, but you know, I mean," she stammers, "that's just not something he would do."

"Well, clearly it is," I snap. "Since that's exactly what he did."

"I'm sorry, honey," she begs. "You're totally right. Forget I said anything."

We go back to the table.

"You okay, babe?" asks Ethan, putting his arm around my waist.

"Uh-huh," I sigh, burrowing into his shoulder and wishing that Nate Sullivan would stop ruining everything so I can just get on with my life. It's time for me to be happy with someone else, someone who actually deserves me.

CHAPTER 22

It's overcast as I leave for the bar Wednesday night. "You'd better take the car," my grandmother sighs. "It's supposed to storm. Make sure you don't leave the top down." It's hard to hide my shock: I've never seen either of my grandparents lend their pristine, vintage Mercedes convertible to anyone. My grandfather used to let me ride in his lap when I was little and help hold the wheel, and that's the closest I ever thought I'd come to driving it.

Heather is on the dance floor when I pull up so she sees me. "Ooooohweeee, we got the Benz tonight! Come on y'all. We're going cruising!" she shouts to the table.

"No we're not," I correct her. "This is the first time in 22 years my grandma's trusted me with that car. I'm not about to have half the town tell her I was driving down Main with a bunch of drunks hanging out of the back."

"Fine," says Graham, "I'll drive."

"Right," I snort. "Because a drunk at the wheel would make her so much happier."

I'm so worried about the car, in fact, that I don't have a single drink. It has good points and bad. I find that my friends aren't nearly as amusing without a fair amount of beer in my system. I also find that watching Nate talking to girls, giving them that knowing look, that crooked grin, is more sickening than normal.

On the upside, I have slightly more control over my desire to go slap him in the face.

I am pondering this as I realize there is suspicious giggling going on around me. I look up and see Graham and Heather heading out of the bar, and realize my keys have disappeared.

"Graham!" I shout. "Give them back."

He grins mischievously and starts running. I jump up from the table. It's a joke to them but my grandmother will kill me if she hears they've been driving the car. And Graham was drunk when I arrived.

"Graham!" I shout in the parking lot, catching up to them at the car's door. "Give them back, damn it!"

"What's it worth to you, Maura Leigh?" he taunts, a little suggestively. He holds the keys high over my head.

He is laughing, and just as I realize I have no recourse if he decides to go, someone is behind me, a solid wall of heat and muscle, close enough that my hair brushes against his shirt. "Give them back, Edwards," says Nate.

"Fuck you," Graham sneers. He turns to Heather. "Get in."

Graham turns toward the car but Nate is faster. He snatches the keys and puts them in my hand. Graham glares at him, but Nate is looking at me, as if he's shocked to discover who he was defending.

"Thank you," I whisper, still astonished that of all people, Nate is the one being kind.

There's a flash of something in his face, a flash of the old Nate, the sweet one, who looked at me adoringly, trustingly. And then it's gone.

As I drive home I feel almost drugged by that look. I think of the last time Nate and Graham got into it, when Graham crashed into me on his jet ski. I think about how scared Nate was, how he couldn't let go of me, how there was nothing he wouldn't do to keep me safe. I remember those things and I *know*, no matter what came afterward, that he loved me once. And it's ridiculous, but I think about the look on his face tonight, and wonder if he still might.

* *

The rumble of thunder wakes me sometime before dawn. I spend exactly two seconds feeling relieved that I put the top up on the car before I remember that I left the windows down.

"Shit," I hiss, stumbling out of bed. I fly out the back door in nothing but panties and a UNC t-shirt that doesn't quite cover them, and come to a dead halt, as does Nate, who is just climbing out of his truck. The first drops of rain hurl me back into action, and I'm grateful for it, grateful that there's no time to contemplate that I'm half-naked in front of him, or the fact that he's just coming home right now. I run to my grandmother's car, willing myself to ignore the fact that my t-shirt is flying halfway up my ass with every step I take.

The rain is really coming down by the time I get to the car. I fling open the driver's side door and slide onto the seat to roll up the window. To my surprise the passenger's side opens too, and Nate is there, beside me, taking care of it. We both jump out of the car at the same time. "Thank you," I tell him for the second time in a matter of hours, so flustered by the change in him that I'm almost stunned into inaction. I run to the house, but when I get to the door I turn to find that he is standing exactly where I left him, watching me. And for the first time since I've been back he looks young, and kind of lost.

* *

On Friday my whole family arrives – my parents, Jordan, Mia and the baby.

I am immediately suspicious. "What's up with the family reunion?" I ask my mom.

"You're not the only person who enjoys the beach, Maura," she chides.

I could counter that she didn't seem to enjoy it for the 13 years she sent me here alone, but I don't.

"Don't make any plans for tomorrow night," she adds. "We're having the Mayhews over for dinner."

I sigh deeply. "Why?"

"You and Ethan are getting serious, honey," she replies, looking puzzled. "This is just what's done."

"No, we're not 'getting serious' Mom. And this is not what's done when you're just dating. It's what's done when you get engaged."

"Maura, don't be ridiculous. He's practically family."

"So is Heather but I don't see you trying to marry me off to her!"

Her good humor, her attempt at mediating, evaporates. She pinches the bridge of her nose as she scowls. "Maura, must you be contrary about everything? If I told you that you *couldn't* see him anymore, the two of you would be at the justice of the peace by tomorrow morning."

"You're probably right, Mom," I retort. "Because if you told me I couldn't see him it'd just mean you'd found someone even wealthier to whore me out to."

"Maura Leigh!" my father yells. I hadn't even realized he was in the room. "Apologize this instant."

I look at them both flatly and walk out of the house. I go to the shed, realizing that really, I have nowhere to go. If I was younger, I'd pull my bike out and tear off on it as fast as I could. How is it that I'm finally an adult, but feel far more trapped than I ever did when my choices weren't my own?

The last time I biked like that – barefoot, no helmet, breakneck speed – I was racing Nate.

"What do I get if I win?" he'd smirked.

I shrugged. "What do you want?"

I remember his heated glance, the way it ran the length of me before flickering back over my mouth. "I think you know."

And just the look he gave me, the low pulse of his voice, set something off inside of me, made my legs feel boneless, my stomach a tight knot of need.

"Fine," I grinned.

"And what do you want in the unlikely event that you win?" he asked.

There was no helping it. There was no other answer for me now. I gave him the same look he'd just given me. "I think you know."

He stood stock-still for a moment, his eyes serious and feral. And then he leapt on his bike and took off.

He was waiting for me by the shed as I pulled up. I expected him to crow and gloat and smirk for a while, but he did not. Instead he came over to me, fierce and determined, and lifted me off of my bike. It fell to the ground, and I barely noticed, because his mouth was already on mine and he was pulling me to the far side of the shed, where we couldn't be seen.

I wonder if he remembers that anymore. I wonder if he remembers how much he wanted me once. He was my best thing, my sweetest thing, and he wasn't really mine at all.

The sun is going down, the yard is losing its light. And all the things that were good and sweet and pure are withering away, slipping from my grasp.

* *

My parents seem to sense that they have pushed too hard, and they say nothing about the fight or my mysterious disappearance when I come back. My mother looks politely away from my tear-stained face. "We saved you some dinner," she says.

When Ethan comes to pick me up, Jordan walks out with us. "Isn't Mia coming?" I ask, looking back into the room.

"Nah," he shrugs. "She'd rather stay with the baby."

"I can stay with Catherine if she wants to go," I offer.

He rolls his eyes. "She won't leave Catherine with anyone. Don't worry about it."

Friday at Oak is more of a throw-down than normal because Jordan is here. Jordan is big and loud and we hover around him like satellites, unable to help ourselves. Nate is there with friends, but he stays on the far side of the room. It doesn't stop me from watching him. He is standing by the pool table with a girl in a tiny miniskirt who seems to find innumerable opportunities to bend over. During one of these bending maneuvers, he slides his hand under her skirt, grinning slyly at her. And of course her only response is to press farther into his hand. They leave not long after.

Ethan and I stay late, but Jordan still isn't ready to go. He's fairly drunk, incredibly boisterous, and the whole table is treating him like some kind of celebrity.

I sleep poorly, poised on the edge of wakefulness, waiting for the slightest noise to warn me that Nate is coming home. But at 6 a.m., the noise that wakes me isn't Nate. It's Jordan, coming home from a bar that closed four hours before.

* *

A catering truck sits in the driveway from early afternoon on.

I play with Catherine in the side yard and try to ignore the upheaval, try to pretend this is all nothing, that every action my family and Ethan's take isn't somehow tying me further into a contract between us that I'm not interested in.

"Here you go," I coo to her, as she grasps my fingers and tries to walk with me. Her shaky, lumbering little steps make me laugh despite my bad mood. I lie on my back and hold her aloft on my raised legs swinging her to and fro while she screams in delight. Poor little Catherine seems to be the only member of her family who is happy today. Mia is even more withdrawn and pale than usual, Jordan is surly and tired and hung-over even though he didn't wake up until 11.

"Going up!" I shout, flinging her upward. "Going down!" I say as I bring my legs down quick. She screeches and drools on my face and I laughingly try to swipe it off without losing my grip on her, still floating above me, perched high on my outstretched toes.

In the quiet of the moment I realize that we are not alone. I look over, with Catherine still aloft, and see Nate. His brow is furrowed, as if he's never laid eyes on me before and can't figure out why me and this baby are laying in the yard. Finally I see the question leave his eyes, replaced by disgust.

"What's up in number 11?" he asks coldly, glancing over at the catering truck.

"Dinner party," I reply, lowering Catherine to the ground and swinging myself up so I'm seated. I don't even know why I'm answering his questions. It's not as if he answered any of mine a few years back.

"Oh, I must have missed the invite," he says. "Let me guess: your family and the Mayhews?"

I hate, *hate* that he is correct. I pull Catherine into my lap like she's a security blanket. "Don't you have someplace else to be?" I hiss. "Surely there's some slut in a mini-dress waiting for you with bated breath."

He looks at me assessingly. "For someone in such a serious relationship, you're sure keeping a close eye on me."

I'd tell him to fuck off if Catherine wasn't with me, but she is, and with my luck it'd be her first word.

"I'm not keeping an eye on you, Nate. You just make such a spectacle of yourself every night it's hard not to notice."

"Strong words for someone who practically screws her boyfriend every time she hits the dance floor," he snarls back.

I stand then, with Catherine in my arms, and begin to walk away. I look over my shoulder. "Now who's keeping a close eye?" I ask. I go inside. I got the last word, and yet feel completely defeated.

* *

It is an engagement dinner, without the engagement. There are flowers and champagne. The parents exchange a constant stream of references to the future. Toasts are made to our two families, to grandchildren, to how wonderful everything is and will be. My smile is strained, but Ethan's is broad and relaxed and proud.

Someone toasts Jordan and Mia and the baby too. Mia smiles, but her mouth is pulled tight at the corners, like a marionette's. It holds not an ounce of actual joy.

The whole experience creates a compelling, contrary desire to separate myself, to stand up and announce that I will never come back here, that I will never be a part of this. But I don't, because I was raised by these people, I'm one of them. And people like us don't do things like that.

Everyone is talking about the destruction of the public walkways. Actually, "talking" is the wrong word. "Crowing" is more accurate.

"But aren't they just going to build them again?" asks Mia.

Ethan's father laughs. "Yes, and it'll cost them thousands of dollars, and as soon as they've got every single one completed, they'll be destroyed all over again."

I smile, because Ethan is watching me. "So you're arguing that the state only owns up to the water line and everything in front of it is private, right? What if the state disagrees?"

"Then we'll just maintain that the road is private," he says, entirely confident. "It won't stop people from walking, but it's the only road with a shoulder wide enough to park on, so no one will be able to drive here. That'll get rid of most of them."

Everyone nods, and that desire to stand up and announce that I want nothing to do with any of them? It's so strong I find that I'm digging my nails into my thighs to stay seated.

The only consolation of the whole evening is that there is no sign of Nate when we go to Oak later. But it's only a relief until I begin to torture myself, wondering if he's on a real date this time.

I thought listening to Maura Lite moan through my windows was as low as it could get, but I discover that the thought of Nate in love with someone is much, much worse.

Ethan pulls in front of the house but puts his hand on my mine when I reach for the door. He's leaving early the next morning to take Jordan and Mia home. "I can't say goodbye to you properly with your parents hovering right inside the door," he says.

"You're just scared Jordan will see us," I tease.

He laughs good-naturedly. "I'm a little scared of that as well."

He pulls my chin toward him, running a thumb over my cheekbone and then over my mouth. "I'll miss you this week," he says. He leans over to kiss me. It's a sweet kiss, gentle and loving, the kind of kiss he probably could give me in front of Jordan without risk of bodily harm. My lips part, I feel a gust of breath in my mouth, his tongue moving gently, his fingers still on my cheekbone like I'm made of glass. The sound of my door being opened is so incongruous that it doesn't register at first, but then there's a strong hand locked around my elbow. My first thought is that it's my dad or Jordan, only as illogical as the fact that the door's been opened at all.

"Hey Ethan," says Nate, ducking his head down so we can see him. "Thanks for bringing her home safely. Her grandmother was worried."

"What the hell, Nate?" I hiss, snatching my elbow out of his hand. "It's not even midnight!"

"You know how she is," he shrugs, and grabs my arm again.

Ethan's got the door open and one foot out. "Now I've fucking had it," he hisses.

I stop him with my hand on his arm. "It's okay. I'll deal with this."

"Fuck that, Maura. I've had it with his shit."

"Please Ethan. My parents are here. I'll handle it."

"I'll deal with him quietly," he says.

I arch an eyebrow. We both know that any confrontation that

occurs right now with Nate will drag every person within 200 yards out into the street. "Please," I beg.

He sighs. "I don't like it."

I kiss his cheek. "It'll be fine. I'll talk to you tomorrow." Ethan glares at Nate as I shut the door.

"What the fuck is your problem?" I ask as Ethan drives off.

He shrugs, and starts heading toward the carriage house. He chuckles to himself as he walks away. "I was just making sure you got in okay," he calls over his shoulder.

"Bullshit, Nate." I walk after him as quickly as I can in my heels and don't catch him until we're in the side yard. "Why are you doing this?"

He comes to a stop, and faces me. He is no longer laughing, and my breath stills in my throat. The look on his face could only be described as malevolent. I never could have imagined seeing him like this.

He steps close, so close I can smell his soap, I can feel his breath. "I just want to make sure no one is forcing you to do anything against your will," he sneers.

"What the hell are you talking about?" I argue, feeling equal parts angry and confused. "Did I *look* like I was being forced?"

"No," he says bitterly. "You definitely appeared to be enjoying it."

He starts to walk away, and I clench my fists, enraged, no longer thinking. Seeking, like a child, to hurt him in any way I can. "Your mom would be so proud, Nate!" I call after his retreating back. "You've turned into a stupid townie just like all the whores you bring home."

I regret it immediately. I know, before the words are out of my mouth, that I've made a mistake, gone too far. His body stiffens before he's even come to a halt. And then he turns and strides back toward me so quickly that I gasp, so quickly it seems he might not stop before he walks right into me.

The air swirls against his size and speed as he pushes me

against the side of the house, his chest bearing down, pressing against me so that I am trapped. "You know what I remember, Maura?" he asks. His mouth hovers an inch from my own, and I try to stay angry but the proximity is maddening. I can't take my eyes off his lips. "I remember the way you begged for it the last time we were together. God, you begged. So if you begged for it from a stupid townie, what does that make you?"

I gasp, feeling him open up the wound that never really healed right, that feels as raw as it did years ago. "I never begged you," I snarl.

"Oh? What would you call it? 'Oh, God, Nate, please, please…' " he mimics me.

There is the high, thin sound of a hand across a face, and I register the sound before I realize it is my hand, his face. He grabs my wrist in mid-air, grabs the other as it begins to rise, and pins both to the wall behind me. And then his mouth is on mine, angry and demanding, as punitive as it is needy. His whole body is pressing against me, and I am responding. I am so angry, I so badly want to hurt him back for what he said tonight and for all the things he did but I can't because I am drowning in my need for him, gasping for air as I kiss him back. He pushes into me as if we can meld together, and I arch against him. He's hard. I can feel it through my dress, through his jeans, and all I want in the entire world is for him to lift my dress up and slide inside of me.

He pushes off of me as suddenly as he started. Air rushes into the space he's just left vacant. "Still want to claim you never begged?" he asks, turning to leave. I'm numb now. He's walking away. It was just a game, just like last time, and I fell for it again.

My arms and legs are shaking so badly that it's hard to walk to the back door, hard to steady my hand enough to find the key, but I will myself to do it, and when I finally get inside I collapse on the kitchen floor in the darkness and cry. I feel completely violated. Not because of what he did, but because he did it without really wanting me at all. And I can't say the same.

CHAPTER 23

I sleep fitfully, and wake at daybreak. It's low tide and the water is calm, perfect for swimming. I take off for the sandbar, and I swim until my pain and my thoughts of him lose their distinctiveness and begin to blur and dull.

I've almost regained my equilibrium by the time I get to Peter's office. His eyes light up the moment I mention Stephen Mayhew's name. I tell him what Stephen said, that if the beach is ruled public property, they'll insist the beach road is private.

He rolls his eyes. "That's a ridiculous argument. The state took that land away from them and built the road nearly a century ago."

"And the other thing," I add, "is that they plan to tear up the public walkways once they're rebuilt. I got the impression they'd do it just like they did last time – all at once."

"Now *that* is good information," he grins, slapping his hand on the desk. "If we could catch them at it, it might be enough to end this nonsense – it would certainly make some very wealthy people look very, very bad."

My smile is slight. Because that's kind of what I'm afraid of.

* *

I spend the entire week consumed by equal parts arousal and humiliation when I think of Nate, and I hate myself for the part that is aroused. I go to Oak on Monday. He's playing pool, leaning over some girl while he makes his shot. It's so overtly sexual that I feel sick to my stomach. He glances over at me as they walk out, and for once he looks torn rather than angry.

I'm beginning to think that I need to leave — not just the bar, tonight, but Paradise Cove entirely. My apartment is available in August, and I can always fly back to Charlotte for Elise's wedding. It will hurt my grandmother, and Ethan, but I'm not sure how much more of this I can stand.

* *

Ethan calls on Wednesday to tell me he has to go to Houston for work and won't be able to make it down for the weekend. I didn't realize, until now, how much I appreciated having him here as a buffer, an extra layer to stand between me and Nate. I could really use that extra layer right now, too.

"Why don't you come with me?" he suggests.

My heart leaps at the idea, for about two seconds. "Aren't you going to be at a conference all day?"

"Well, yes, but I'll be free at night. Once the dinner thing is over."

I laugh without much humor. "So basically I'd see you from 10 p.m. to 11 p.m. on Friday night, and then the flight home."

"I can see where that's not the greatest deal for you, but I'd make that one hour the best hour of your life."

"Really?" I laugh.

"Okay, maybe the best hour of your month."

So for the first time, I'm at Oak on a Friday without Ethan. For once, when Nate arrives, he doesn't have a girl clinging to him like a damp shirt. He walks to a pool table, and I hate what I notice. I hate that I notice his ass in his jeans, the way his tricep moves as he draws his arm back. The way he scrubs at the back of his neck when he's deciding on a shot. Someone who's treated me the way he has doesn't deserve my attention, and yet I can't seem to stop giving it to him. I remain so much more conscious of him than the conversation around me that I become the joke of the night.

"Poor baby," teases Kendall. "You just fall apart without your man, don't you?" This is probably the least raunchy of the comments — the bulk of them implying that I require sex in order to function outside of my home.

I let them think it. I certainly can't tell them that it's the energy I expend tracking Nate that is draining me.

"I'm calling it a night," I finally say.

Graham rises. "I'll take you home."

I am so tired of having this conversation with him, a conversation I never seem to win. I face him with resignation. "Thanks, but I brought my bike."

"You shouldn't be biking this late," he argues, gathering his stuff.

"Graham, there hasn't been a crime in Paradise Cove since… I don't know. Has there ever been a crime here? I'm fine."

"Absolutely not," he says. "Leave your bike and I'll bring you back to get it tomorrow."

"I'll take her," says the voice behind me. The voice that belongs to Nate and for once isn't laden with scorn. "Her bike will fit in my truck."

Graham looks at him sourly. "Come on Maura," he says, as if Nate is so beneath contempt we don't even need to acknowledge him – the same way he and my brother treated Nate when we were kids. And it infuriates me. I probably would have refused Nate on my own, but now I can't. In spite of everything he's done, for some inexplicable reason, I'm still worried about his feelings.

"It's okay, Graham," I say. "Nate lives right there."

I watch Graham struggle to craft a new argument, before finally giving up. "Fine," he says tersely.

I'm walking beside Nate Sullivan for the first time in so many years. It's unreal in a way, and yet nothing could feel more natural.

I think back to the last time we did something like this. That if someone had told me then that it would be five years before I'd walk beside him again I'd never have believed it.

There are a hundred sounds – distant laughter from the bar, the shuffle of our feet over uneven ground, the layered song of crickets in every direction, the wheels of my bike rolling beside me – but we remain silent. He takes the bike from me and puts it in his truck without saying a word.

I wonder if we'll continue like this, in absolute silence. In a way I hope we do. I'll pretend I'm 16 again, and that I still have everything I want.

We climb in, but instead of starting the truck he grabs the steering wheel, as if bracing himself.

"I'm sorry," he says quietly, staring straight ahead of him, not meeting my eye. "Last week. What I did. I'm sorry."

I don't know what I was expecting, but it wasn't this. After weeks of hostility, this apology sits awkwardly, out of place and also woefully insufficient. How can he apologize for something so minor, but not at all for what he did to me five years ago? I don't respond for a moment, as my head swims with the need to know *everything*, to ask him questions I probably don't want the answers to. How could he have chosen the girl at school instead of me? What did she have that I didn't? Did he ever really love me in the first place, or was the whole thing fake?

And did he ever regret it?

I hate that it matters now, but it does. Far too much. I know the wrong answers are going to make me wish desperately that I hadn't asked.

My voice sounds small and childish to my ears when I finally reply. "Why did you do it?" I ask. I really mean so much more, but I can't bring myself to ask, not yet.

"I don't know." He pauses, and his face clouds over. "I didn't think... I didn't think it was going to be like this."

"Like what?" I ask.

"I thought I would hate you. I thought I wouldn't see you the way I used to," he says grimly, still looking out into the darkness. "But seeing you here... it's hard. In spite of everything you did, it's hard."

Surprise morphs into anger before I even have time to register it. "What *I* did?" I seethe. "What exactly did *I* do, Nate?

He closes his eyes and draws his jaw up tight. There is rage in the movement. It rolls off him while he remains frozen. When he finally speaks, his voice is lethal. "Are you really going to pretend you don't know what I'm talking about?"

"I have no idea what you could be talking about," I hiss. "Because I've never done *anything* as awful as what you did to me." My voice teeters on the edge between tears and fury. I don't want to cry over this now, not in front of him, but I don't think I can help it. I feel my throat closing in. "To let me believe all those things and just leave..." I begin, but I can't continue.

His response is explosive. "I didn't leave you! You told your grandmother I *raped* you, Maura!" he shouts, slamming his hand against the steering wheel. "Why the fuck are you acting like this is news to you? I would have done *anything* for you. Anything. I loved you so much, Maura, and you fucking stabbed me in the back."

His words wash over me as if they are made of something I cannot absorb. "I told my grandmother *what*?" I ask incredulously.

He continues as if I haven't spoken. "Do you really not understand how that destroyed me? I trusted you more than anyone alive," he says, his eyes alight with rage – a storm at its worst point. "I had to leave home. I only saw my mom once before she died. *Once*. I lost my scholarship. All because of you. Can you not even be honest about it now?"

"I don't have any idea what you're talking about!" I cry. "I never told my grandmother that."

"Fine. Let's play it your way," he snarls. "Why don't you tell me what you *did* tell her the night we slept together?"

I gasp. "Why would I *ever* tell my grandmother *anything?* You know what she's like. I'd *still* be locked upstairs if I'd told her that." The idea is so preposterous that an unhappy laugh bubbles out of me as I speak.

This entire conversation is illogical, as if we are discussing two entirely unrelated events. His conviction almost makes me doubt myself, but I *know* none of this happened. I see the first whisper of doubt intrude on his rage.

"So how exactly did she know that we'd slept together?" he challenges me. "You expect me to believe it was a lucky guess?"

"She didn't know!" I shout. "She still doesn't know. This has got to be some kind of mistake."

"Maura, I was there when your grandmother came to the house," he says. "And believe me, she knew."

I shake my head, as if to dislodge the barrier that is blocking me from comprehending this. "Why would I tell anyone you raped me?" I ask in disbelief. "We'd been together for years."

"So are you really telling me you didn't say anything to her or anyone else?" he asks warily.

"Of course I didn't!" I cry. "You knew me better than anyone, Nate. How could you have believed that?"

He still doesn't meet my eye as he replies, speaking slowly, as if weighing each fact as it leaves his mouth, his anger replaced by uncertainty. "Because she knew. You were so angry at me that night…and she knew. It *had* to have come from you."

I shake my head, blinded by tears and feeling as if there's some major piece of this that's eluding us both. "Someone must have seen us," I say. "But why didn't you even check? If you thought I'd done it why didn't you at least confront me?"

"Because your grandmother said I had to leave immediately. That you'd agreed not to press charges as long as you never saw or heard from me again, but if I made any attempt to contact you the deal was off."

"You could have gone to the police though," I argue. "You

had to have known I wouldn't have a shred of proof that it had happened."

He laughs unhappily. "My word against a Pierce? I'd have gotten the death penalty for even suggesting it."

"This all makes no sense. It's *completely* different from what you said in your letter."

He looks at me blankly. "What letter?"

"The one you sent back with your mom," I reply in astonishment. How can he not remember writing something that could so devastate another person?

"I never sent you a letter," he says.

"I still have it!" I argue. I take a deep breath, remembering, willing myself not to cry as I retell it, because it still hurts as badly as anything I've ever experienced. "You said you were going back to your girlfriend and that you only cared about me as a 'friend'."

He looks stunned, as if he's been punched and isn't quite sure whether or not he's going to fall. "Maura," he breathes, "I never said that. I never wrote you anything. I wasn't *allowed* to write you anything. And *you* were my girlfriend – my only girlfriend."

"Then why didn't you ever call me back?" I cry. "I called and texted you so many times, an embarrassing number of times, and you never replied. In fact, that's what you said in your letter. That I should stop embarrassing myself."

"There. Was. No. Letter," he repeats. "And your grandmother took my phone, which I never understood until right now."

"I even tried to call your apartment and some girl answered and… " my voice is raspy, broken at the end. "I wanted to die. That whole summer, I just wanted not to exist anymore."

He looks so stunned, and so guilty, that I wish I'd said nothing. He pinches the bridge of his nose and closes his eyes. "Jesus," he says, his voice rough, turning toward me almost desperately. "You've known me since I was two, Maura. Did you really think I could have lied to you or left you like that? You really thought I could have cheated?"

My words are so quiet they are barely audible. "I didn't know what I was doing. It made sense to me that I'd been bad at it. You'd slept with those other girls and… "

"Until we fought, it was the best night of my life."

It was mine too. It's still the best night of my life, but I don't tell him that. I sit back in the seat, curled up like a little girl with my face pressed to wet knees, the tears warm against my skin. I only want to undo everything that happened — I want to find the loophole that will take us back, let us relive the past five years and make all these things right — but there is none.

"I still don't understand," I finally say. "Even if someone saw us, why didn't my grandmother just ask me? If she really thought I was raped, don't you think she would have talked to me about it?"

"Maura," he says gently. "She made it up. She must have found out we slept together and decided to get me out of the way."

I shake my head adamantly. "No. She'd never do something like that."

He looks at me with sympathy. "I think she would."

"She's strict, not evil," I argue.

"Then who left the note?" he asks. "Why did she take my phone and make the school change my email address?"

I have no answer. He's right. I look back and see only now how oddly she acted, how smoothly she told me about Nate leaving, with more detail than she would have been privy to. The story she concocted so I wouldn't ask Mary why he'd left. How I asked her if there was a letter and miraculously, one is produced the next day.

I struggle to reconcile the two versions of the person I call my grandmother – the loving but stern matriarch I've known all my life, and the person who could have been so cruel, so deceitful. "This can't be right," I say. "I need to talk to her."

If he's right, then she's taken something from me that I will never, ever get back. Nate was it. He was my best friend, he was the person I would have stayed with forever. And that's gone now.

Neither of us are the people we were then. Five years ago, he was sweet and earnest and loyal and ambitious, like me in every way that mattered. Now he's angry and reckless, and as far as I can tell his only goal is to sleep with as many women as possible. Somehow, in five years, everything I loved about him has evaporated, and our lives and dreams are so far apart it almost feels like we are in different countries.

And there's Ethan now, though it comes to me almost as an afterthought. It might not be the most exciting relationship I've ever been in, but you only get to be a 17-year-old in love for the first time once. If I made Nate my standard for all future relationships I'd be single for the rest of my life.

We ride home in silence. I can't stop myself from sneaking glances at him, looking into his profile for the boy I knew. Can I still find him there, even a little bit? I look at his mouth and think of the way he kissed me last weekend, the exquisite torture of being pressed against him, the way I responded.

He walks me to the back door, and I flush, because I'm still thinking about it. I want to relive that kiss. Just once more. We have both changed, but in this moment that doesn't matter to me at all. I want to step back toward him, into him, and forget that five years have passed.

He looks in my eyes, his own gray and cloudy and inscrutable, hesitating, as if he wants to say something. "I'm sorry it turned out this way," he finally tells me, and he walks away.

CHAPTER 24

At night all of the small, terrible pieces of this story entwine in ways that don't make sense. I dream that I'm watching Mary fall to the kitchen floor while I talk on the phone, but I do nothing; I dream that my grandmother has caught Nate and I together in her room and she is telling us both we can never come back. And the worst – that I'm still 17 and I see him leaving, but when I try to shout for him no sound will leave my throat.

It's a relief to wake up from it. There's no sign of my grandmother when I go downstairs. That may be for the best. I don't think I can have a rational conversation right now.

I go swim, trying to clear my head, burn off the fog that lies there. I can't stop reconstructing the past, wanting to create a different outcome as if it's a puzzle whose pieces I can shift to create a prettier picture. I want to go back in time and beg him to shout for me, throw gravel at my window, insist I come downstairs and set things right. I ask myself, again and again, why my grandmother never asked me about it, how she could have jumped to the ridiculous conclusion that she did, how she could have allowed me to suffer like that.

When I finally hear the creaking of her floorboards, I go upstairs. It's not a conversation I really want to have in front of Rebecca and Stacy.

"Yes?" she snaps when I knock, already annoyed.

I open the door. "I need to talk to you," I say.

She sighs her irritation. "Can't it wait? I was just about to bathe."

"No it can't," I say, feeling my temper flare. "I talked to Nate last night."

Her mouth draws together. It's a subtle movement, but it tells me that she's disturbed. I wanted to be wrong about this, to discover that this was all some vast misunderstanding, but with that small change to her face I begin to lose hope. "Yes?" she asks, placid again.

"Did you accuse him of raping me?" I ask, my voice growing angrier, more appalled, with each word.

"I was trying to protect you," she says coolly, without remorse. Her chin raises, just a hair, in defiance. "You were a little girl with a crush, and he took advantage."

"Where are you getting your information, Grandma?" I cry. "Because I was 17, which isn't so little, and let me assure you, I didn't do anything I didn't want to do!"

"It doesn't matter where I got my information."

"Then tell me, did your source tell you I was 'forced' or did you just decide that on your own?" I spit out, wondering how it's possible that she feels no guilt about this.

"It doesn't matter. You were too young to be making those kind of decisions for yourself, and he was an older boy who used your crush to his advantage."

"What about the note?" I hiss. "Were you behind that too?" Her lips close tightly, as if holding a pin right in their center, telling me all I need to know.

I remember my grandparents together when I was little, how she was always more formal, less approachable. But I'd never doubted that underneath her crisp surface there lied good things. Now I can only stare at her, knowing that I will never see her that way again.

"I guess you've answered my question," I say, walking out and slamming the door behind me.

I go to the carriage house. In the years since I was last here, the yard has gone wild. Mary's rose bushes still bloom profusely, but they're lost in a jungle of weeds and plants that have managed to flourish without care. I knock on his door, and watch so many things cross his face – surprise, hope, grief, resignation. They pass so quickly I'm not certain any of them were there at all. I wonder, with a hopefulness I shouldn't have, if he sometimes looks at me and forgets the years have elapsed. If he looks at me and just for a single second, wants me again.

He steps aside to let me by and gestures to the kitchen. "Do you want some coffee?"

"No thank you," I murmur. He hasn't changed anything here. I sit at the kitchen table and trace the pale green boxes laid out on the orange vinyl tablecloth, the same one that was here when I was a little girl. Nate and I played board games here when it rained, and sometimes Mary rolled out dough for us and let us make Christmas cookies in mid-summer.

He sits across from me, and I slide him the battered note that I've kept all this time.

He opens it and I watch his face fall as he reads. He looks at me in horror when he finishes. "Maura, I never… "

"I know," I tell him. I choke on the next words I say, feeling all of my sadness welling up in my throat. "It was all my grand-mother. She knew you didn't force me. She said I was a little girl with a crush and you took advantage."

His eyes glitter with anger. He looks over at my grandmother's house and draws in a breath. "It wasn't even that we slept together," he says, pressing his fingers to his temples. "It's just that I wasn't good enough."

I shake my head and begin to argue, but he cuts me off. "Tell me she would have done the same thing if someone caught you with Ethan instead of me," he says.

My stomach lurches, because he's right. I rest my face in my hands to breathe through it. My grandmother did a terrible thing

– to him, to me, to Mary – and it wasn't even out of misguided concern, but something far uglier, and less forgivable.

"Are you all right?" he asks, and when I look up there's concern in his eyes. It's the Nate I knew, as if he never left.

"I'm so sorry," I whisper, and then I begin crying in earnest, covering my face again.

"Don't," he says helplessly from across the table. "Don't apologize for her."

"Who's going to if I don't?" I ask, taking a deep breath and willing myself not to fall apart in front of him. The last thing he should have to do right now is console me. "She's not even sorry."

"Her being sorry wouldn't change anything anyway."

"She owes you, Nate. I don't know what, but *something*. She can't just get away with it."

His face is grim, and he looks down at the table. "That's not how the world works, Maura. People like your family and Ethan's, they get away with whatever they want."

"That's not true," I argue, a little surprised that Nate, of all people, seems so defeated.

"And they take whatever they want, even when it doesn't belong to them," he adds, looking at me with sudden despair. "And the rest of us have to sit back and watch them take it."

His eyes hold mine. The way he is looking at me – desire and need and grief — makes me feel boneless. I can't look away, and the very air between us is suddenly strung so tight that it hurts. *He sleeps with everyone*, I remind myself. *Don't pretend this makes you special.*

I will myself to push away from the table, to stand. I can't sit three feet from him in an empty house when he looks at me like that. "I should go."

He walks me to the door. I have no reason to be here anymore, but I wish I did. It feels as if no time has passed at all.

I step back into the blinding sunlight, and he makes no move to stop me.

"See you around," he says quietly, and I hear the door shut behind me before I'm halfway down the path.

* *

With a bouquet gripped in my left hand, I bike to the far end of the island, where my grandfather and my great-grandparents are buried. Ethan's too. I pass those graves and keep walking, until I find one of the newer ones, the marble unblemished and shiny. I sink to my knees and place the bouquet in front of it, tears streaking down my face before I'm even fully to the ground. I look at her year of birth and her year of death. She was only 38 when she died. She always seemed so much older than us, but she was only 38.

"I didn't do it Mary," I whisper hoarsely. "I'm so sorry. I didn't do it. I hope you can hear this. I hope you know I would never do that to him."

And then I cry, openly, for the way her life ended, and my life too, and for all the ways my family is responsible for both.

CHAPTER 25

I collapse on the sand the next day after a long swim, and fall into a deep sleep, worn down by all the drama and two nights straight of terrible dreams. When I wake the sun is going down and the beach is clearing.

Nate is sitting next to me, fully clothed.

"You snore," he says.

"I do not," I argue, groggily pushing up onto my elbows. I look at the heavy boots kicked off in the sand. "Were you at work?"

"Yep, carpentry. It's been pretty steady, so that's good."

My stomach drops. Nate wanted to be an architect his entire life. Even that fort we built as kids was a work of art, its peaked roof the result of many hours of careful placement. I still remember that almost adult look he'd get on his face as we built it, the way he'd tear something down and reconstruct it time and again in order to make it perfect. He would have loved being an architect, was born for it, and it's entirely possible that it didn't happen because of me.

"What happened to your scholarship?" I ask tentatively.

He shrugs. "I blamed you the other night, but it was my own fault. I went back to school and did a lot of things I shouldn't have. I lost my scholarship, and I deserved to lose it."

"The Mayhews wouldn't... ?" I begin, hesitating. It would have been so easy for them to help him. He could have gone to them. He could have shamed them into it if nothing else.

"No," he says angrily. "Do you really think I'd take a dime of their money?"

"I'm sorry," I reply. I can't stop wanting to fix this for him. "You could get loans," I venture.

He sighs. "Maura, it's over. I'm 24. I'm not going back. You look down on me for it. In your world it's unthinkable not to go to college, but I make a decent living and I don't mind the work. That's more than most people can hope for."

"I don't look down on you," I murmur.

"Yes you do. Or have you forgotten calling me a stupid townie last week?"

I exhale, ashamed once again. "I was just mad. I wanted to hurt you and it was all I could come up with."

Our eyes meet and his darken. Suddenly I can think of nothing but his response to my words, the way he kissed me, his hands in my hair, his body pressing hard against mine. How, in that moment, I would have done anything for him. I know the look of desire on Nate's face, I've seen it a thousand times before.

I'm seeing it now.

I scramble to think of something else. "I don't understand why you'd ever want to come back here after what my grandmother did."

"Well I own the carriage house, so it was kind of the logical choice," he says.

I gape. "You *own* the carriage house? How is that possible? It's on our land."

"Your grandfather bequeathed it to my mom in his will. When she died, it went to me."

"But why would he do that?" I ask. "I mean, that house, the land — it's got to be worth a fortune. How did I not know this?"

"I didn't know either, until after my mother died," he says, and then he pauses. "Maura, I don't want to offend you, but I think it happened because your grandfather had a pretty good idea of who he was married to."

"What do you mean?"

"If your grandmother's the kind of person who would have lied about you being raped, then she's probably the kind of person who would turn my mother out with nothing if it suited her."

In light of what I've learned about her in the past day, I can't even argue with him. The picture of my family keeps shifting, and each movement makes it uglier. I hate the person I see in my grandmother, and I hate that my grandfather may have known it all along.

"Why not just sell it?" I ask. He could do anything with the kind of money he'd get out of that land. "I'd think you would never want to see my family again after what happened."

He's slow to reply. "Well, first of all, I can't sell the house," he says. "The way it was written into the will, the carriage house can only be sold if the main house is sold as well. I guess I could have rented it out, but I just... " he glances at me and stops himself. "It's complicated."

I nod, and let it drop, unsure how to proceed. I don't know how to be with a Nate who is neither my enemy nor my friend. Every question I ask him seems to imply that he's done something wrong – by dropping out of college, by staying here – so I just stop asking.

"Come on," he says, pulling me to my feet. "Let's see if you still know how to bodysurf."

I laugh. "You're not really dressed for it."

He takes a quick, slightly heated glance at my bikini. "Neither are you, but I bet you'll still do it."

He pulls his shirt off and it takes me an extra breath to regain my ground. God, he's beautiful. I already understood why girls threw themselves at him, but seeing it firsthand is another matter entirely. There is nothing about his body that isn't defined, skin pulled taut over hard muscle, the way his broad shoulders taper to narrow hips. I force myself to look away as we walk into the water.

We push out into the surf, diving under the small waves to

get to the bigger ones farther out. It's hard not to stare at him – as he dives, as he stands and shakes the water out of his face. Everything about him, every movement, makes me feel more vulnerable. I focus on the waves with an intensity they couldn't possibly warrant.

But just as I did when I was a lovesick 14-year-old, as we talk I can almost forget about the response he provokes in me. Each thing I learn, each thing I tell him, eases the strain away from the situation until we become something like our old selves with each other.

He asks why I gave up studying architecture, what kind of law I want to practice, why I chose Michigan, if I've got my class schedule already. Ethan has never asked me a single one of these questions, and the realization doesn't surprise me much. Sometimes it feels like he doesn't even see me as an individual, but some kind of placeholder for the things he wants, with all of my interests and quirks an unfortunate handicap he's forced to overlook.

I like hearing Nate talk about his company, seeing all the ways that the little boy who loved to build things got his wish. And it makes me sad too, because the fact that he should have been an architect couldn't be clearer as he discusses the parts of his work he loves the most.

The last sliver of sunlight slips away and we watch as the sky comes alive with faint stars that will soon grow bright.

"It's getting dark," he teases. "Remember how you used to worry about sharks?"

"Yeah, until you told me they don't feed at night."

He grins sheepishly. "I vaguely remember telling you that."

"Why do you have such a weird look on your face, then?" I ask suspiciously.

"Because it was a complete fucking lie," he laughs. "They totally feed at night. Why would you believe an eight-year-old anyway?"

I feel a sudden clench of fear in my stomach, and look down as if I might find fins circling as we speak.

"Time to get out," I say briskly, and begin wading to shore. I hear a splash behind me, and before I can even turn to find him something is grabbing my ankle, pulling me under. Teeth sink into my skin lightly before they let me go. I know it's him but that doesn't entirely quell my panic.

I come up gasping for breath, and he is laughing his ass off. He grins. "I couldn't resist."

My glare reluctantly gives way to a smile. "You never could," I say. The words, so innocent when they were in my head, do not sound innocent when they come out. Our eyes meet and there's a moment, friction, a muscle low in my abdomen tightening as I watch something shift across his face. We both turn away quickly.

* *

It's odd that so much has happened, and yet I can't really tell Ethan any of it – he's not going to want to hear how I had sex with his cousin on the beach, and that our resulting breakup was just a terrible mistake. I return his call reluctantly after my swim with Nate. He sounds tense, and my own silence can't help.

"I've got to ask you something," he says.

"Okay." Trepidation stretches the word out an extra beat.

"Graham called today." He waits, as if this should tell me everything I need to know. When I remain silent he continues. "He said you went home with Nate on Saturday night."

My laugh is half-humor and half-exasperation. "No, I didn't 'go home' with Nate in that sense. He just gave me a ride back. I can't believe Graham freaking called you about it."

He is quiet for a minute. "I thought you hated Nate."

I sigh. I so don't want to tell him this story and I get the feeling he's going to force the issue. "We had a misunderstanding, and it's resolved."

"So you're what – friends with him now?" he snarls. It's the first time I've ever heard him openly hostile.

"No. Maybe. I don't know." I stutter. "Probably not. But we don't hate each other. I'd like to be his friend again."

"Well I'm not comfortable with that, Maura," he says.

"Ethan, you're being ridiculous. I have guy friends. I see Teddy and Robert and Graham almost every night."

"The difference is that they aren't trying to sleep with you."

"Neither is Nate!" I argue, astonished that he's so jealous of someone he hasn't seen me friendly with in years.

"Bullshit," Ethan snaps. "He does nothing but stare at you when we're out. We get on the dance floor and he's immediately right there next to us. And he's sleeping with the one girl he could find who looks anything like you."

"He's sleeping with half the girls in town, so odds are one of them was going to look a little like me at some point."

"And you want to be friends with someone like that?"

"Yes, because the key word is 'friends', Ethan. I don't want to date someone like that. I don't want to date someone like Graham either. That's why I can be friends with him."

"You weren't always friends," he mutters.

"What's that supposed to mean?"

"I know you slept with him," he hisses.

"And how exactly would you know that?" I snap.

He hesitates before answering. "You don't date someone as long as you did and not sleep with them."

I sigh. "Do you really want to start exchanging our sexual histories? Because I'm sure yours is a lot more interesting and varied than mine."

"The difference is I'm not 'friends' with any of them," he says acidly.

"You slept with Heather *and* Kendall *and* Maura Lite. I'm not sitting around crying about it. And speaking of Heather, she's picking me up in 45 minutes so I've got to go."

I hang up, fuming, and jump in the shower. I put on a semi-sheer cotton sundress that ends just below my ass, solely because my grandmother will hate how revealing it is. Normally even I hate how revealing it is.

"Where are you going?" she demands when I come downstairs.

I stop in place with a look that dares her to continue this conversation. "Out," I say, and then I leave without another word. I've spent my entire life slightly cowed by her, wanting to do things just right, never sure when I'd violate one of her lofty standards of behavior. The one good thing to come out of what happened between me and Nate is that I no longer give a damn what she thinks.

Graham takes one look at my tense face when Heather and I walk into the bar and gets me a gin & tonic.

"Thanks," I say, unsmiling. "This will be refreshing while you explain why you called my boyfriend and told him I went home with someone else."

"Well," he equivocates. "You did go home with someone else."

"There is a world of difference between getting a ride with someone and going home with someone and you know it," I hiss.

His face grows contrite. "I'm sorry, Maura. I was just worried. Ethan really likes you, and you know, you and Nate... have a history."

I sigh. "You don't need to worry about me and Nate, and neither does Ethan. Okay?"

"Okay," he agrees.

Graham is annoyingly attentive for the rest of the night, to the extent that I wish I hadn't chastised him in the first place. The second my glass is empty he's got another drink in my hand. Things grow pleasantly hazy. Graham pulls me to my feet to dance, and at last my anger at him and my grandmother floats away. When the song ends, Graham pulls me in for a hug.

I laugh when he doesn't let go. "Jesus, Graham," I finally say, shoving him off of me. "Even my parents don't hug me that long."

Of course, my parents don't really hug me at all, but that's sort of irrelevant. When I push back I see Nate. He's sitting at the bar, watching us, and he's scowling.

Guilt rolls over me. For all of my tears and apologies yesterday, what my grandmother did wounded him far more than me, and here's the proof: I'm out tonight laughing and dancing with our old friends, and he's sitting at the bar alone, watching. Here after a week at work while all the rest of us, tan and indolent, prepare for another day spent wallowing in money we didn't earn.

I walk over to him. "Hey," I say hesitantly.

"Hey yourself."

"Do you want to sit with us?"

He shakes his head and looks over at the table, where several of my friends are watching, Graham in particular. "I don't think I'd be welcome."

"Of course you would," I breathe. "They're your friends too."

He shakes his head again. "That's okay. I'm meeting someone anyway." I wonder if it's a girl. Of course it's a girl. My stomach knots, and I'm embarrassed I came over here at all.

"Do me a favor, Maura," he says, looking back at our table. "Watch out for Graham."

"For Graham?" I laugh. "He just drinks too much. He doesn't mean any harm."

"I think you've spent so much of your life around him that you can't see how he's changed," Nate says. "I don't trust him."

"That's silly," I smile. "It's because I've spent so much of my life around him that I know I *can* trust him."

Nate prepares to disagree just as Graham walks over and puts his hands around my waist. He steers me back toward the table. "Go sit, Maura. I'll get the drinks." He means well. It makes his big-brother-like condescension difficult to object to.

I sit and pretend to rejoin the conversation. What I actually do is watch Nate with scientific observation as he waits for his "friend." When she arrives, my gin and tonics threaten to come back up. She's blonde and cute – the kind of girl he might actually date, not just sleep with. He kisses her cheek and pulls out her stool, glancing back at me as he does it. I quickly look away.

I guess I should be happy for him. I've found someone, and maybe he's found someone. He deserves a little peace, a little happiness. *Just not with her*, I think. Let him wait to fall in love until I've left for school, until I'm far enough away that I don't ever have to come back and see it firsthand.

I try not to watch the way she rests her hand on his thigh. The way he grins at her knowingly, the way he once grinned at me. I try to listen to my friends as they drunkenly argue about the shittiness of one college football team versus another.

But at a certain point, nothing can be achieved by feigning happiness. After about 30 minutes, I'm at that point. I stand to leave, and Graham stands too. "I'll walk you," he says.

"You don't need to," I sigh.

"Of course I do," he insists.

I walk quickly, trying to march off some of my irritation at Nate, as misplaced as it is. The old Nate, the one of my youth, had so much sweetness about him. His devotion, his focus, was fierce and unrelenting. And it was mine. I need those things to stay gone. I can't afford to think about what it would be like if they were mine again. And I can't stand to think they might be someone else's.

"God damn, you walk fast Maura!" laughs Graham. "Where's the fire?"

"I'm just tired," I apologize, without slowing my pace. "It's been a long day."

"Long day laying around on the beach?" he teases.

"You're one to talk. Shouldn't you be working by now?" I hadn't given it much thought, but Graham doesn't seem to be moving on with his life the way his friends have. Ethan has his MBA and a good job and he's talking about buying a house. Jordan and Sammy are married and have kids.

"I'm just taking some time off," he says vaguely.

We get to my grandmother's house, and I sense his hesitation. He seems to waver, stepping closer to me instead of heading back down the street. Nate's warning echoes in some distant part of my brain and I move away quickly, walking into the yard. I wave airily over my shoulder. "Thanks Graham!" I call, relieved to see that he isn't following me.

He sounds a little disgruntled as he says good night.

I'm tired, but not tired enough to sleep. I lay in bed listening, listening, listening. The sound of Nate's truck never comes.

CHAPTER 26

I'm just returning from a run the next morning when he pulls in. I draw in a deep breath, trying not to hate him for doing exactly what any other 24-year-old male would probably do if he could score the way Nate does.

"Want to swim?" he asks with his lopsided smile. He's in an unusually good mood, at least compared to mine, and it only pisses me off more. I have a pretty solid idea about the source of his good mood.

"You're still in last night's clothes," I say sourly. I clearly didn't try hard enough to dampen my irritation, and that this pleases him only irritates me further.

"Come on," he says. "You know there's nothing you like to do more after you run, and besides, it'll cheer you up."

"I'm surprised you have the energy after your *long night*," I say pointedly, kicking myself as the words leave my mouth. I sound bitter, jealous even.

His smile widens. "Five minutes. Loser buys breakfast after."

I groan, but even as I do so my heart is picking up its pace. He knows I can't turn down a challenge. I race upstairs without a word to anyone, not that I'd speak to my grandmother anyway, and am back down in less than four minutes. He's already there, as I knew he would be, his smile unabashed. I feel young again, as if things never changed. I feel alive again too, bursting, excited. It's been so long since I felt like this I'd almost forgotten it was possible.

By unspoken agreement we swim out to the sandbar. The waves that break here are much larger, and it used to be that if you caught a good one it would carry you all the way back to the shore. I'm still tired from my run, not sure how many return swims I have in me, so instead we go further into the waves and tread water.

"So what happens with Ethan when you leave in August?" he asks.

"What do you mean?" I ask, a tad defensively. I'm growing tired of the assumption that I should change my plans for a guy I've only dated for four months.

"Is he going with you?"

"No, of course not," I reply too quickly. "His job is in Charlotte."

"But you guys seem pretty serious."

I shrug. "I don't know. You know how it is here. We all know each other too well. Assumptions are made."

He's grown oddly still in the water. "It's pretty easy to clear up those assumptions if you want to."

He doesn't understand. I can't explain that it's comforting to have Ethan here, while I'm so consumed with wanting things I can't have. That I like Ethan a lot, and I have five years of dating behind me to support the fact that what I feel for Ethan is probably all I'm capable of feeling anymore.

"I don't know," I repeat. "I'm leaving in less than two months. That should take care of things all on its own." He looks dubious, and I don't blame him. I'm a little doubtful myself.

* *

We go to the diner my grandfather always took us to, where they used to make Nate's eggs and bacon into a smiley face, and my pancakes into Mickey Mouse.

"I'm not going to miss a lot about the south, but I'll miss this," I ruminate, looking around. Unlike other areas of Paradise Cove, I have only good memories associated with this place.

"You make it sound like you're never coming back," he says quietly, watching me. I find the color of his eyes fascinating. I always have. They soften his face, remind me of the sweet boy I knew. It's hard not to just stare sometimes.

I focus on the mug in my hands. "I'm not sure I plan to," I tell him. "There are a lot of things here I'd prefer to avoid."

"Like what?"

I take a sip of my coffee. "Just all the expectations. My mom's already disappointed in me for not being engaged. If I stay here I'll end up married and pregnant, and the next thing I know I'll be just like her, hanging out at the club all day, playing tennis and planning auctions."

He watches me. "Which of those things don't you want?"

"I don't know if I want any of them," I say. "Name one happy marriage."

He rests his head against the back of the booth, observing me like he's just uncovered something. "I've seen people happily married."

I sigh. "I wish I could say the same, but I can't. I don't want to be my parents, or my grandparents. And I definitely don't want to be Jordan and Mia."

"But you don't have to be any of them," he says adamantly. "Don't you want to know that there is one person in the world who knows exactly who and what you are and loves you because of it and in spite of it?" he asks. "Don't you want to know that there's someone who will fix you when you're broken?"

This is the sweet side of him, the earnest side. I'm touched by it, and I don't want to be. "Beautifully spoken by the guy who goes home with a different girl every single night," I tease.

"Maybe I'm just trying to deal with the fact that I can't have the one I want." For just a moment his face is serious, stricken, and then he washes it away with a crooked grin.

I don't know if this is the emergence of the old, sincere Nate, or the new one – the one who will say or do anything he thinks might get him laid. But I seem to be susceptible to both, and that's not a good thing.

* *

Ethan calls that afternoon. "I'm sorry," he says immediately. "You were right last night, and I was totally out of line."

"It's okay," I reply, perhaps made more amenable by guilt. I spent two hours straight with Nate yesterday, and more than that today.

"So you and Nate are… friends?" he asks hesitantly.

"Yes," I answer firmly, recognizing as he must that my lack of certainty on this topic has disappeared completely. "We're friends."

"And now that you're friends is he going to stop staring at you?" he asks snidely.

I sigh. "Ethan, he never did stare at me, and he can't stop doing what he never did in the first place."

"Whatever," he says. "Even if you're not, I'll be keeping an eye on him."

* *

Two days later Nate is waiting for me again when I return from my run. Thankfully, this time he's not just coming home.

"Swim?" he asks.

I laugh. "Don't you have a job?"

"Really?" he asks, smiling. "*You're* giving *me* crap about not working?"

Each day we seem to stretch out the time a little more. Our swim takes longer, our breakfast takes longer. While we eat, a girl comes over to our booth to talk to Nate, eyeing me curiously. She's cute but not at all Nate's type. Of course, based on what I've seen this summer that doesn't necessarily mean he hasn't slept with her. "I'm Beth," she says, reaching across the table to shake my hand. I'll give her points for being both polite and ballsy if she *did* sleep with him.

"Maura," I say, shaking her hand.

A smile crosses her face. "*The* Maura?" she asks Nate with an eyebrow arched. She looks delighted with this for some reason.

Nate sighs. "Yes," he mutters, shooting her a warning glance. "Beth is a bartender at a place in town I go to sometimes."

"*Sometimes?*" she laughs. "You were there every night of the year until this summer." He shoots her another look, and a secret smile crosses her face as she looks back to me.

"It's so nice to finally meet you, *Maura*," she says with emphasis, grinning at Nate one last time.

She leaves and I look at him, waiting for an explanation.

He says nothing.

"Well?" I ask.

"She's a friend," he mutters, not meeting my eye. "Your name may have come up once or twice."

He looks so embarrassed by the whole thing that I resist the temptation to give him shit about it. I settle for being quietly pleased.

We leave the diner and he takes a meandering route back home, from one end of the island to the next. When we approach the graveyard I feel him hesitating.

"It's okay," I tell him. "Go ahead. I'll wait here."

"Why don't you come with me?" he asks. I pause, because it seems like such a private thing, before I agree.

We walk past the graves. I trail my fingers over my grandfather's, a quick hello to him on my way. Nate stares at it for a moment.

"I miss him," he says simply.

I sigh. "So do I." Especially now. He's the anchor my family needs. Without him, we all seem adrift.

We get to Mary's grave and Nate stares at the flowers there, just beginning to wilt.

"You came here," he says.

I feel ashamed, as if I've been caught at something. "Yes," I reply reluctantly.

"Why?"

"I miss her too, Nate," I almost whisper. "And I wanted to apologize."

"*You* didn't do anything wrong," he says.

"But she didn't know that."

He never looks over at me, but his fingers reach for mine, entwining again as if things never changed. We stand there wordlessly, still holding hands, and when we leave it feels like some of the weight has been lifted. It feels like she really knows now.

* *

That afternoon I head over to Peter's office and begin culling through relevant briefs again. I'm beginning to wonder if this isn't just busy work he's created for me out of pity.

He comes out of his office and sits on my desk. "I have a favor to ask, and it's a little awkward."

I nod warily.

"Work is beginning on the new walkways. The problem is we don't know when, exactly, they'll attempt to destroy them again."

I dread the request I know is coming.

"You're dating Stephen's son," he says. "You may be the only chance we've got of finding out what they have planned. I'm hoping you'll just keep your ears open."

It's a whole new level of duplicity, one that could potentially lead to the arrest of Ethan's father. What Mr. Mayhew's doing is wrong, but I'm not sure it's any more wrong than what I'm about to agree to. "Okay," I tell him reluctantly. "Although I doubt I'll be much help. It's not the kind of thing they're going to discuss in front of me. Couldn't the police just stake it out?"

He shakes his head ruefully. "Police aren't touching this with a ten-foot-pole. Whoever's behind this has deep pockets, and probably has enough power to make sure our chief-of-police is out of a job if need be. They'll try to shove it under the carpet. Probably won't even send out a patrol if we call it in."

"If the police aren't going to help then what's the point in trying to catch them?" I ask.

"They can still help us if we play it right. If an officer on our side just *happens* to be driving by, just *happens* to see it and arrest the guys doing it, and it just *happens* to gets leaked to the press, it'll force the issue."

"This sounds kind of farfetched, Peter," I say. "What are the odds the right cop is going to be driving by just as it happens?"

"Don't worry about that part of it," he assures me. "If you find out when they're doing it, I promise you the right people will get there."

CHAPTER 27

E than calls on Friday afternoon. He doesn't even say hello. "Are you wearing that red bikini again?" he growls.

I laugh. "I'm afraid not, baby."

"Please be the cut-off shorts, please be the cut-off shorts," he says, almost like a mantra.

"Sorry, dude. I'm sitting on my front porch with Jordan and Jackie and a pitcher of margaritas and I am fully clothed."

"Jordan and *Jackie?*" he asks, clearly unhappy. We haven't seen each other in two weeks. I suppose it's reasonable he'd be less than thrilled that I have a friend visiting.

On my end, having her here is a relief. Every time I see Ethan, every time he pulls me into his lap, holds my hand, climbs on top of me... it feels like I'm slipping a little further into a hole I won't be able to climb out of. Jackie will help me keep my footing.

And my isolation here is beginning to make me question everything – why am I the only one who doesn't feel this whole marriage thing with Ethan is a little premature? I need someone, anyone, to tell me I'm not crazy.

"Yeah, they beat you by an hour."

"They rode down *together?*" he asks.

"Yep," I say. "Are you almost here? Do you want to swing by?"

"Sure," he says, sounding remote. "Be there in five."

I watch Ethan climb out of his car with new eyes, with Jackie's eyes, because I'm trying to imagine what she sees. Ethan is hot.

He's tall, he's got a good body, a great smile, clear blue eyes. In his suit pants and his button-down with the tie pulled off he is irresistible. I realize in this moment that Jackie isn't going to be the voice of reason. If I tell her what's going on she'll be yet another voice of shocked reproach – "*he's gorgeous, he's perfect, you're so lucky, what the hell is wrong with you?*" And how many people need to say it before I should consider that they might be right?

He smiles at me, and I can't say I'm not happy to see him. I want him cuddled up beside me on the porch swing, I want the feeling of his leg pressed against mine, the way he'll take my hand once he sits.

"Are you okay?" I ask. "You sounded a little off on the phone." He grabs a beer out of Jordan's cooler and sits beside me.

"I was just disappointed about the bikini," he grins. "You're wearing way too much clothing right now." His smile falters a little, though, as he looks at my brother.

Jackie fits right in when we go out at night — helped, no doubt, by the four beers she pounds within the first hour.

"Holy fucking hotness," she moans, looking over my shoulder. I feel my stomach sink at her words. Nate isn't the only guy who could elicit those words from her mouth, but he's the most likely to. And sure enough, there he is, sitting at the bar. He smiles at us both when I look over my shoulder. It's not his real smile. It's his dirty smile, the one that offers you five minutes with him in a bathroom stall, and as far as I can tell it works 100% of the time.

"I'm in love," she sighs, flinging her hair over her shoulder and trying to maintain eye contact with him.

"Don't," I say, far more sharply than I intended.

"Wuh – what?" she asks, seeming to sober suddenly as she looks at me in confusion.

I try to soften my voice, checking to make sure Ethan isn't listening. "Please, Jackie. Not him," I say quietly.

"Why?" she cries, a little distraught.

"Please," I beg. "I'll tell you later. Please just don't." I look her in the eye to let her know I'm serious, to see her confirm that she understands.

"Okey dokey," she sings, raising a brow at me. She looks back over at Nate. "You and him, huh?"

"Not here," I hiss, as Ethan turns back toward us.

"God damn I want to be reborn as you, Maura," she laughs.

We stay at Oak far later than I would like, and we do so for only one reason: I'm not leaving here without Jackie, and she doesn't want to leave. She's had a lot to drink, and when I imagine her failing to keep her promise about Nate I feel like I can't breathe.

"Ready to go, baby?" asks Ethan, kneading my shoulders.

"I can't leave Jackie," I say.

"Jordan'll take care of her," he says.

I look nervously at Jordan. He's not much of one to take care of people other than himself.

"Jordan!" calls Ethan. "Make sure Jackie gets home, will you?"

My eyes flutter from Ethan to Jackie like a bird at the sound of gunshot. He's now put me in an impossible situation, because I absolutely do not trust Jordan to take care of this, but I'll look nuts if I complain.

"Go ahead, Mom!" shouts Jackie drunkenly. "I'll be home by morning."

Yes, but what will she have done before then?

Ethan drives me home, but as we walk through the yard he tugs me sideways. "Come here," he whispers.

"What are you doing?" I ask, pulling slightly against his hand, trying to head to the back door.

"Come on," he tugs again. I go reluctantly. He pulls me behind the shed, and then grabs my hips and pulls me into him.

"You look so unbelievably hot in that dress," he murmurs against my ear, his mouth moving over my neck while his hands lift the hem and rise beneath it.

"Not here, Ethan," I say, squirming a little without actually moving away from him.

"Maura, I'm a grown man," he says, his voice muted against my skin. "It's been *weeks*, and I can only stand so much hand-holding, especially if you're going to dress like that."

I don't want this. My stomach churns thinking about Jackie coming home with Nate. And it churns thinking of the way Nate once kissed me here, pulling me off my bike like he would die if he waited a moment longer. I thought then that it was a beginning. The first of thousands of memories, each better than the one before it. I didn't know there'd come a day when I would hold that memory in my hand like something pristine and priceless, knowing nothing ahead of me would even come close.

"I'm sorry," I beg. "I can't do this here."

He's pissed. His jaw clamps shut while he tries to master the emotion. "I drove all the way down here to see you," he says tersely. He leaves the second half of the sentence unsaid, but we both hear it anyway: *and I deserve to get laid. Any other girl would do it.*

I'm so relieved when I escape him that a fine sheen of sweat breaks across my hairline as I go to my room. My relief is short-lived, however, as I lie awake waiting for Jackie. Finally it's so late that there's only one conclusion I can come to, and then I just wonder why I didn't hear him bringing her home.

She comes in just before dawn. My whole body is rigid. I sit up and stare at her, trying to determine how I can get through the rest of the weekend hating her the way I do at this moment. I would like to send her home, and I know I can't, particularly since she rode here with Jordan.

"Why are you staring at me?" she mumbles through heavy-lidded eyes.

"I can't believe you did it," I hiss, and even I am surprised by the venom in my voice. It wakes her up immediately.

"Did what?" she asks, but she looks frightened enough that it's an admission of guilt all on its own.

"You fucking slept with him!" I cry.

"Um," she mumbles nervously. "Sorry?" she says, flinching at the look on my face.

"I begged you, Jackie. I begged you," I say, and I feel tears forming.

"Wait," she says, confused. "Who are you talking about?"

"Nate!" I hiss. "How could you? What have I ever asked of you, in all these years, aside from that one thing?"

Realization dawns on her face. "I didn't sleep with Nate."

"Then what were you apologizing for?" I ask.

Her eyes widen and she remains silent.

"Who did you sleep with, Jackie?" I demand.

She looks down at the mattress, and still says nothing.

"Did you, or did you not, sleep with Nate?" I ask, voice rising. I realize now that I am too angry to keep her here. I am too angry to ever look at her face again if she slept with him.

"I did not sleep with Nate," she repeats, still not meeting my eye.

"Then who… ?" I ask, trying to puzzle it out. She slept with someone, clearly, and it's someone she thought she needed to apologize for.

"Ethan?" I ask, my voice more surprised than upset.

"No!" she gasps, shocked. "How can you even ask that?"

And then I know, because there's only one other person it could possibly be.

"Jordan."

She says nothing.

"Did you sleep with Jordan, Jackie?" I ask coolly.

"I'm so sorry, Maura," she pleads. "We were really drunk and

I didn't even think about who I was with until we were in the middle of it and then it was too late."

I spend all of 10 seconds being stunned that it happened, and 20 more being stunned that I didn't figure it out sooner. Them riding here together. Her on Jordan's lap at graduation, Jordan not coming home that night, and Ethan's strange reaction to them yesterday. "This wasn't the first time, was it?" I ask.

She hesitates, not meeting my eye. "Please don't say anything," she begs. "I know it was a mistake, and he knows it was a mistake. Please don't make it worse."

"A mistake is something that happens once," I tell her. They traveled here together. There's no way this is as unintended as she wants to make it sound.

We go to the beach with Ethan, and by midday Jordan joins us. I don't meet his eye. My loyalty should be to him, not to Mia, I tell myself. But also I remember how he failed to come home the last time he and Mia came to the beach, and I think about how withdrawn she's become.

That's when I realize I don't need to tell Mia. I'm pretty sure she already knows.

CHAPTER 28

"I'm going to explode if we don't find a place we can be alone together," Ethan tells me over the phone on Monday night.

"That's super romantic," I say dryly.

"I'm sorry," he says, "But if you don't want to have sex against the shed or on the beach you're going to have to start coming on business trips with me."

I laugh. "That'd probably be a little more appealing if all your trips weren't to Houston. See if you can get sent to Paris next time instead."

"Do you want to go to Paris?"

"I like Paris, but it was just a joke."

"Let's go this weekend."

I laugh. "We can't!"

"Why not? Because you're just dying to hang out at Oak for the 45th consecutive night?"

He has a point. I'm torn, although I'm not sure why. Surely not because I enjoy the strained silence of our house, where my grandmother and I continue to ignore each other. Not because seeing Nate out with other girls is any more tolerable. Suddenly Paris seems like a spectacular idea.

On Tuesday afternoon, Nate catches me in the side yard. "Going out tonight?"

"No," I say, squirming a little. "I'm going out of town in the morning, so I need to stay in and pack."

He holds himself very still. "Going home?"

I push my hair behind my ears, embarrassed on a number of fronts. Primarily because I feel like a spoiled little shit jetting off to Europe on a whim. "Paris, actually," I say with obvious shame.

"With Ethan?" he asks quietly.

"Um, yes," I reply. "It's pretty uncomfortable around my grandmother right now." It's a lame excuse.

He calls me on it, with a smirk. "Sure, that's how I deal with discomfort too. I run off to Paris with my boyfriend."

"It's just the weekend," I shrug, not helping the situation at all.

"Have a good trip," he says coldly, and he turns and marches off to his truck.

* *

Ethan and I fly out separately and meet at the gate at LaGuardia. His smile is huge and unabashed when he sees me, and I fall into him. He feels safe. He is the one person this summer that I've been able to count on. The one person who hasn't hurt me in some way. That's worth something. Certainly it's worth more than innuendo from the guy sleeping his way through Paradise Cove. I'd be an idiot to act otherwise. I doze on Ethan's shoulder all night, and he never complains or moves me once.

The porter sets our suitcases on the luggage stands, and I go out to the balcony, looking over the Champs Elysées, watching morning rush hour unfold before me. He comes out and wraps his arms around my waist, resting his chin on my shoulder. This is what it would be like to be married to Ethan. Just like what it was to grow up a Pierce – flying first class, staying at the best hotels, having things miraculously taken care of. Is it so wrong that I like these things? I like the lemon-scented hot towels in first class. I like not having to carry my own luggage, taking a limo in from the airport instead of the train. Perhaps it's not the hearts and butterflies I imagined as a teenager, but doing this with Ethan is a hell of a lot better than doing this with my parents.

I rest against him. "Where to first?"

Laughter rumbles in his chest, and his hands slowly lower onto my hips. "I think we've got some things to take care of here first."

"Did you seriously fly me across the Atlantic just to have sex with me?" I laugh.

"Are you seriously surprised?" he grins.

We don't get out of the room until the afternoon. We've both been to Paris before, so there's no pressure to do much of anything at all. We wander the streets, hand in hand. I buy a ridiculously expensive dress for Catherine at Chanel, and we find a place where we can sit outside for dinner. We linger over it, and the night is really pleasant. In spite of all the great things I imagined adulthood would be, lingering over duck confit and a nice bottle of Côtes du Rhône on the Left Bank is probably as good as it's going to get.

Over the course of the next two days, we spend so much time in bed that we might as well have stayed at his townhouse in Charlotte. It's a lot of time and expense for something we could have done just as easily at home, particularly since it hasn't been all that satisfying for either of us. I haven't finished once all weekend. He hasn't mentioned it, but I can tell it bothers him.

A few hours before we return to the airport, he lays beside me, wrapping a coil of my hair absent-mindedly around his finger.

"If we were married it'd always be like this," he says.

I smile. "You clearly haven't spent enough time with Jordan and Mia. If we were married I'd be pissed at you all the time for not helping with the baby, and you'd be pissed at me for not being any fun."

He grins. "I'm not Jordan and you're not Mia."

"That's how married couples always are."

"Not us."

"That's because we're not married."

"Fine, when we do get married, it won't be us."

I say nothing. He's venturing into dangerous territory, and I can't think of a way to transition out of it.

"You know I'm going to propose eventually," he says quietly.

"You know I'm leaving for Michigan next month."

"I can wait. Or you could transfer back. There's a law school in Charlotte."

My whole body tenses at the suggestion. I can already divine the rationale behind his words: he thinks it doesn't matter where I go to school because he assumes one day I won't be working. The logic Brian uses with Elise will be used on me as well – *we don't need the money you make, Maura, so why would you do that to our kids?*

"Michigan is one of the best law schools in the country," I say. "I'm going there."

"That's fine," he replies. "Like I said, I can wait."

"I'm worried you're expecting something that isn't going to happen Ethan," I tell him. "I *want* to work. I'm never going to be like my mom or yours."

"That's fine," he assures me.

I don't want to hurt him, but I can't help it. My chest feels like it's caving in. "I just feel like this is moving a little quickly for me."

"I love you, Maura. We'll go as slow as you want." It's the first time he's said those words to me, and I can feel his expectation lingering between us. He's waiting for me to say it back.

Of course I love him. I've known him my entire life. He's practically family. It's not a big deal to tell him I love him, to make him happy, is it? This is what I tell myself as I say it back, even as I feel the noose tighten further around my neck.

He rolls on top of me then, kissing me slowly, pulling up my t-shirt, gripping my nipple between his teeth. God knows he's good at this, but it all feels distant somehow, as if he can't really reach me. He isn't going to stop trying, and I have a feeling there isn't a single trick in his arsenal that's going to work.

So, at last, I give in to the thing I've denied myself all weekend, the one thing he most wouldn't want me to do. I think of Nate, and I come less than a minute after I allow him into my head.

CHAPTER 29

I get back to the beach fairly late on Monday night, but I slept for most of the flight home, so I have the driver drop me at Oak and take my bags on to the house. I don't question the impulse to go to a bar and a group of people I'm somewhat tired of.

"Where's your little beret and easel?" asks Graham sourly.

I arch a brow, a little surprised at the attitude. "In my suitcase."

Nate is playing pool. The sight of him seems to heal something in me, some slight abrasion I tried to ignore all weekend, not realizing until just now how much it bothered me. I see him look over at us, and he lifts his hand in a tepid half-wave. He approaches with clear reluctance when I go to the bar. He looks exhausted.

"You forgot to shave," I tell him, touching a finger to his jaw line. He flinches and I withdraw my hand.

"How was your trip?" he asks. His voice is neutral, but something unhappy, detached, lies beneath it.

"It was fine."

"Yes," he says sarcastically. "That's how people always describe Paris: 'fine'."

I smile. "Isn't that the slogan? 'Paris, the most adequate city on earth'?"

His smile is so slight it's barely evident. "So no ring on your finger yet?" he asks, glancing down at my hand.

"No!" I say, astonished. "Is that what you thought? That we were going there to get engaged?"

His face shifts then, as if a storm has blown away. "It crossed my mind," he says. "Kind of the place for it. It's the kind of thing he'd do."

Nate is totally right. Ethan is sweet and romantic and thoughtful and generous. That would be just like him to fly me to Paris to propose.

"There is no ring. There will be no ring," I say adamantly. "I'm leaving in six weeks. I don't even want to get married."

"To him, or to anyone?" he asks.

I don't know why he feels the need to persist with this line of questioning. "To anyone. It's a crappy, pointless institution. Just a lot of hype to disguise the fact that a year later, you the wife are sitting home by yourself with a squalling baby while your husband goes on like nothing's changed."

"You didn't used to feel that way."

I flush. The two of us had once named our children, settled out how we would watch them while we ran our architecture firm, all in the simplistic way of people who haven't ever worked or discovered the harsh realities of parenting.

"That's because I hadn't seen Jordan and Mia in action then."

"Not everyone is Jordan and Mia." It's the second time I've heard this in 24 hours. It makes me wonder if the words are somehow encoded in the Mayhew DNA.

"I'll probably come around at some point," I sigh. I suppose in a way the decision has already been made. I'm probably going to end up married to Ethan eventually – our conversation this morning was no longer about "if" but "when". I'll wait until after law school, but it's going to happen. And it'll be good. Paris was good. Certainly better than the time I've spent here. I'm stronger than Mia and Elise, strong enough to make a life in Charlotte that doesn't involve giving up everything I want.

"You don't sound happy about it," he comments, meeting my eye.

I shrug. "It'll be fine."

His face clouds, suddenly. "So there will be an engagement. You're just trying to tell yourself that you don't have to face it right now because they're letting you leave for school."

"You make it sound like I'm imprisoned or something. No one is 'letting' me leave. I make my own decisions."

"Right," he smirks. "Tell me that next summer when you've deferred for a year to plan a wedding."

Something in me hardens at his words. I want to tell him he's wrong, and yet behind my anger is the fear that he is completely correct. The girl he was standing beside in the pool room is shooting me daggers. It's a good time to leave before I say something I'll regret. "You'd better go. Your girlfriend of the night looks like she's about to break a bottle against the wall and stab me with the glass shards."

He frowns, eyes narrowing. "What do you mean by 'girlfriend of the night'?"

Just thinking about it, looking at her, makes me angry. "You know, the parade of girls you bring in and out of the carriage house."

"I'm not that bad," he argues, still frowning.

"Please," I snap. "You've fucked more girls so far this summer than most guys do over the course of their lives."

His eyes widen slightly. He looks surprised and irritated and maybe a little ashamed. Then the look grows lascivious, the grin sly. The same look he gets on his face when he's flirting with one of those girls. "You didn't used to have such a dirty mouth, Maura. It's kind of hot."

"Fuck off," I snap, and I stomp away.

CHAPTER 30

I go to Peter's office the next morning. "I haven't heard anything," I tell him. "But I was out of town, so I might have missed it."

"You haven't missed anything," he says. "Only four of ten access points are done. We've got a few weeks, I imagine. But I've already warned the guy on my end. He'll stake it out once you have some idea when it's going to happen."

I grow still. "You're not going to tell him where you're getting your information, are you?" I stammer. "That would make things a little awkward on my end."

He rests a reassuring hand on my shoulder. "Don't worry, Maura. No one will ever know."

I pray he's right. Because it could make for a very uncomfortable summer if he's not.

On Wednesday evening my grandmother stops me in the foyer as I'm leaving. "I'd like a word with you," she says. It's not a request. She points to the parlor and walks in behind me, slamming the pocket doors shut.

"How much longer is this attitude of yours going to continue?" she asks coldly.

"I don't know, Grandma. How much longer are you going to act like you've done nothing wrong?"

"It was my duty to protect you and I did it. I have nothing to apologize for."

"Did you not have a duty to Mary and Nate? He did nothing wrong but got yanked from his mother anyway. Mary did nothing but serve you for nearly two decades and in response you took her son away from her. He lost his scholarship. You devastated an entire family, all because you didn't want me sullying myself with the help."

I watch as my words wear away at her, watch a slight crack begin in her stern façade. "He's done just fine," she snaps. "He's got a job and he's living in my carriage house without paying a penny."

"*His* carriage house, grandma. It's his."

"It shouldn't be," she hisses.

I want nothing more than to see that self-righteous look on her face shatter into a million pieces. "I'm glad Grandpa isn't here to see the person you've become," I tell her. "Or maybe he already knew. Maybe that's why he left the house to Mary."

"Enough!" she snaps. "How dare you speak to me this way, after everything I've done for you?"

"I'm just telling the truth," I say without emotion, turning to leave the room. "Which is more than I can say for you."

"Your parents have supported every action I've taken!"

I freeze. "My parents knew what you did?"

"Of course they knew!" she says triumphantly, as if this fact alone trumps all else. "Do you really think they wanted you with *Nate*?"

It's been five years since I felt so abandoned. My parents too. I'm surrounded by liars, by people who do whatever serves them, without remorse. She sees my shock, the look on my face that tells her I want to fall apart right now, and she thinks she's won.

"I can send you home, Maura Leigh," she threatens. "I'll send you right back to Charlotte, and you will never be welcome here again."

In an odd way, it's freeing to no longer respect her – the complete lack of fear is nothing but a relief.

"You could, but you won't," I say icily. "Because you and my parents are desperate to see me end up with Ethan, and you know if I leave here I'm headed straight for Michigan, and if I go I won't be back." I fling the pocket doors open and glare at Stacy and Rebecca, who stand less than a foot away, listening, before I walk out of the house.

I am still fuming when I get to the bar. Nate sits at a table with a girl, the same darling, fragile little blonde he brought here a few weeks ago. Rage spirals in my stomach, now directed entirely at myself. I'm the one who gave him shit for sleeping around, and he listened. Now he's going to date. He's going to date this girl and marry her and I'll be watching their darling blonde babies toddle all over the lawn of the carriage house in a few years.

Graham sees my mood and drags me onto the dance floor. I allow myself to be pulled along with my mind a million miles away. He brings me a gin and tonic afterward. "Looks like you could use it," he says.

I give him a wan half-smile, and I pound it.

Graham wants to dance again, and I agree, but this time there's a viciousness to it on my part. I brush past Nate and his future wife without glancing at them, knowing he's seen me. When the song ends Graham leans in toward my ear. "Want to get out of here?" he asks.

I do, I definitely do. I do not want to watch Nate leave here with that girl, his arm around her back. I don't want to lay in bed waiting to hear her giggles, her moans, coming from the carriage house.

But at the same time, I feel unnerved. I remember Nate's warning and have to admit that the way Graham asks, the feeling of his breath on my ear and his hands on my waist, worries me.

"Let's see if everyone wants to go to the beach," I suggest as we walk over. His face falls.

No one wants to go to the beach, so we stay. I have another drink, and I watch Nate with that girl. I watch the way they laugh together, the way she keeps touching his arm. I hate watching him fondle the girls he meets here. I hate even more that he's *not* doing it to her, as if she's special. There's pressure building in my head and in my chest. I need to leave. "I'm going home," I say, surprising even myself.

"I'll drive you," Graham offers, a little too quickly.

"That's okay," I say, waving him off. "I feel like walking anyway."

"Fine," he says. "I'll walk you then."

Oh my God, must we go through this every freaking night? I look at him stonily. "Graham, that's sweet but this is the safest town in the world. I'll be fine."

"Your brother would fry my ass if he found out I let you walk home alone," he says, standing up and clearly not planning to budge.

I roll my eyes and walk out with Graham at my heels.

We walk and I think about Nate until I realize Graham is asking me about Ethan.

"I'm sorry," I say. "I didn't hear you."

"You and Ethan? Is it serious?"

I shrug. "I don't know what you mean by serious."

"Like, what's the plan? Summer wedding? One boy, one girl, one dog?"

I laugh humorlessly. "No."

"It sounds to me like you're not that into him."

I sigh. "We just started dating last spring. It's too early to be deciding on anything, one way or the other."

It's too early for me, but it's sure not too early for Ethan. Which begs the question: is it too early for Nate? He has a job, he has a house. He might be totally ready to settle down, and maybe it'll be the girl he's with right now.

Graham's still talking about Ethan. "I think if he was the right guy, you'd know by now," he is saying. He's right. I should know by now. Not that I should know if I want to marry him, but I should know if I even want to be with him.

"It's just early," I sigh. I'm hardly about to share my doubts with one of Ethan's best friends, and my mind is elsewhere. I wonder if Nate has left. I wonder if he's going to her house or if he's bringing her to his. I'm not sure which would be worse, more devastating. I decide, finally, that it's worse if he brings her to his. If he doesn't come home I can imagine other possibilities. If I have to see her straggling out tomorrow morning with her underwear wadded up in her hand and just-fucked hair it'll be hard to rationalize. Or even worse, maybe she'll stay. Maybe she'll make him breakfast and they'll walk out around lunchtime, swinging hands on the way to his car.

Graham is stopping me. His hands are on my waist. It seems like his hands have been there a lot tonight, and it strikes me that this is not particularly big-brother-like. I don't think Jordan has ever put his hands on my waist, unless you count punches.

"I've liked you longer than Ethan has," he is saying. I try to back away, but his hands tighten and he leans toward me.

"Graham, don't," I protest, pushing at his chest. His hands are in my hair, holding my head so tightly that I can't move.

His mouth is on mine. I refuse to open my lips in response, and I push against him again, but he doesn't budge. He grinds his teeth against my lower lip. My surprise gives way to horror as I realize that this isn't some awkward incident with Graham I need to finesse my way out of.

I'm paralyzed by the realization, my limbs immobilized by fear. It's not until I feel him pulling my dress up that I move, jamming my knee between his legs. I just make contact before he grabs my leg and yanks so hard that I lose my balance.

I hit the ground, unable to break my fall because he's still holding my leg. I only make it onto my elbows before he is pinning me down, his hands gripping my wrists, his knee an immovable weight on my thigh.

"Get off me Graham!" I shout. I try to lift my arms and my legs and it's useless. He outweighs me by a hundred pounds. I begin to scream, and he presses down on my mouth and nose with his hand. I fight for air.

"Stop screaming!" he yells. "I'm sorry, okay? I'm gonna take my hand off but you've got to stop… "

And then all I see is Nate's face, his rage consuming him. Graham's hand disappears as he goes flying backward. Nate throws him to the ground with so much force that I can feel the impact in the sand beneath me. Graham strikes back, but he's no match for Nate, who is larger and more agile. Nate holds him to the ground with a knee in his chest and a hand around his throat, punching him in the face once, twice, three times. Graham stops fighting back, but Nate continues, his anger endless and all-consuming. I'm not sure if he even realizes that Graham is now motionless, and it's only this that forces me to shake off my stupor.

I run to them, grabbing Nate from behind, throwing my arms around his. "Stop!" I feel him straining against me. He could easily throw me off if he wanted to. "You're going to kill him!"

"Are you fucking protecting him?" he yells, jumping up and spinning to face me. His jaw is clenched, his hands still in fists as if the fight isn't over.

"No, I'm protecting you! You'll wind up in jail if you keep going!"

Suddenly the adrenaline has deserted me, and I sink to the ground. My whole body is shaking. I wrap my arms around my knees and curl into a tight ball to contain myself.

He falls to his knees beside me. "Oh my God. Are you hurt?"

"No," I say weakly, still huddled. He pulls me into his lap, cradling me against his chest.

"Everything's alright now," he whispers. I feel his lips brush my hair. "I'm sorry I yelled at you," he murmurs. "I'm so sorry." I want to curl up into him until I disappear. I remember the feeling of Graham's hand over my mouth, draw a panicky breath just to convince myself I'm okay.

"I couldn't breathe," I tell him, the only words I can say. I can't stop remembering it.

"You're okay now," he soothes. "I'm never going to let him touch you again, Maura, I swear it."

"How could he do that?" I cry. "He's known me since I was a baby." My throat is choked with tears I can't seem to will away.

"He's not the same guy he was when you were a kid," Nate says. "He's been following you around like a puppy all summer. Even back when we were teenagers he was always watching you."

I shake my head. "I thought he was just trying to take Jordan's place."

"No," Nate says. "He was trying to take Ethan's."

I press my face into his chest, breathe him in, let him fix me because right now I could not be more broken. All the people I thought I knew – my grandmother, my parents, Graham – none of them are who I thought they were. And the person I thought had betrayed me the most is here now, keeping me safe.

"How did you know?" I ask. "How did you know to come out here?"

"I followed you," he says quietly. "I didn't trust the way he looked at you, the way he's always trying to get near you."

I start shaking again, and then weeping into his shirt in huge gasping sobs.

"Baby, you're okay," he croons, sounding a little desperate.

"I know," I say, taking deep breaths and trying to calm myself. "I just can't believe how lucky I am. He's taken me home so many times this summer but tonight was the night you knew to follow him."

He stiffens slightly. "Not exactly," he says. "I've followed you every time he's taken you home."

"But…" I shake my head. "You hated me."

"I never hated you, Maura," he sighs. "I just wished I did."

I feel as if I am rising up on top of a wave, weightless, suffused with sunlight. Nate still cares about me, even if he doesn't know it. I lean into him, my face against the shirt that is wet with my tears. My shaking stops, but I stay in place, listening to his heartbeat, feeling his breath on my hair. I should let him get up but I want to hold on to him, just for one more minute.

I lean in farther, breathing him in, pretending this is a place I can stay forever, memorizing the feel of him, the smell of his soap. It's the same soap he used when we were younger, when I'd run out the back door and find him waiting, straight out of the shower. For a *date*. My euphoria dies a sudden death.

"What happened to the girl you were with?" I ask.

He sighs. "I left her at the bar."

I climb off of his lap and stand on shaky legs like a foal. He's not mine anymore. "I should let you get back."

He stands with me. "Not until I've gotten you home safe."

I don't want his pity. I don't want him walking with me out of obligation while all he wants is to get back to her. "I'm okay now," I say, taking a breath to steady myself. I still feel dizzy, slightly disoriented, but I take a small, staggering step away from him. Once he leaves I'll find somewhere to sit until I can walk home. "Thank you so much Nate. I'm sorry I messed up your date."

He grabs my elbow, looking incredulous. "Are you out of your damned mind? Do you really think I'm going to let you walk home alone after that?"

"I'm fine," I say, trying to sound calm, trying not to sound bitter and jealous. "Your date is waiting."

"I'm sure she's gone by now," he shrugs.

"I'm sorry."

"I'm not," he says, and a tiny bit of my happiness returns.

I take a look over at Graham, who has been moving slightly, and moaning, for a few minutes. "Do you think he's okay?" I ask. "Should we call for someone?"

He looks at me with his brow raised.

"Again," I say testily, "I'm not worried about him. I just don't want you to get in trouble."

"He's fine," says Nate grimly. "But we need to call the police as soon as we get you home."

I swallow hard, avoiding his eye. Graham's father is one my dad's biggest clients.

"You're not going to call, are you?" he asks, a flash of anger crossing his face.

"I don't know. I need to talk to my parents first."

I watch him struggle with his irritation. "Then call them as soon as you get in," he finally says.

I head toward my grandmother's house, and he follows. At the door, under the glare of the kitchen light, I turn to thank him and watch his face change from appalled to enraged.

"You said you weren't hurt," he says through gritted teeth. "What did he fucking do to you before I got there?"

"Nothing," I say, confused. "I mean, nothing more than what you saw."

Nate raises his fingers over my cheekbone, and even the slightest brush makes me wince. I must have hurt it when I fell. "That's not '*nothing*'," he hisses. His fingers move to my mouth, and in the same moment that it hurts I'm aroused by it too. How can I be feeling this after what just happened? We exchange a look and his hand falls away. Nate steps back and looks at me — at my arms, already covered in small bruises, the press of Graham's fingerprints, at the large bruise on my thigh, where I fell, another on the leg he pinned down with his knee.

"I'm going to fucking kill him." Nate's body is vibrating with rage, and I sense the energy that is building. I know he's going back to the beach for Graham.

I climb back down and wrap my arms around him, calming myself, trying to calm him. His arms go around me too, and he rests his chin in my hair. "Everything's alright now," I whisper, repeating his words back to him. "You did everything you could do. If you go back, Graham wins because he can get you arrested for it. You can't let him walk away from this the good guy."

We stay like that until his body relaxes and the pace of his breathing slows. But when I back away the tortured look on his face – some combination of longing and grief and restraint – unmoors me. His eyes flicker to my mouth, and mine to his. I've spent the whole summer fighting this impulse and I am beaten. It doesn't matter what his intentions are, it doesn't matter that he'll be with someone else tomorrow night. I need this too much.

"Maura," he says softly, hesitantly, placing his hand on my cheek as he steps back toward me. I lean into the heat of his palm.

And then the upstairs lights turn on, flooding the backyard. His shoulders sag. "You'd better go in," he sighs.

I pause, just for a second. These are the last moments of us being us – of the thing we once were, and I wish I could climb into this space and hide here forever.

But instead I walk away.

CHAPTER 31

I call my mother in the morning and tell her what happened. The first words out of her mouth let me know how this will go.

"Are you sure you're not misconstruing things?" she asks. "You were walking on the beach with him after a night out. I can certainly see where you might have given him the wrong impression."

"He held me down and covered my mouth to keep me from screaming, Mom," I snarl. "Does that sound to you like something I could have 'misconstrued'?"

She sighs, as if this whole thing is just me being petulant and dramatic for no good reason. "Well, I'll need to talk to your father."

I stay inside all day. I'm scared I'll see Graham, and I'm also scared I'll see Nate – he's going to push me to call the police again and I just can't until I've heard back from my mom. When she finally calls, there are no surprises. "I'm sure last night was upsetting for you," she says patiently, as if speaking to a child. "But since nothing actually happened, and a very valuable relationship is at stake, we think it's best to just let this go."

"So what would have to happen for it to be worthy of pursuing?" I ask. "If he suffocated me to death, would it be worth risking your 'valuable relationship' then?"

"Don't be ridiculous, Maura," she says. "What exactly do you think is going to happen? The courts will laugh in your face if you pursue this. You were out with him, drinking I assume, and you went for a moonlit walk on the beach afterward? It sounds to me like you led him on, and if your own mother thinks so, what would a stranger think? The whole thing makes you sound a bit loose, if I'm being honest."

She isn't saying anything that I hadn't thought myself. But just once, I wish they'd be outraged on my behalf, the way they would be if something happened to Jordan. I've spent my whole life trying to please them, trying to get a small taste of that unconditional adoration they feel for my brother. I swipe away angry tears after the call ends. Thank God I'm leaving. Maybe the distance will allow me to stop waiting for something that's never going to happen.

I don't tell Ethan. I struggle with it all day, knowing he'll call that night. I have no desire to protect Graham, but if we're going to pretend this never happened, I need to minimize the number of people who know it did. And am I really going to explain that it was Nate who saved me? And that he knew I was there because he's been following me home all summer?

So when we talk, I say nothing, and I hope my bruises have faded by the time he gets here.

On Friday morning I'm woken by a rock at my window. I grin, knowing it could only be one person.

"You know, I do have a cell phone," I shout down to him. "You could just text me instead of vandalizing my house."

He grins. "Get your lazy ass out of bed and come swim with me."

I pretend to grumble but can't stop smiling as I do it. "Five minutes."

"Two," he counters.

"Three," I argue.

"Fine, but I'm throwing more rocks if you're late."

It isn't until I fling off my t-shirt and begin pulling my suit on that I remember the bruises — still there, and then some. I wouldn't have agreed to go outside in a suit if I'd looked first. I put on a long-sleeved shirt and Bermuda shorts to cover it up.

When I open the back door he has a rock in hand and his arm is poised.

"I'm here!" I cry. "Stop!"

He grins. "Good to know that even at 22, that threat still works."

Neither of us mention what happened. It feels too raw still, and in the light of day I need to not feel that same kind of closeness with him. I look back on Wednesday night with horror, and not just because of what happened with Graham. Nate almost kissed me, and I know if he'd started we wouldn't have stopped. It can't happen again.

At the beach I start to undress, hoping I can get into the water fast enough that he won't notice.

I don't.

"Goddammit," he hisses, staring at my arm.

"Stop," I say quietly.

"Did you tell your parents?" he asks.

I wish he hadn't brought it up. There's no way to tell him what they said without making them sound like terrible people, and I'm beginning to wonder if I really have much proof that they're not. "They asked me not to say anything. Graham's dad is a major client, and it's not like anything would come of it if it went to court."

That muscle in his jaw pops. "And Ethan?" he asks. "What did he say?"

"I didn't tell him."

"Why the fuck not?" he snaps.

"If I'm going to have to go through the rest of my life running into Graham I don't need everyone in the world knowing it happened," I tell him. "And how am I going to explain that you were there to save me? Ethan's jealous enough as it is."

"This whole thing is insane," he spits out. "What is it with you people? You'd think you were in the Mafia the way you all cling together."

I huff, feeling defensive although I'm not sure why. I've thought the same thing myself, often enough. "You just don't understand how things are."

"No," he turns on me. "You're the one who doesn't understand. You've got such tunnel vision, Maura. It's bad enough you're letting them push this shit with Ethan, but now you won't even protect yourself? You could have been raped. Do you understand that? He could do it again! Or he could do it to someone else! Is that what you want?"

"Of course that's not what I want!" I cry, and to my horror I feel my eyes welling up.

He sees it and his anger fades into regret. He takes a step toward me, and then stops himself. He runs two fingers over the bruises on my arm, focusing on them and avoiding my eye. "Please don't cry," he begs. "I'm gonna drop it. But please think about what I'm saying."

I nod, just to end this argument. The truth is that he is wrong. There is only one way of doing things here, even if we both wish it wasn't so.

"Do you think he'll be there tonight?" I ask Nate tentatively.

Nate rubs at the back of his neck. I remember this habit of his. It's what he does when there's something he doesn't want me to know. "You will absolutely not see him for the rest of the summer. Not here, and not in Charlotte."

I eye him suspiciously. "How are you so certain of that?"

He shrugs. "There are some things you're better off not asking." It's all he will say.

* *

I wear jeans and a long-sleeved shirt that night when Ethan picks me up. He laughs. "Feeling a little chilly tonight?"

I shrug. "It's not that hot."

"It's got to be 95 degrees," he argues.

"I'm so used to 105 that it feels cold," I joke, hoping he'll let it go.

We approach the table. Graham's absence is the first thing Ethan asks them about, and they merely shrug.

"I heard he's staying at his parents' place in Vail for the rest of the summer," says Robert.

Ethan's brow is furrowed. "I can't believe he didn't even tell me," he says quietly, his voice hurt. I'm so relieved Graham's gone that it's hard to feign sympathy. As they continue to discuss it, I slip off to talk to Nate, who sits at the bar. Ethan looks unhappy as I go, but says nothing.

"Nice outfit," Nate says snidely when I approach.

I roll my eyes.

"At least there's one weekend where you're not sleeping with him," he mutters.

"Why do you care who I sleep with?" I snap. "It's not like you're doing without."

"I just think you shouldn't be sleeping with the guy if you can't even tell him his best friend tried to rape you," he snaps back.

"Right," I hiss. "Because you have such a level of intimacy with all the girls you bring home."

"No, I don't," he replies. "The difference is that I'm not pretending I do."

I have no response to that, and I'm saved from creating one by Ethan, who comes up, wrapping a possessive arm around my waist. Nate's jaw is set but he says nothing.

"Everything okay, baby?" he asks, leaning down to kiss my temple. Nate's eyes flicker to the movement, the gray glinting like metal when they meet Ethan's. I can't see Ethan's face, but I'm guessing his isn't too friendly either.

"Everything's fine," I tell him.

Ethan's hand slides to my ass and gives it a quick squeeze, an action he undertakes solely to remind Nate who I'm with. "Come back to the table," he says.

I resent him for trying to take me from Nate, for interrupting our conversation and pulling me away like I'm his property. But there is a look on Nate's face that I've seen before – it's the look he gets about five seconds before he throws a punch. It's best for all of us if I go.

CHAPTER 32

By Wednesday, I'm ready for the rock when it hits my window at 7 a.m. He's done it every morning this week.

I throw open the window. "Already dressed," I laugh, and his crooked grin – sheepish and pleased — makes my stomach flip, like it did when I was 14. These mornings, the 30 seconds it takes me to fly down the stairs, are like stepping back in time, to all the mornings when I shot out of the house to find him, to all the nights when he was just getting out of the shower and so was I and we'd cling to each other as if we'd been apart for years.

Stopping myself before I reach him feels unnatural. I lurch to an awkward halt.

When we get to the beach he dives in immediately. I let myself watch, though I shouldn't. Despite his breadth he's impossibly lithe and graceful like this, in the water with the sun glancing off his arched back. Those stupid girls at Oak, falling for his cocky grin and his swagger when it's here that he's himself. It's here he's irresistible. He emerges, grinning at me like a boy again, the water glittering on his chest, his trunks pulling low, and I feel carved clean inside, aching and empty for something that can't be mine.

"You coming?" he laughs.

"You know I'm a wader," I sigh. Even water as warm as this takes me a minute.

"Guess I have to fix it the old-fashioned way," he grins. I know exactly what he means and I extend a hand to ward him off, as if

Nate would ever allow himself to be warded off. He scoops me up without effort, holding me tighter when I flail, silencing me with the sudden feel of his skin beneath mine, warm and damp, before he launches me into the waves.

I stagger to my feet, laughing and scowling simultaneously. "How old do I have to be before you stop manhandling me like I'm five?"

"I'll still be doing that when you're 80," he says.

"If you do that when I'm 80 I'll break a hip," I retort.

Silence overtakes both of us as we realize we're discussing a future that isn't ours. I keep forgetting I'm not with him. And each time I remember it feels like a small death.

On our way home we discuss the upcoming weekend. Elise and Brian are having their bachelor/bachelorette parties two weeks before the wedding, at Mrs. McDonald's insistence. I'm not sure what kind of mayhem she thinks will occur, but one week is cutting it too close for her.

"So how big a tantrum would your boyfriend throw if you rode up there with me?" he asks.

Pretty big, I think. But my only other options are to ride in the tiny backseat of Heather's convertible, which isn't even fit for a child, or ride with Mrs. Mayhew, which would be even worse.

My lack of options is entirely unrelated to the reason I agree to go with him.

* *

I'm outside promptly at 2:00 on Friday. Ethan never asked how I was getting to Charlotte and I didn't volunteer it, which makes this afternoon feel like a gift. A gift that isn't wrong in any way, if you ignore the fact that I am going to make sure my boyfriend and my family never find out.

I emerge from the kitchen and watch in surprise as Nate's face falls.

"Seriously?" he sighs, looking at my outfit. I'm wearing cut-off denim shorts and a tank top, which seems fairly appropriate. Did he think I was going to wear a ball gown and tiara for a four-hour car ride?

"What?" I ask. "It's not like you're all dressed up."

"You're practically naked," he says.

I laugh. "That's insane. I'm wearing more clothes than any girl I see you out with at night."

He shakes his head and grabs my bag. "Yes, but none of them look like you," he mutters.

I blush, wondering if he means it before I begin to scold myself. He isn't the same boy I knew. I know that boy is still in there somewhere, but he's also slept with half the girls on the island by now. Flirting is probably so engrained in him it's like a switch that's flipped the minute he sees breasts.

But as we drive, I forget. I forget that he's changed, and that I've changed too. It feels like I'm 16 again. We drive with the windows down despite the heat, just like we did then. And for some reason I like it. I like the sweltering press of it, making my shirt cling to my skin, with a breeze that still smells like flowers though the heat should have killed off everything this late in the summer. We don't talk about the future. We don't even talk about the present, really. We just talk about absolutely nothing, ponder the origins of "Butt Hollow Road" and "Cuckold's Landing", sing along with the radio and talk about the summers behind us.

His profile, his hand on the steering wheel, the way he glances at my legs every time I move — they make me forget we aren't together. I find myself imagining, again and again, how easy it would be to slide my leg over and…

I catch myself, shaking my head as if I can dislodge the image.

Our ride goes too fast. Three hours into our trip we see the first signs appear for Charlotte and I feel sick, already mourning the end of something that isn't close to being over.

"Are you hungry?" he asks suddenly, too quickly. We both have dinners planned tonight with our friends, in just a few hours.

"Yes," I reply, also too quickly.

His shoulders relax. We find a diner. The marquee out front boasts that it is "sanitary".

"Always the sign of a fine dining establishment," he laughs.

It's not until we've parked and are walking inside that I catch my reflection in the restaurant's window. "I'm a mess. I can't believe I'm going in like this," I groan, running my hands through my hair.

"Maura," he says, stopping in place to look at me. "You are the single prettiest girl who has ever or will ever set foot in this diner." Small smile. "Even with that hair."

We get cheeseburgers and shakes, and we eat slowly. We play tic-tac-toe on the placemats, draw the worst possible portraits of the other we can.

I realize I was wrong, earlier, when I was with Ethan in Paris, thinking life doesn't get much better than dinner on the Left Bank. Because this crappy diner with its questionable health code grade and greasy food has it beat hands-down.

* *

The yards and houses grow larger and more elaborate as we approach my neighborhood, and I begin to squirm. I don't want him to see my house. I want us to remain here, in this space where all things are equal and the distance between our two worlds seems insignificant.

In fact, I don't want to go home at all. I don't want to get out of the car, I don't want to leave him. If my grandmother hadn't taken the actions she did five years ago, maybe I wouldn't have to.

"Do you ever wonder where we'd be now if my grandmother hadn't lied to us?" I ask.

I watch the subtle grind of his jaw before he responds. "I figure we'd have ended up where we are now no matter what," he says.

His answer hurts. In my mind we were perfect, inevitable. It never occurred to me that he might see it otherwise. "Why do you say that?" I ask.

Something grim settles over his face, anger that hasn't been subdued at all by time.

"Do you remember when Ethan and I fought? The baseball game?" he asks. I nod. "He said no Pierce was gonna end up with white trash like me and as soon as you figured it out he'd be the one... with you every night."

I cringe. "I'm sorry," I say.

"Don't apologize," he says, his eyes focused ahead of him. "I hated him for it at the time, but he was right."

"He wasn't right!" I gasp. "You know that. That isn't why we broke up."

He frowns, struggling with his answer. I hear the sadness in his words when he finally speaks. "It would have happened eventually. You grew up with things I could never have given you. You would have gotten sick of that at some point."

"Is that who you think I am?" I demand angrily. "You think I'd have chosen some mansion in Charlotte over you?"

"It's not just the house, Maura," he says with resignation. "It's everything – you're so used to things that are outside of the norm. Regular people don't just hop over to Paris for the weekend, they don't just go buy whatever they want. Even if you'd been able to put up with it, I couldn't have stood to be the reason you had a crappy life."

"I think I could have had a really good life without the trips to Paris," I say quietly. My eyes sting, and I look out the window so that he doesn't see.

He hesitates. "Maybe," he says reluctantly. "But you'd have a better one with Ethan."

I don't respond, because I can feel the sadness welling in my throat, and anything I say right now would lead to tears. We enter my neighborhood in silence. I give him the gate code and we head down the lane toward my house. When it finally comes into sight, he says nothing, but I feel the shift in him, a wall that is descending, separating us.

He pulls into the circular drive. My father's Range Rover is parked in front. "Do you want to come in?" I ask. Bringing him to meet my parents would be disastrous. I want him with me in spite of it.

All of his light-heartedness is gone. "I'd better get going," he says. He's grown completely aloof over the course of two minutes.

I want to beg him to come back to me, to be the person he was just minutes before, but I can't find the words. I could tell him that it's all meaningless, and that my parents don't care where he comes from.

But it's not entirely meaningless, and they absolutely do care.

* *

Mrs. McDonald, desperate as always to have her fingers in every part of this wedding, has invited all of Elise's friends and their mothers for a dinner that couldn't possibly be a less fun start to a bachelorette weekend. It is held – predictably – at the club. Do they *never* get tired of being here?

My mom is already there, huddled on a couch with Stephanie Mayhew. They call me over. It's an effort to walk toward my mother, knowing what I do, to look at her without scowling.

"You're late!" my mother scolds. "What happened?"

I can't even pretend to be apologetic. "Other things came first."

"I thought you were riding up with Heather," she states, clearly expecting an explanation for that too.

"I never said that," I reply, watching both of them fight the impulse to ask who I rode with.

"We were just talking about how nice a spring wedding would be here," says Mrs. Mayhew, who looks slightly alarmed by the unexpected tension. "It's just too hot in Charlotte for a summer wedding."

I manage a smile. "I'm sure Elise's wedding will be just fine."

"Oh, I wasn't trying to imply that it wouldn't be," she demurs. "But don't you think, given the choice, a spring wedding would be lovely?"

I shrug. I see where this is going, and I can't come up with a single polite way to steer it in another direction. "I guess."

They seem satisfied by that, and as I walk away I tell myself I haven't agreed to anything, though the weight in my stomach tells me differently. I escape to my friends, and they are hardly better. Our friend Cristina is there, just back from her post-graduation cruise – and as I approach she starts singing "Here Comes the Bride."

"I think you've got the wrong girl," I say with a strained smile, throwing an arm around Elise. "This is the bride, remember?"

She winks at me. "Yes, but from what I hear you're next."

I grab a drink and go out to the pool. Rounds of ten are set up for dinner, complete with twinkling lights. It's beautiful, but Mrs. Mayhew is right. It's way too hot for a summer wedding here. I begin sweating the minute I get outside.

Ethan has texted, suggesting we cut out of our respective dinners early and meet at his townhouse. And the funny thing is that I want to do it — I want to escape from all of this and forget, even though in a way he's the thing I want to escape from. I don't reply right away. Instead I feel the tug of rebellion, the fervent wish that my life contained something more than it does.

I text Nate: I HAD FUN TODAY. JUST LIKE OLD TIMES. THANKS.

He replies right away: ME TOO. AND JUST LIKE OLD TIMES, YOU STILL CAN'T SING FOR SHIT.

I laugh out loud, the sound echoing off the cement deck, too loud, too joyful. A moment later, he sends another text: HOW ARE THINGS OVER THERE?

I reply: STIFLING IN MORE WAYS THAN ONE.

He answers immediately: SHOULD I COME SAVE YOU?

I WISH YOU COULD, I respond.

He answers: I COULD IF YOU'D LET ME.

My heartbeat speeds up, just a little. I wonder if he means it, and I wonder at the impulse that lies behind it. Does he want me? Is he just being a friend? Am I merely a challenge because I'm with Ethan? I have no idea.

I want to say yes, but I don't, because I already know it's not possible. He can't save me from tonight – with my mother and her friends and my friends all expecting me to play my part. And not tomorrow, or next year either, because they will always expect it. And I will always give in. I don't know any other way to be.

* *

We are not entirely successful in ditching our mothers until Saturday night. After countless bars, and countless drinks, Elise and I are in the suite we checked into earlier in the day. She lays on the couch with her feet in my lap while we wait for the rest of the girls to stagger back.

"It's funny how it's all worked out, isn't it?" she muses, a kind of drunken melancholy in her smile.

"What do you mean?"

"Do you remember all the shit we planned when we were teenagers?" she asks. "We were going to have this awesome loft in New York City and I was going to be an executive and wear really cool suits with a short skirt and stilettos and be a total bad-ass, and you were going to be an architect, and then we were going to have a double wedding at St. Patrick's Cathedral – me and Brian and you and Nate."

She is no longer smiling, when she concludes, and neither am I. Her lip trembles. "At least we each got a little of the dream. You're still going to be a big shot somewhere."

"And you're marrying Brian," I add, trying to sound cheerful.

But suddenly she is crying, huge gasping sobs, her face buried in her hands.

"Oh my God, Elise," I cry. "What's wrong?" It came out of nowhere. I must be the worst bridesmaid ever — somehow I've made her cry at her own bachelorette party.

"It's all happening so fast," she sobs.

It's really not been fast at all. She's been planning this wedding since she was 16.

"What do you mean?" I ask.

"I just don't know if I'm making the right decision," she weeps. "I'm never going to leave. You know that right? I'm never leaving. Brian doesn't want me to interview now. Not even after the honeymoon. I was getting my resume ready and he said, 'Why are you bothering? You'll be pregnant by Christmas.'"

I understand exactly what she is feeling – the sensation of being swept away by a current you can only fight for so long.

It's not supposed to be this way. In movies, you stand your ground and this miracle occurs where everyone else discovers the error of their ways. But in real life, you stand your ground and the people who loved you just a moment before now think you're petulant and selfish and unreasonable. And when that happens, you don't stand your ground for long. At some point you let the current take you, because over the long haul it's too hard to fight.

Maybe we've both given up. She's just been swept farther to sea than I have.

I try to comfort her, saying the only things I can, things I don't really believe. "You're imagining life would be so much better in New York or someplace, and it's probably not. And you can always tell them no. It's not too late."

She just shakes her head, raising her tear-stained face to me. She looks sober all of a sudden, her face a mask of sad recognition, as if she's been handed a death sentence and accepted it. "Of course it's too late," she answers, regarding me with what looks like sympathy. "It was always too late."

* *

On Sunday I ride home with Mrs. Mayhew and Lily. She drives the speed limit the whole way, the radio on an easy listening station that makes me want to stab my own ears.

I could be riding with Nate. I caved to the pressure, as always, and now I'm paying the price. But it wasn't just the pressure. I think about my response to him, the thoughts he can inspire without even looking at me, the way I wanted to beg him to keep driving after we'd reached Charlotte, and it just seemed safer to avoid a repeat. I texted to tell him I was riding with Mrs. Mayhew and he never responded. I guess he's hurt, and I guess I can't blame him.

Mrs. Mayhew spends roughly half the drive talking about weddings – how she thinks tulips are "so common these days they're almost like carnations", how she likes the idea of having a groom's cake, how strapless wedding gowns are "unseemly", how destination weddings are "thoughtless" and outdoor weddings are "too dicey." I suffer through all of it, trying to neither agree nor disagree.

At some point, to my infinite relief, Lily cuts in to begin grousing about the bachelorette events she wasn't invited to, insisting that she shouldn't have had to leave the beach at all since she couldn't go out with us.

"I still don't see why I couldn't just stay at the beach with Daddy," she says.

Mrs. Mayhew clucks her tongue. "He was just very busy with a project he's working on this weekend. We've gone over this."

"What project?" Lily demands. "His office is in Charlotte. It wasn't even open this weekend. What could he possibly have to do?"

"It was a special thing," Mrs. Mayhew says, with a wary glance at me. "You'll see him tonight."

"But what could he need to do at the beach?" Lily persists. "He *never* works on weekends."

Mrs. Mayhew glares into the rear view mirror. "Lily," she says with finality. "That's enough."

It could mean anything, but it's definitely strange. I dial Peter's number before I've even entered the house.

* *

Nate is nowhere to be found. Not at Oak, not at home. On Tuesday morning, his truck is in the driveway but there's no sign of him. On Wednesday there's still no early morning rock against my window. Finally, unable to stand the strain, I text him:

I'M SORRY ABOUT SUNDAY. ARE YOU MAD?

His reply sets me somewhat, but not entirely, at ease:

NOT MAD, JUST BUSY. SEE YOU SOON.

It's the kind of reply he'd send if he were busy. It's also the reply he might send if he were mad.

On Thursday morning, Peter calls. "We caught them," he says, expelling a long breath. But he doesn't sound particularly happy about it.

"Them?" I ask. "Mr. Mayhew and who else?"

I hear the disappointment in his exhale, before he's said a word. "It wasn't Stephen Mayhew. Police rounded up about 16 guys – migrant workers, all of them here illegally. The case is being turned over to Immigration."

"Oh," I whisper, as my stomach sinks. "But they'll still be questioned, right?"

He sighs. "I think someone's trying to shove this under a rug. My contact is talking to a reporter he knows – if the press presents this the right way it may force the issue. But I'm not too hopeful."

I hang up and rest my face in my hands. I thought I'd feel guilty if Ethan's dad got arrested, but this is so much worse. My family and the Mayhews are selfish and entitled and greedy. But none of them have ever gotten anyone deported.

CHAPTER 33

"**D**on't be mad."

It's never a good start to a conversation.

"You're traveling again, aren't you?" I sigh.

"I'm so sorry," Ethan says. "You have no idea how much it pisses me off, especially with you leaving for Michigan in a few weeks."

I'm legitimately disappointed that he won't be here. Though my relationship with him has felt slightly risky all summer, it's nowhere near the level of danger I feel in my friendship with Nate. I think about our ride to Charlotte, how much I've missed seeing him this week. The truth is I would give up almost anything to be with him. I know that now. But if he tossed me aside, if he treated me the way he treats those other girls, he'd destroy me. He'd destroy me in ways I wouldn't recover from.

The safest thing I can do, the thing I absolutely have to do, is stay away from him. But without Ethan here, I'm not sure I've got the strength.

* *

Any good intentions I may have had grow shaky the minute I see Nate smile at me from across the room on Friday night. If he was mad before, he seems to be over it. I've sworn to myself that no matter what he says I'm going to avoid him until I leave the beach, but the minute he gives me that lopsided grin I begin to falter.

"Where's your boyfriend?" he asks.

"He had to go to Houston for work again," I reply.

"You sure it's work? Maybe he's got a secret family down there."

I roll my eyes. "Shut up."

"You're right," he says. "Ethan's too boring to have a second family."

"Are you done?" I sigh.

"Insulting Ethan?" he asks. "No, probably not. So what are you going to do without him lapping at your heels all weekend?"

I should make up plans. I should tell him I'm packing, or seeing my friends, or something, anything, that means I'm not free. But already I'm standing here with him and I don't want to walk away. It's too late. My resolve is absolutely, positively gone.

"Nothing much," I say.

"Meet you outside at 8:00?" he asks.

I nod, my smile guilty and elated at once. I *so* shouldn't be agreeing to this.

"Sun-up to sun-down, just like old times," he states, but there's something tentative in the statement, bravado masking a real question.

Maybe he's joking about spending the whole day together. But damned if I won't be outside at 8:00, ready for an entire day, just in case.

I return to my friends, enveloped in a haze of slightly inebriated joy, though I've only had one drink. I hear Nate's truck pull in shortly after Kendall drops me off, and to my immense happiness, there's no extra door slamming, no second pair of feet.

**

The moment my eyes open the next morning I bolt out of bed, put my swimsuit on under shorts and a tank, fix my hair, brush my teeth, and I'm out the door. Nate sits on the bumper of his truck, waiting, that crooked smile spreading over his face when he sees me.

After we've gone swimming, we head to the diner. We've been here together so often in the past few weeks that they know our order. He's grabbed today's paper off one of the stools by the counter, and the front page catches my attention. The lead story is about the destruction of the walkways. I see the story's subtitle –

"INS Says Detainees Will Be Questioned" – and I can't hide my pleasure.

He looks at me curiously. "What are you smiling at? This is bad news for you."

I shake my head. "Not really. I'm glad they were caught. Old Cove has no right to close those walkways."

There's something tender in the way he looks at me then. "You're more like your grandpa than you know," he says with a small smile.

I flush with pleasure. It's the nicest thing anyone has said to me in a long time.

"So what happens after Elise's wedding?" he asks, grabbing the bacon off my plate he already knows I won't eat. "Are you coming back here afterward?"

"I hadn't really decided," I say tentatively. It really doesn't make much sense to come back down. I probably ought to pack, spend a few days at home.

"Your flight doesn't leave until the 18th," he says. "That would give you almost another full week at the beach." He focuses on stirring his coffee, avoiding my eye.

I told him the day of my flight over a month ago, and he remembered. Even my parents and Ethan can't seem to remember it, though I've told them multiple times. Suddenly the idea of leaving him after next weekend is untenable.

"I guess I'll come back then," I tell him.

He looks so relieved and happy and sad in response that I

don't know what to say. I'm staying only for him, and he wants me to stay, and we are not together, so why do either of us care?

After breakfast we bike down to where Paradise Cove ends, crossing the narrow, one-car bridge that leads over to North Shore, which is bigger and more modern. The people here live in condos. If there were mansions here once, they are gone now and nobody seems to miss them.

I didn't come here much as a kid. I wasn't allowed to cross the bridge when I was younger, and by high school I no longer wanted to, sucked into a kind of unconscious snobbery about the higher standards of Paradise Cove. But today we do, heading to the boardwalk, where there are probably more shell shops and ice cream stands than there are people.

I like walking with him here, where no one knows us, where our combined appearance isn't something that will induce whispers and concern. I like that not a single one of the crappy little storefronts sells anything with arugula or herbs. There's a small amusement park on the boardwalk now. It wasn't here when I was a kid or we would never have followed the rule about the bridge.

We go on the Tilt-a-Whirl and the Octopus and the Scrambler, all rides that involve centrifugal force spinning you uncontrollably close to your partner. I do my best, the first time, not to crash into him, not to create another moment we have to awkwardly ignore. But I'm fighting a losing battle, and by the second ride I give up, allowing myself to be pressed hard against him.

His arm goes around me, holds me in place, and I tell myself that it is fine, what we are doing, because it will stop when the ride ends. It does stop, but then we choose the same kind of ride again and again, and each time I curl into him a little more, memorizing the feel of it, the smell of his shirt and his skin. His hand grows familiar, the way his fingers press against my arm, his breath on my neck when he turns to glance down at me.

Every action he takes reminds me of who he was when we were young and how there was a time when I was incapable of distrusting him. For so many years I've looked back on it as poor judgment, the way I never dreamed that he would cheat. But here I am, knowing what I know, and I find myself wanting to trust him in spite of it.

"I want to ask you something," I breathe.

He stops walking and turns to me with a small frown. "Okay."

"That fight we had, that night on the beach when you were in college…" I begin, watching him grow suddenly wary. "Look, I realize it was unrealistic to think you wouldn't sleep with anyone else all those years when we weren't even in the same place but I…"

"Maura, I never slept with anyone while we were together. Never."

If I didn't know better I'd stake my life on the fact that he's telling me the truth right now. Except I know that would be impossible. "You admitted it! It clearly wasn't your first time."

"That doesn't mean I slept with someone else when I was with you. You weren't my first girlfriend."

Yes, this fact I remember quite clearly, but it doesn't exonerate him. I shake my head in disagreement. "You had condoms. Are you trying to tell me you were still carrying condoms around from previous *years?*"

He sighs and sits on a bench to the side of us, resting his forearms on his thighs before looking up at me. "I never wanted to push you, Maura, but just because we weren't sleeping together didn't mean I wasn't praying we would. I kept waiting for you to be ready, and for a long time you just… weren't."

"So you'd been carrying them around for years?" I ask.

He nods.

"No," I insist. "You cheated. It was all over your face that night. You were so guilty. In fact, the reason I ran off was because you were insisting on telling me about it."

In a way I need to believe he cheated. I need to believe there's a silver lining to losing him, that there's some possible way I'm better off for it.

He flinches. "I didn't sleep with anyone but yeah, there was something…" He trails off. "Are you sure you want to hear this? Because I can tell you right now that I'd rather cut off a hand than hear you describe being with someone else."

"I want to know."

"There were these girls… they were kind of like baseball groupies."

I nod. We had them at UNC too, the girls who hovered around the athletes. I never saw them without thinking of Nate, without assuming he'd been with any number of those kind of girls.

"They came to all the games and they came to the parties after and I always avoided them. But one night I got drunk off my ass and passed out and the next thing I know this girl is in my bed. She kind of looked like you, I thought, although when I saw her later on campus she really didn't. But she had your coloring, your mouth. I honestly don't know what happened, but I thought I was dreaming about you – that we were hooking up – and the next thing I know this girl is screaming at me for calling her the wrong name. I was still dressed, and probably too drunk to have done much, but I guess I did something. And after that I never had more than a beer or two if there were girls around."

I feel sick. Not over what he did, but that it could all have been avoided. "You could have told me, " I say quietly. "You know, when it happened. I would have forgiven you."

His shoulders sag. "I know," he sighs. "I figured you would but I was just insecure, I guess. I spent so many years hearing from your brother and his friends that I wasn't good enough and that you were gonna move on and I just didn't want to give you a reason to."

"But if I'd known," I say, "or if I just hadn't flown off the handle the way I did maybe none of this would have happened. You wouldn't have been kept away from your mom that whole year."

"Among other things," he says, meeting my eye. "I wouldn't have been kept away from you either. But the truth is I'm not sure it would've mattered. It's not like your grandmother knew we'd fought. She'd have accused me either way."

"But you wouldn't have had a reason to believe her," I argue.

We both sit in silence. My stomach twists with the desire to go back and set things right despite how futile it is.

"I've had that conversation with myself a thousand times," he says, as if he knows what I'm thinking. "There's no way to fix it." He pulls me to my feet. "Let's go swim."

Something has changed. From the moment our conversation ended something is different between us. Being around him, before, was a slippery thing, a constant balancing act of getting close but not too close, carefully studying my steps to make sure they fell on level ground. That's gone now. Now I feel charged, sure-footed. That uncertain piece inside me is gone and in its place is the old feeling of knowing that Nate is my safety net, my soft landing. That as long as he's beside me nothing else can matter.

The beach is far more crowded here, and yet it feels intimate, because suddenly that old tie is there, binding us. I don't look away when he meets my eye. He picks me up and throws me in the water, and doesn't even pretend not to watch as I try to adjust my bikini.

He's all I can see. It's been that way all summer, but this is the first time I don't pretend otherwise. It's as if we've wrenched this small moment out of our history, out of the present, and none of our actions count.

We bike back as the afternoon winds down. There's a party on the beach tonight that I promised Heather and Kendall I'd attend. It seemed like a good idea at the time, a welcome reprieve from the same drinks, same table, same people at Oak. But now I resent it, the way it looms with finality at the end of our day. We roll our bikes into the shed, and I look at him wordlessly, feeling distraught at the prospect of parting from him.

"What?" he asks.

I shake my head. "This was a good day," I reply, my voice hushed, containing all the things I want to say in its place.

"It was the best day I've had in a long time," he replies. Neither of us move.

"Are you going to the party on the beach tonight?" I ask.

He looks at me, unblinking. "I hadn't planned on it."

I nod, trying and failing to hide my reaction.

"But I might as well," he says with a small smile, watching my face. I don't just smile. I glow, and when he sees it, he does too.

CHAPTER 34

I put on music. I dance while I shower, while I dry my hair, while I moisturize and put on mascara. I put on my too-short sundress. I bounce down the steps when my friends walk up.

"Someone's in a good mood!" shouts Heather, raising high a cup full of something I'm certain violates our state's open container laws. There are at least a hundred people at the beach when we arrive, and most of them appear to be in line for the keg.

"Nate's here," says Heather, under her breath. I follow her eyes and find him, across the way, in khaki cargo shorts and a tee-shirt that isn't tight but is certainly fitted enough to document how good he looks when his shirt comes off. I've never actually failed to notice how good-looking he is, but watching him from afar, in a new setting, makes my pulse erratic.

"Goddamn, he's hot," moans Kendall. "I can't believe you never slept with him." I don't correct her.

He watches as I approach, his face serious. "You're stunning," he breathes. "You know that, right?"

I blush and shrug, as pleased as I am uncomfortable. "I'm glad you came," I tell him.

"So are you allowed to dance when your boyfriend is out of town?" he challenges.

"I'm allowed to do whatever I want," I say back, perhaps more saucily than I intended. He raises a brow.

"Okay, maybe not *whatever* I want," I laugh. "But I'm allowed to dance."

He grabs my hand and pulls me into the sea of swaying bodies on the left-hand side of the fire pit. His hands rest on my hips as we dance, and he tugs me into him.

The way Nate dances, the way I dance when I'm with him, is something Ethan wouldn't be happy about. But after a day spent brushing up against him, wanting him, catching the way he looks at me again and again, this doesn't feel inappropriate at all. It feels inevitable.

We move in sync with each other, with the music, the movement and our proximity ensuring that this is something we shouldn't be doing in public. But our anonymity from earlier has carried over in our minds, if not in reality. I forget that we can be seen, and that I can't be seen like this. He's so close that I can feel his breath on my face as we move, that when he looks down he can see straight into my dress. And he repeatedly looks down. The crowd surges around us, and we push closer, his shirt brushing my collarbone, his hands tightening around my hips. I look up at him and watch his face change – suddenly hesitant, his mouth softening. I'm only on my first beer, but I feel drugged in a way. I shift into him, meeting his eye and for once not looking away. He leans in just as I am yanked backward.

"What the fuck, Maura?" yells Jordan, glaring at me and Nate as if we were just screwing right in the middle of the dance floor. And I guess we weren't that far off from it.

"Why are *you* here?" I seethe, more angry than guilty.

"The better question is why you're dirty dancing with your ex the minute your boyfriend is out of town!" he yells.

I hate him for being a hypocrite. I hate him even more for interrupting us.

"I think my dancing is a lot more respectable than what you did with my roommate a few weeks ago, you cheating prick!" I shout back, shoving him away from me.

He blanches, his face growing still and shocked. "I don't know what you're talking about," he says stonily.

"Bullshit, Jordan! How long have you been cheating on Mia?" I shout.

He grabs my arm again, looking around him in surprise. "Jesus fucking Christ, Maura, keep it down."

"You want me to keep it down? Don't come over here moralizing to me when you're the loser who can't keep it in his pants," I hiss. He lets go of my arm with a shove that sends me toppling back into Nate, and storms off.

"What was that?" Nate asks at my ear, still holding onto me.

"Exactly what it sounded like," I sigh, my anger drained.

"Come on." He pulls me away from the crowd, refilling our beers before he leads me over to a log to sit. "Now tell me," he says.

I summarize the situation, beginning and ending with Mia's unhappiness, how withdrawn she's grown since Catherine was born.

"Why does she stay with him?" he asks, aghast. "She's young. She's what, 24? She has her whole life ahead of her."

"They've only been married for two years, Nate. They had 400 people at their wedding. Everyone knows them. There were four different baby showers held for her. She can't leave."

"Of course she can leave!" he exclaims. "That's complete bullshit and you know it."

I shake my head. "No it's not. Her parents and my parents go way back. They're all in the same circle. Them splitting would be a disaster. We have all the same friends. They'll be spending holidays together when they're in their 90s. It would be awful."

"You know what?" he says. "This whole thing you've got going on at home is ridiculously fucked up. I listen to you and it's like England in the 1600s or something. She doesn't have to stay in Charlotte. She can go anywhere."

"But she won't," I say decisively, and as I say it, I know that this is why I haven't spoken to Mia about it. Not out of loyalty to Jordan, but because I knew it wouldn't change her outcome in any way.

"Is that what you want?" he asks harshly, his anger taking me by surprise.

My eyes open wide. "Of course not. But what am I supposed to do? I can't make him stop."

"No, not what you want for *her*, Maura. What you want for *you*. Because that's where you're headed with Ethan and you know it. Your families act like you're engaged and you allow it."

"I can't stop it!" I exclaim, throwing up my hands. "They do what they want no matter what I say."

"You could stop it, but you won't," he hisses. "You don't even want to be with that guy and yet here you are! One day you're going to find yourself married to him and you're not even going to know how it happened. But I'll tell you how it's going to happen: he'll ask, and you won't want to upset everyone and hurt his feelings and it's so comfortable that it seems like a decent idea and before you know it you've fucking agreed."

I stand up with tears pooling in my eyes, inexplicably hurt.

"That's not going to happen!" I argue, swiping at my eyes angrily, with the back of my hand.

"It's already happening, Maura!" he shouts, standing to face me. "Name one thing that's happened this summer that indicates otherwise!"

My anger at him and what he has said is irrational and misplaced. I know it, even as I react, even as I tell him to fuck off, even as I stomp away to find my friends.

My regular crowd stands hovered around Jordan. I've recovered myself enough by the time I find them that they don't seem to notice anything is amiss. Either that or they're too drunk to care.

"Where's your wife?" I ask Sammy, with unnecessary acidity. He looks at me in surprise.

"Home with the baby."

"Of course she is," I reply, looking back and forth from him to Jordan. "The two of you have a pretty sweet deal, don't you?"

"Shut it, Maura," says Jordan, with a warning glance.

"You need a drink, girlfriend!" shouts Heather, dragging me toward the keg.

A drink is probably the last thing I need. I'm usually a happy drunk, but somehow the night and my mood have headed in an irreparably unhappy direction. I take a drink anyway, because I'm certainly not improving my mood by *not* drinking.

I no longer see Nate. I'm sure he's moved on, working that devious grin on some girl who can barely stop herself from undressing at the sight of him, and it makes me sick. I don't understand my own volatility around him. Was there a single thing he said that wasn't true?

I had him all to myself and I lost him. And for what? Because he was absolutely right about how ridiculous my family is and what outcome I'm heading toward? I've lost him again and it's entirely my fault.

The hand that wraps around my hip brings me out of my thoughts and my distress. He stands at my back. "I'm sorry," he says quietly, against my ear. "I should have let it go."

I want to weep with relief as I turn to face him.

"No, I'm sorry," I reply. "You were right. I was mad because you were right."

His eyes are locked on mine, and in them I see something that hasn't been there all summer – a sort of urgency replacing his uncertainty. He grabs my hips and backs into the crowd, away from my friends, into the middle of a throng of people dancing, where we might be less likely to gain attention.

He pulls me tight against him, his hips pressing against mine as we dance. It's as close to having sex with him as it can be without actually having sex with him. It's more erotic than a single moment I've ever spent with Ethan.

Our argument should have made us distant to each other, but

instead it has gone the other way. There is something desperate in me now, something that wants to beg him for other things. He pulls at me, and I pull at him, as if we can't get close enough, and suddenly we aren't dancing any more, but clinging. His thumb brushes my lower lip, rests there. He stares at it for a moment, as my shaky exhale grazes his skin. His eyes flicker to mine, and for once I don't look away, I don't hide. I know who he was and I know who he is now and the truth is that I love them both. There was nothing I wouldn't give up for him at 17. There's nothing I won't give up at 22.

His hands slide into my hair, cradle my face as his mouth lowers. I feel the heat of him, the softness of his lips, and for only a second there is no haste, as if it's merely an experiment.

And in the space of that single second the world falls away and there is only him. Our uncertainty is gone. There's no longer anything tentative or gentle in our actions. His mouth on mine is demanding, relentless. Anyone can see us, can tell Ethan, and I don't care. My hands go around his neck, and I sink into the feel of him. He's endlessly familiar and yet this is all new, the way I crave him. The way I no longer care about anything beyond this moment.

He groans against my mouth, pulling me away from the fire to where the light is dim. "God I've missed you, Maura," he whispers, his mouth fervent against mine. "I've missed you so much."

It's as if I've been ill for so long that I forgot what it was to be well, and in this moment I suddenly remember. His kisses grow harder and more demanding. I arch into him, press against him and feel how ready he is. We keep moving, our bodies attached the entire way until the sound of the music is distant and we are in complete darkness.

There's an urgency in both of us, as if this can't possibly happen fast enough, as if the entire day, the entire summer, has been foreplay.

"Get on your back," he says roughly. I drop immediately and

he follows, sliding his hands along my thighs, lifting my dress as moves forward to hover above me. His hands are everywhere, on my hips, in my hair, on my thighs, until finally his fingers glide between my legs.

"Nate," I cry, arching into his hand.

"I need to be inside of you," he says, almost apologetically, the words a plea.

"Yes," I groan, unzipping his shorts, moving him toward me. This feels as necessary as oxygen, like a hand reaching into the pool to save me from drowning. He pauses, his face strained, to meet my feverish eyes with his own. "Please," I beg. He pushes hard then, groaning once he's all the way in, and it takes me by surprise, the almost painful fullness of it. I gasp and he stops moving.

"Are you okay?" he asks between gritted teeth.

"Yes," I breathe, my hands already pulling him toward me, demanding that he continue. He responds, and his thrusts grow fast and hard at my urging, his mouth against my lips, against my breasts.

"Maura," he growls, and I am building, building, unable to slow myself down or slow him. I cry out as I clench around him. He buries his mouth in my neck as we both come, clinging to each other.

I hold on to him tightly, my whole body shaking with the impact of it. I don't want him to leave me. I want to cling to him, hold him here in any way I can. I try to savor the last seconds of him inside of me, the feeling of being clasped against him, but already the truth is edging in.

I can't keep him.

He's not the boy he was. He moves from one girl to the next with blinding speed. Even if that changed, even if I were the exception, I'm leaving and I know he's not going to wait three years or more for me to return.

Five years ago I was in this exact position, staring up at the stars with him above me. I was about to lose it all, though I didn't know it then. This time I do. I'm going to lose him, this time for good.

His lips are pressed against my neck when he feels my tears. He pulls away, his face suddenly wary. "Did I hurt you?" he asks. "Did you not want…?"

I shake my head. "I'm fine," I whisper. I can't tell him the truth. It's too pathetic, too clingy. "I don't even know why I'm crying."

The sweetness of his face, his concern, it disappears suddenly, like a mask he's discarded. His eyes grow distant as he pulls away. "This shouldn't have happened like this," he says. "I shouldn't have… I wasn't thinking."

I'm too dumbfounded by the change in him to be coherent. "What do you mean?"

He pinches the bridge of his nose, squeezes his eyes tightly shut as if searching for words. "I wasn't thinking," he says again as he tries to find his clothes. His voice is clipped and cool. "After the whole day together, I just got carried away."

I expected several things from him afterward, but I didn't expect this: his immediate, unmitigated regret. His sudden distance is a knife to the chest.

I would laugh at myself if I weren't crying so hard. I really thought, for half a second, that I was special to him. Maybe he thought I was too, only to discover his mistake before he'd even pulled out. With no protection, either, but that's secondary to everything else at the moment. He's slept with more women than I can count in two months' time and I just added myself to the list.

And then there's Ethan. I just cheated on my boyfriend for a guy who's apologizing before he's even zipped up his pants. "I cheated," I whisper in horror, more to myself than to him, my voice breaking. "I cheated on Ethan."

He pauses. "I won't tell anyone," he says tersely.

I shake my head. It's not enough. "I'll still know I did it."

He stands, buttoning his shorts, and finds my panties and throws them into my lap.

"I'm sorry, Maura. It shouldn't have happened. There's not much more I can say beyond that," he says icily, as if we are strangers.

I can't believe he's doing this to me. I can't believe I've done this to Ethan.

"You want to go back to the party?" he asks gruffly.

"I'll be there in a minute," I say without meeting his eye.

He pauses for just a second, just enough time for me to realize how badly I want him to tell me that this meant something. And then he walks away, blending into the darkness before the breath has caught in my throat.

I stay where I am for a long time, leaden with a sadness so heavy and pervasive I can barely move.

CHAPTER 35

I wake, I remember. And then I am flooded by guilt, and by hopelessness. There is a sense that I've made a fatal error, though the world looks unchanged when I open my eyes. I am still going to Michigan in the fall. I still am not with Nate, nor will I ever be. Nothing has changed, so why does it feel as if there is no point in getting out of bed at all, not now, not ever?

I know I will have to break up with Ethan — Heather and Kendall probably saw me leave with Nate, or took an educated guess as to our sudden disappearance. Even if they didn't, I can't go through my life feeling like I'm harboring a secret that might blow up in my face. But I also can't tarnish Elise's wedding with all the distress and drama our breakup will create. Which means I will have to spend the next week pretending I've done nothing wrong while barely able to look Ethan in the eye.

When Heather calls I consider not answering, and then change my mind. If I'm going to need her to keep her mouth shut for a week, she'd better know it sooner rather than later.

"Hey," I say cautiously.

"Hey," she says, slowly, expectantly. I assume she's waiting for me to confess, but I say nothing. "You left early."

"It was just kind of a bad night." If she knows I wish she'd just say so.

"I saw Nate later but he didn't know where you were."

"Was he with a girl?" I ask.

She laughs. "He's always with a girl." I want to fold in on myself, as if I've been stabbed. Not even for one night was I enough for him.

"Things got a little crazy at the party," she tells me.

I'm barely listening. I can't believe he was with someone else so soon after me.

"I'm just going to come out and say it," she says, and my heart starts beating harder. "Kendall got super drunk and I think she... she left with Jordan."

I groan.

"You can't tell them I told you," she warns.

Poor Mia. I never thought when he married her that I'd feel like this – like she was the one who got a raw deal, who'd married down. But now I do. Some people peak when they're older – they pull together a career and a family and build it all into something strong and beautiful. But Jordan is not one of those people. Jordan peaked in high school, or maybe college, when he was popular and good-looking and everyone wanted him. I'd always assumed that life was a race that he just had a huge head start on. But now I see he was just farther along on a much shorter track. He will spend his entire life trying to get back to being the person who was ahead, who was best, not realizing that the minute you start looking backward you've lost the race entirely.

I can't face anyone. Not Nate, not Jordan, not my friends. I stay in bed. It's so unusual that by 10 a.m. my grandmother has come to check on me. "If you throw up in that bed you'll be washing the sheets yourself," she snaps.

I have an entire day to think about what has happened, to imagine Nate going off with some other girl last night as soon as he'd finished with me. I still feel stunned by his behavior, as if it's not possible that he could have turned so callous, yet I've got nothing but proof that he has.

And I also have an entire day to let the guilt I feel about Ethan ratchet up. When he calls that night I can barely stand to answer the phone. "Are you okay?" he asks gently.

"I'm fine," I assure him. "Just a little under the weather."

"I'm sorry baby. I wish I was there," he says.

Every word out of his mouth increases my sorrow. He's a good guy, and he's been nothing but decent to me. He wants to give me everything, but I withhold myself from him. Everything he wants is what I only want to give to Nate, Nate who wants none of it.

My relief that he doesn't know is short-lived. He calls back 30 minutes after we hang up, something he's never done before.

"I'm in the car," he says. "I'm on my way down there."

"Why?" I croak out.

He hesitates, and when he speaks he sounds like he's on the verge of breaking down. "It's my dad," he says. "He's just been arrested."

* *

The next morning I'm in the courthouse with him, waiting for his father's bail bond hearing. He holds my hand tightly. "It's going to be okay," I whisper.

He gives me a slight, sad smile. "I know. I'm really glad you're here though." I want to shake myself. *How* could I have cheated on him? And *why*?

When Mr. Mayhew's case is called before the judge, the excitement in the courtroom grows palpable. There's a small commotion in the back of the room when the DA walks in. I turn toward it to see Peter Folz standing against the wall, and beside him, of all people, Nate. Our eyes lock for one horrible moment, neither of us able to turn away fast enough. That he doesn't want me, that he will never be mine, feels like a death. I will mourn this for years, all the while forced to pretend I mourn nothing at all. No matter what I told myself, there must have been a part of me that hoped we might work. To have that hope obliterated feels like too much to stand.

I turn back toward the judge quickly, stunned by the loss. Ethan senses my sudden tension and squeezes my hand. It's wrong that I'm allowing him to comfort me after what I've done, yet here I am.

Mr. Mayhew comes over to us after bond is set, hugging his wife, and then Ethan and me in turn. I stand with them as if we are a family. Except I've cheated on one of them and gotten the other one arrested. I looked down on Jordan for cheating. I looked down on Mr. Mayhew for his greed. But look at me: I'm the equivalent of them both combined.

Ethan spends most of the day with his father and his father's attorney, but he comes over at sundown before he heads back to Charlotte. We sit on the front porch and I lean against him.

"Are you okay?" I ask.

He nods. "I think we'll be able to fix this." I'd like to know what he means by 'fix', but I don't ask. I've done enough damage. "How are *you*?" he asks.

"Me?" I ask nervously. "I'm fine."

"Jordan said you knew about him and Jackie," he says. "I thought you might be mad I didn't tell you."

"Why didn't you?" I ask.

"He swore me to secrecy, Maura. What was I supposed to do?"

"So I guess you know about him and Kendall too?" I ask, not hiding my scorn.

"Yes," he sighs. "I tell him the same thing every time and he never listens."

"What do you tell him?"

"I tell him to pull his head out of his ass and go home and try to be a decent husband for once."

I blink away tears. Ethan is a decent person, and a loyal one. He's not the type to fuck me on the beach and walk away. He is so, so good, and he deserves so much better than me. It makes me want to turn over a new leaf, to stop fighting the tide every step of the way and grow into someone who is worthy of him. I've tried taking the illogical, reckless course and I saw firsthand how that turned out. Perhaps it's time I began making decisions based on reason rather than emotion. I squeeze his hand and resolve that, if at all possible, I'll make this up to him somehow.

CHAPTER 36

I stay in all week. I cannot stomach seeing Nate with the long line of girls at Oak who wait for their turn with him. I can either get back in line or I can watch the other girls take my place, and I won't do either.

I'm going to make this up to Ethan, all of it. And the first step, the most important step, is to avoid Nate.

I pack everything. There's no reason to come back here after the wedding, and a thousand reasons not to. The Mayhews take my bags since they won't fit in Heather's car.

On Friday morning I go downstairs to say goodbye to my grandmother, who dismisses me as if I'm someone she barely knows. It doesn't sadden me so much as it does simply confirm what I'd already guessed – to her I'm nothing more than a piece on a chess board, something she's only pleased with when I've been moved into the right position.

I walk into the side yard then, the wet grass beneath my bare feet reminding me of all the mornings I met Nate here as a girl. The insistent buzz of the cicadas, the sun warm on my back, the heat-pressed smell of honeysuckle – suddenly so redolent of childhood that when I finally look at the carriage house I am blinded by tears. I'll return here but this – childhood, contentment, Nate – is never coming back.

Heather and Kendall are bouncing with excitement for the weekend — Kendall clearly unaware that I know about her and

Jordan. I do my best to feign happiness, but the truth is this weekend will be a trial from start to finish. The rehearsal tonight, the wedding tomorrow, the brunch on Sunday — it will be me, Ethan and Nate every step of the way. I lean against the headrest and tell myself that if I can just live through this one weekend, everything will turn out all right.

* *

My dress for the rehearsal is a simple sheath in kelly green. I blow my hair out straight, put on the makeup I don't usually have time for. I'm doing this because I'm supposed to, but I can't say it has nothing to do with Nate either. Tonight and tomorrow are it, the last times I will see him for many years. And if I do see him again, I'll likely have my own children in tow, and so will he. The thought creates a pain so real that I lay my hand over my heart as if I can stop it.

I want him to remember me like this, the polished woman in the green dress, and not like the pathetic girl he left crying on the beach. Maybe someday he'll look at pictures of the rehearsal dinner or the wedding and, just for a moment, he'll regret what he did.

"Very nice," clucks my mother. Her approval, so rare, should mean more to me than it does. Maybe she and my father and grandmother were right – Nate hardly seems to be the stellar human being I once thought he was. But it doesn't change the loathing I feel for her right now.

Ethan drives me to the church, and my stomach churns. I have no idea what I will find when we arrive – if Nate will act like we're friends and nothing has happened, or if he'll treat me like the one-night stand he can't get away from fast enough.

"You seem tense," Ethan says, reaching over to grab my hand.

Tense is hardly the word for it. I'm wound so tight right now that it feels like I can barely breathe.

Outside the church, the bridesmaids and groomsmen are gathered into two small clusters. I train my eyes on the girls, standing around a wedding coordinator who is doling out instructions as if this is the Battle of Normandy. Her face falls just a little as Elise introduces me. "You're very tall," she says, almost accusingly. Her eyes flash to the groomsmen, standing together a few feet away. "Thank God one of them is too."

I don't have to look over to know who she means. And I shouldn't look over, but I can't seem to help myself, can't control my start of surprise when I find he is already looking at me. His head turns quickly, but not before I see what was in his face. Not disdain, not regret, but grief.

The coordinator pairs us up, two by two, until she eventually gets to me and Nate. He stands stiffly beside me, saying nothing, while I try to find an explanation for the look on his face. Does he feel guilty? Does he regret leaving, or does he just regret sleeping with me in the first place?

We link arms and begin our walk down the aisle, silent and awkward under Ethan's watchful eye. But just as we reach the altar, just as he prepares to drop my arm and move off to the right, he speaks — so quietly I barely hear him.

"This should have been us," he says. My steps falter as he sends me off to Elise's side, numb with shock.

Through the rehearsal, through the dinner, I think of nothing else.

Why is he doing this to me? I ask it again and again, my fury ratcheting up each time, never finding an answer. He left me crying on the beach and moved on to another girl. It's too late for him to be remorseful, if that's what this is.

But behind my fury is pain, so sharp I can barely move around it. Because more than anything, I just wish he'd meant what he said.

CHAPTER 37

Even inside the dressing room, the heat is unbearable. My anxiety is unbearable. I tug at my bridesmaid's gown – strapless, fitted red satin — knowing I'll earn another dirty look from Mrs. McDonald. She's mad that I skipped the final dress fitting, and I guess for once she was right.

On the outside, I am buffed and polished, as perfect as I will ever be. On the inside, I am raw and torn by Nate's words. I help attach the train to Elise's dress, relieved to have a thousand tiny pearl buttons demanding my attention.

At least Elise is calm.

"Only you could be this relaxed on your wedding day," her older sister teases.

"Why would I worry?" she asks. "What's done is done." Everyone seems to think this is a happy sentiment, but I'm not sure it is.

* *

We stand in the foyer as the groomsmen make their way back to us. I've never seen anything as beautiful as Nate in this moment, in his tux. My throat tightens painfully. This is the last day he and I will walk down an aisle together. He catches me staring, and today he doesn't look away.

The coordinator sends Elise's younger sister down the aisle, and Nate comes to stand beside me. Her cousins go next, and then the coordinator nods at us. He glances at me, his face strained and serious, and offers his arm. Despite all my best intentions I can feel myself clinging to him, as we wait, as we walk, as we part at the altar.

All through the ceremony, and following it, there is no sign of Elise's regrets. She is beautiful and flushed and impossibly happy when they turn back toward their guests as husband and wife. It seems possible, watching her today, that she might wind up happy in spite of her compromises.

Nate takes my arm for the last time. We make the walk, but we slow as we reach the end, coming to a stop at the moment we should part, neither of us moving or letting go. I am frozen, unable to take the step away from him I should. I see the wedding coordinator come rushing toward us. We have only seconds left.

"You were right," I tell him.

"About what?" he asks.

"It should have been us," I reply.

The wedding coordinator grabs my arm but he stands immobile, looking shaken and lost. As she pulls me into the dressing room I take one last glance back at him, and he remains exactly where he was, still watching me go.

* *

"You were stunning up there," gushes Ethan as he drives to the club. He's oddly keyed up tonight, a stark contrast to my own leaden grief. "You're going to be the most beautiful bride that's stood at that altar in two centuries." I squirm but I don't correct him. I've turned over a new leaf. I'm going to be worthy of him. I'm going to stop fighting it.

Once we are seated and wine has been poured, the toasts begin. Elise's dad talks about how proud he is of them. He tells us that Brian went to USC, that he's the youngest vice president in his company, that there is no limit to the wonderful things he will do. And then he tells us all about Elise's beauty and her kindness and her infectious laugh, the way she used to wear her Cinderella costume to the grocery store and how good she is with children. He never mentions her degree or how she won our high school mathematics competition two years in a row, or anything else that attests to her intellect and ambition. I suppose because Mr. McDonald, like everyone else in this room, knows that those things are no longer relevant. Ethan shifts restlessly beside me as the toast continues, his fingers nervously drumming against his leg.

There are other speeches – from Elise's sister and Brian's brother, Brian's dad and Elise's aunt.

And then Nate stands.

I feel Ethan tensing up beside me, and I have to will myself not to clutch his hand.

I stare at Nate. It's the first time all weekend that I can do so with impunity, and though I shouldn't allow myself to be so weak, I can't seem to stop. I wish I could absorb him, memorize him, find a way to carry some little piece of him inside me when I head north.

He talks about Brian at 16, telling him he thought Elise was pretty but stuck-up. And at 17, when he suddenly became incapable of talking about anything but her. He talks about the time they broke up in college and how Brian ate three boxes of Captain Crunch over the course of six hours that day.

He addresses Brian. "You were apart for a long time. I've seen the two of you fight, and complain, and disagree, and even break up, but it's never worried me. Because Elise is the person you were born to be with. And I really believe that once you've found that person," he says, turning from Brian to lock his gaze onto me, fierce and unapologetic, "then no matter how many times you're separated, you'll find each other again and again."

The room breaks into applause, a rush of noise I barely notice as Nate holds my eye, as I stare back, unable to look away.

Ethan's hand grips mine hard as goose bumps break out across my arms. "What the fuck was that?" he hisses.

I barely hear him. I don't know what it was. I don't understand how Nate can look at me like that, say the things he's said, after what happened.

"It's time he learned once and for all you're not his girlfriend anymore," says Ethan.

His words drag my eyes from Nate. "What?" I ask distractedly, but I am too late. He is already jumping to his feet. "Ethan," I whisper anxiously, tugging on his jacket to make him sit. "What are you doing?"

He ignores me, tapping a spoon against his champagne flute to get everyone's attention. The room falls silent quickly. "I don't want to take anything away from Brian and Elise's night, but let's face it," he says, grinning at their table, "you just have to look over there to know that nothing can take away from this night for them." The crowd chuckles, but I don't. Because this doesn't sound like the beginning of a toast, and I know exactly what it *does* sound like. *No, no, no, no, no,* I intone desperately to myself. *He wouldn't, he wouldn't, he wouldn't.*

"Brian found his perfect match seven years ago. I found mine then too, although she wasn't aware of it," he says, turning to me. The room becomes impossibly still, as if all of the real, breathing humans have been replaced by wax figures. My racing pulse is the only thing in this room that's still moving.

"It's been a long wait. And I'm standing here now, in front of all of the people that she and I love, to say that I don't want to wait another day for her to be my wife." I don't look at Ethan. I look at Nate, and I see my panic reflected there as he returns my gaze. Suddenly all of this feels like a game of pretend gone horribly awry. I don't know how I've allowed it to get this far.

Ethan drops to his knee, placing a box in a hand I can't even feel, his face proud and assured and hopeful. "Maura Leigh Pierce, will you do me the immense honor of becoming my wife?"

The room begins to lose its stillness then as women sniffle and someone claps — as if I've already said yes. Perhaps because they're aware, just as I am, that Ethan has created a situation in which it is impossible to say no. I can't embarrass him, embarrass my family, in front of all these people. I can't ruin Elise's wedding. I see my parents and Ethan's parents beaming, both of our mothers' faces shiny with tears, and know the choice has been made. I didn't want it this soon, but I guess we all knew it would happen eventually.

I take one last, pleading look at Nate. To tell him goodbye. To tell him I'm sorry. In spite of the way he treated me, I'm asking him to forgive me for what I'm about to do.

He is pale and drawn, bracing for pain, as if he's going into a battle he knows he won't come home from. My sweet boy, the one I loved for my entire life. The one I still love. His face is stoic, but he is breaking apart in front of my eyes.

I stand and place the box on the table. No matter what he's done to me, he's the one person in this room I refuse to hurt.

"I'm so sorry," I whisper, before I flee from the tent, into the darkness.

CHAPTER 38

I run, but I have nowhere to go. The golf course is pitch black, the night endless. I've done an awful thing, the worst in a series of awful things, and every person in that tent hates me for it. Even my own family will want nothing to do with me right now. And I don't blame them.

I run to a point where the sounds of the tent grow dim and I don't have to hear the shock and outrage directed entirely at me. Where am I going to go? I can't face those people again. I don't even have a ride out of here. I'm paralyzed by indecision.

There's a shadow moving quickly across the green. I watch, my heart beating hard from something — fear or anticipation or maybe both — as it comes near.

I know who it is by his size, by the way he moves toward me — the same way he once came for me off the baseball field, relentless and focused, as if he'd plow down anyone who got in his way. He never slows as he approaches. And this moment scares me more than any I've endured this weekend. Because he is the only thing I want in the entire world, which makes him the only person who can give me everything, or take it away.

He walks right into me, grabbing me with his hands entwined in my hair, kissing me like I'm something he's starved for.

"You said no," he breathes, his mouth against mine. For a minute I am consumed with him, mindless in my response. For a minute there is nothing in the world I care about more than his soft lips and his firm hands.

And then I remember. "No," I gasp, pushing back though he doesn't let me get far. "You left me on the beach, Nate. You couldn't run fast enough."

His jaw drops. "You were crying about your fucking boyfriend! One minute I think we're back together and it's all behind us, and the next you're *weeping*. Do you know how that made me feel?"

"I wasn't crying about Ethan! I was just emotional. I was sad that we'd lost all those years and that I was leaving. And then *you* said it shouldn't have happened."

He pulls me back to him, and this time I don't fight it.

"I said it shouldn't have happened that *way*," he argues, his voice muffled against my skin. "It shouldn't have been on the beach, and rushed. It shouldn't have been like the first time."

"And what about the girl you were with after me?" I ask bitterly. "Did you not do that either?"

His mouth is on mine again before he answers. "The only girl I even talked to was Beth, the bartender from Stoney's, and I was talking about you. Did you seriously think I could go on to another girl after that?"

"You've spent the whole summer moving from one girl to the next," I say, and my voice breaks. "Why should I believe I'm any different?"

"Maura," he says, pulling back just enough that I can see his face, eyes bright with urgency. "That isn't me. I'm not going to say I've been an angel, but this summer wasn't me. Having you back at the beach was just unbearable, having to watch you with Ethan. I just couldn't think of any other way to move on. You're different because you're the only reason I did it in the first place."

"Why didn't you just say something?" I cry.

"How was I going to compete against Ethan? I'm never going

to be able to give you one of those big houses. Your family hates me. I had no chance."

"I don't care about any of that," I argue. "All you ever had to do was ask."

His eyes glitter in the light, heartbreakingly fearful and hopeful at once. "Then I'm asking," he says.

"And I'm saying yes."

He places a hand on either side of my face, forcing me to see the raw fear in his own. "If we do this," he says, "you can't change your mind."

"I won't," I swear to him.

He backs me up to the tree behind me, pushing into me with his hands still on my face, and kisses me until the tree is all that is keeping me upright.

My mouth moves over his neck while my hands run inside his shirt, beneath his belt.

"Maura," he groans, a pleading noise, as if he's desperate for me to stop, or not to stop. His mouth moves frantically from my lips to my neck, his hands cupping my breasts, his thumbs brushing my nipples, and a small whimper escapes my throat.

"Damn it, if you make that noise again I'm going to take you right here on the golf course," he says, gripping my waist.

"Do it," I beg.

"I'm not going to have sex with you on a golf course," he growls. "At least not right now. For once in our damn lives, I want you indoors, maybe even on a bed."

We are in his car in two minutes, in his hotel room seven minutes later.

He sits on the edge of the bed, watching as I unzip my dress and let it slide to the floor. I step out of it and stand before him in nothing but my heels and thong and a black lace bra so sheer it's practically invisible.

"God, Maura," he says roughly, placing his hands on my waist and running them over my hips. They rise again, resting on the outer curve of my breasts, and his mouth presses against the center of my rib cage. "I've dreamed about seeing you like this every night since I was 16."

"Take off your shirt," I whisper. He stands, never taking his eyes off of me, and I watch him unapologetically. Nate, shirtless in tuxedo pants, should go on posters. He is all muscle, perfect lines and curves. I trail my fingers over his biceps, his chest, his ribs. I gently graze my teeth over his neck, and unzip his pants. I wrap my hands around what must be the most impressive erection I've ever seen, and air hisses between his clenched teeth.

He pushes me onto the bed with sudden ferocity, sliding off my thong, his mouth moving everywhere while his fingers glide inside me. And when his mouth meets his fingers I am arching against him, muscles tightening, crying out as my hips clear the bed. The moment I land he climbs up, until our faces are inches apart and I can feel him nudging between my legs. I move toward him, but he resists me. He hovers there, so close and so ready but unyielding.

"I love you so much, Maura," he says quietly. And then he pushes into me, his eyes never leaving mine. He pulls back slowly, torturously, and I moan my impatience, trying to arch into him, but he resists me again.

"I want to hear you say it," he demands.

"I love you," I reply. "I've always loved you."

He thrusts in hard then, and I feel him everywhere, filling me. I cry out as I pull him against me, my tongue in his mouth, my nails clawing at his back. His movements become faster, less controlled, his hands pulling at my hips with every thrust, the headboard slamming against the wall, mimicking the rhythm.

It's the sound of his groan that puts me over the edge, and he follows me with a cry that sounds like pain but is not.

He buries his face in my neck and I cling to him.

"Are you okay?" he asks. His voice is rough and a little anxious as it brushes against my ear. He pulls back to look at me, warily.

This is the moment I feel we are destined to repeat, again and again: the moment where things fall apart, where he leaves me.

"You don't look okay," he says grimly.

"I'm scared," I whisper. "This is the point where you leave."

There is something pained and broken in his face. "I never wanted to leave you, Maura. You know that."

"I know," I sigh. "It's just hard."

He runs his fingers over my cheekbone. "Maura Leigh Pierce, I swear to you that I will never leave you again unless you tell me to. Never."

My eyes well. He's making promises he can't keep, because in a week we will separate again when I leave for school. But I'm going to do my best to forget that during the time we have left. And I'll just pray that the memory of this week is enough to carry me through all the years I'll spend without him.

Sometime in the middle of the night I wake and am struck dumb by fear of my family's reaction if they don't find me in my hotel room in the morning. There will be hell to pay no matter what, but this would make it so much worse. I climb out of bed silently and feel around the floor for my dress.

"What are you doing?" he asks.

"I'm sorry. I didn't want to wake you," I whisper, coming to sit beside him. "I've got to go back to my room. My parents will freak out if they come in the morning and I'm not there."

"Maura," he says, pulling me down beside him and wrapping the blanket around me. He's so big and warm that I can't help but curl into him.

"Yes?"

"Don't go."

"I have to," I argue. "I'll never hear the end of it if I don't."

"If you leave, something will happen," he says. "I have no idea what it will be, but it'll be something, and you won't come back."

"I will," I promise, despite the fact that his words scare me a little. I feel it too, this sense that everyone and everything in our lives is conspiring to keep us apart.

He flips me on my back, and leans over me, looking in my eyes. His face is raw and scared. It's a face I recognize, the face I saw last night as Ethan proposed. The face I can't say no to. "Please don't go," he whispers.

I know I will pay for this. I'll pay for what I did at the wedding, what I did to Ethan, but I'll pay most of all for the fact that I am with Nate now.

It's a little heartbreaking, his relief and astonishment when I agree. "You're really doing this. It's really going to happen." I understand his awe, because I feel it too. He makes love to me again, but this time it is slow and gentle and it feels like we are sealing a pact.

We go to my hotel room at daybreak and I pack the little I have with me.

"It's going to be an interesting week," I laugh, surveying my small pile of belongings – two pairs of heels, a red satin dress, my cut-off shorts and two tank tops. All the rest of my clothes are at my parents' house, and God knows I'm not stopping there.

We check out of our rooms quickly, before any more drama can unfold, and head back to the beach. His hand never leaves mine. Every once in a while he looks over at me and grins the way he did when he was young and thrilled to be getting away with something. A smile spreads over my face in response, a smile that seems to begin at my very core and emanate outward.

He shakes his head. "I still can't believe you're here."

I laugh. "I kind of can't believe I am either."

* *

I have seven messages on my phone. The only call I return, shame-faced, is the one from Elise, who is about to leave for Bali.

There is absolutely nothing I can do to excuse my behavior, to excuse the terrible way her wedding became focused on me, or the fact that I ran out before dinner was even over. "I'm so, so sorry," I tell her, hating how insufficient my apology is.

"Are you kidding?" she laughs. "I just had the most memorable wedding in the club's history! And even if I didn't, it was Ethan's fault, not yours."

"I'm still sorry," I sigh. "None of it should have happened."

She makes a noise of dismissal. "I'm not calling about that anyway. I'm calling because I want my wedding present."

"Uh," I stammer in surprise. "I had it mailed to your house. It should already have come… "

She cuts me off. "That's not the present I want. I want to hear you tell me why one of my husband's best friends also disappeared from the wedding."

"Oh," I say, breaking into a smile. "I guess that's because he was with me."

"With you in a biblical sense?" she goads.

"Among other things, yes," I giggle, turning red though Elise and I have had far more graphic conversations.

And then all I hear is her joyful screaming to Brian, and him shouting back, his voice growing louder as he approaches. He grabs the phone out of her hand.

"It's about time you idiots got back together," laughs Brian. "Put him on the phone."

I hand it over, only able to hear Brian's excitement, but not his words.

"Yep, finally," Nate says, grinning as he looks over at me. Brian says something else and Nate's smile grows sweeter, more secretive.

"I'm working on it," he says.

When he hangs up, I ask him what exactly he's working on, and he refuses to tell me, changing the topic by running his hand along the inside of my thigh. "You were killing me when we rode to Charlotte together," he says. "You know that, right?"

"No," I reply. "What was killing you?"

"Those shorts! The same damned ones you've got on right now. I had a semi the whole way there."

I giggle, running my hand over his crotch, and sure enough there's something starting there already. "Just let me know if it starts bothering you too much."

He places my hand back in my own lap. "Don't even think about it. I'm not about to kill one of us now that I finally have you back."

I sigh. "I wish it hadn't taken us the whole summer to figure this out. I only have a week left."

Something flickers across his face, but he lets it go. "Me too," he says.

We stop for breakfast in Florence, an otherwise perfect meal were it not for the relentless vibrating of my cell phone, which I put on mute hours earlier. Every two minutes comes another reminder that this happiness comes at a price.

"You're gonna have to talk to her eventually," Nate says, somewhere around the 15th call.

My shoulders sag with dread as I pick up the phone and let my mother's tirade begin. She starts by expounding on the many ways I've injured her — how embarrassed she is, how she can't imagine ever showing her face at the club again – and follows that with questions she doesn't really want the answer to – am I ashamed of myself? How could I have done this to them, to Ethan? Do I understand the damage I've done and how so many people will never, ever recover from my selfish actions? Finally, she demands to know where I went when I left.

"To the hotel," I say. Technically true. I glance at Nate.

When she finally runs out of steam, she slams the phone down without saying goodbye.

"Are you okay?" he asks.

"Yes," I reply. "It was pretty much what I expected."

He pauses. "You didn't tell her about us."

"No. I'm in enough trouble already."

"Are you going to tell them?" he asks.

"We have one week together," I sigh. "I can spend it with you peacefully or I can tell them and get dragged home."

"You're 22, Maura. They can't drag you anywhere."

"I may be 22 but they still pay the bills," I tell him. There's a pleading note to my voice – I don't want him to be hurt but he needs to understand my predicament. "And I've got three years of really big bills ahead. I can't afford to piss them off too much."

Again, he says nothing, but I feel distress in his silence.

* *

We walk quietly into the carriage house. The confrontation with my family will occur soon enough. I'm not going to let my grandmother get a head start on it.

He closes the door and pulls me to him. "Can we go straight upstairs or should I feed you first?" he grins.

"We only have a week left," I say, pulling his hand toward the stairs. "We can eat later."

He pulls back, and all the playfulness has left his face.

"Why do you keep saying that?" he asks angrily.

My exhale is exasperated. "You already know why. Because I'm starting school."

"You starting school is irrelevant. Why do *we* only have a week?" His voice is strained.

"Because I'm *leaving*, Nate," I say. I hate that I am hurting him, and at the same time I feel exhausted by the sheer number of people who think my plans are some kind of childish whim, like an insistence on only wearing stripes or refusing to eat vegetables. "You knew this. Why are you upset?"

"I know you're leaving," he persists. "Why does that mean we end?"

Since the moment we got back together last night, this is the question I've had to continually shove away. I just wanted a week, or even a day, of being happy with this, the little time we have. I want to beg him to take the question back, because my answer will ruin everything.

"Because you're not going to wait," I finally say, choking on the words as they emerge.

"That's why I'm upset!" he shouts, pressing the heel of his hand to his forehead. "Damn it, Maura. I don't want anyone else. I have *never* wanted anyone else, and I don't know what it will take to make you believe it. The reason you're not telling your family about us is because you still don't think this is for real."

"I'll be gone for three years, Nate!" I cry. "That's a long time for any couple, and we've never really been together as adults."

He moves back to lean against the wall, and closes his eyes. I wait, worry and dread overtaking me. I thought I had a week, but here it is already: the moment when it all falls apart.

"Then ask me to go with you," he finally says. Not at all what I was expecting.

"You can't," I argue. "You have this house and your job and…"

"Ask me to go with you," he says, cutting me off. "If you don't want me to go, then say so, but don't try to make my decisions for me."

"Are you serious?" I breathe, incredulous. He says nothing, just waits. "Go with me," I whisper, and I wait for the bottom to fall out.

"Okay," he says simply. As if it's a decision that requires no thought.

Exhilaration and wariness battle each other — really believing him, and then being disappointed, feels like more than I can bear. "What about your business? Your house?"

"Businesses can be started over. The house I can rent, or just board up for now. But you I won't give up."

"Don't say it if you don't mean it," I whisper. "Please. If you tell me this is going to happen and it doesn't…"

He comes back to me, tipping my face to his. "I mean it, Maura." He looks into my eyes, waiting for his decision to register, waiting for me to accept it. I look back at him, blurry through a film of tears, and nod, unable to even reply around the lump in my throat.

He presses his mouth against mine gently, and I can taste my tears as they slide between us.

He pulls back, a little cautiously. "Why are you crying? If this isn't what you want you need to say so. I'm not going to be like Ethan and your family, forcing you in a direction you don't want to go."

I shake my head. "I'm crying," I say roughly, "because you're telling me that I'm going to get the one thing I've always wanted and thought I'd never have."

He pulls me into his chest and holds me tightly, pressing a gentle kiss onto the top of my head. "The real test awaits, Maura. I want you to tell your mother."

I groan. "Are you sure we can't just go and call her from Michigan?" I suggest, only half-joking.

"I'm sure."

I take a deep breath. "Fine. But can we at least wait until tonight? Give me a few hours between her tantrums."

"Promise me you'll tell them."

"I swear it."

"Good," he says, pressing me to the wall with a crooked grin. "Because we have things to attend to here."

CHAPTER 39

The light is fading outside when the banging on the front door rouses us. I forget, for a second, where I am, and feel a shot of joy as I see Nate jumping out of bed. He pulls on his jeans quickly and frowns at me.

"Why are you smiling like that?" he asks. "Someone's trying to break down my goddamn door."

"You're coming with me," I say, unable to put a hold on my joy even if someone *is* trying to destroy the house.

And he smiles back at me, boyish and thrilled. "Yes, I am." He runs down the stairs while I throw on my clothes. I hear shouting, and the moment my shirt is over my head I am running toward the sound.

My father is yelling as I emerge from the stairwell.

"Dad?" I cry. "What's going on?"

Both of my parents are outside Nate's door. My father sees me and attempts to push past Nate.

"Dad! Stop!" I insist. Nate is larger and blocks my father, but he does so looking over at me with uncertainty. Despite everything we have promised each other, this, for him, is the moment of truth – the moment when I choose sides.

I know what I have if I stand with my parents: I have a ridiculously comfortable life, I have money and the power behind it to put me anywhere I want to go. Except there's only one thing I want right now, and it's on this side of the door. I walk beside

Nate, and I take his hand. He squeezes mine tightly, relief echoing in the pressure of his fingers.

"You can't be serious, Maura!" my mother cries. "You're with *him*? You clearly haven't thought this through."

"Mom, I've been in love with him since I was 13. I've had almost a decade to think it through."

"You're 22 years old! What do you know about love?"

"You certainly thought I was old enough last night when Ethan was proposing," I argue.

"This is unbelievable!" she shouts. "First you humiliate all of us at the wedding, then you get Jordan arrested, and now you've chosen some blue collar local over *Ethan*?"

"What do you mean I got Jordan arrested?" I gasp.

"Thanks to your little stunt last night, Stephen Mayhew told the police that Jordan helped destroy the walkways," she says. "So I hope you're happy."

I feel Nate grow tense beside me. "Your son destroyed property and somehow that's Maura fault?" he asks scathingly.

She turns to Nate. "No one was talking to you," she snaps. "You're not a part of this family. No matter how much you steal from us or use our daughter."

Rage surges through me, but Nate speaks before I can. "We both know I haven't stolen anything – you can check your father's will if that's not clear," he says calmly, and then he turns, and he's really talking only to me, "and I'm not using your daughter. I'm marrying her."

My mother's laugh is biting. "Maura doesn't even want to get married. Which shows how little you know about her."

"Actually, Mom," I say, feeling the words rise out of me like tiny, happy bubbles. "I think I've changed my mind about that."

Looking at Nate's smile is like staring straight at the sun. "Really?" he asks, wide-eyed, forgetting my parents completely.

"Really," I reply, forgetting them too.

"When?" he asks.

"I cannot believe I am listening to this!" my mother yells. "Stop that this instant! You two barely know each other!"

I laugh, still looking only at Nate. "I know him better than anyone alive."

"I won't stand for it, Maura," she says.

"You don't have to stand for it, Mom. I'm 22. I don't need your permission."

"What about law school? I seem to recall you insisting you didn't even want to *date* Ethan because you were leaving for school, but now you're ready to get married?"

"Nate's coming with me," I tell them.

"We will cut you off, Maura, without a dime," she warns.

"We don't need your money," says Nate.

"Maybe you don't," sneers my father. "But if she wants to go to law school she does."

"Fine," I reply. "I'll use the trust."

"You can't access that trust until you're 30," he says triumphantly. "So you'd better re-think what's going on here. And fast."

"And you can forget about setting foot in our home again until you've come to your senses," says my mother.

Nate shuts the door and leans against it, pulling me into him.

"We'll find the money, baby, I promise," he whispers into my hair.

I just shake my head. "Where? There's nowhere we can get that kind of money," I say. I can't believe I was so close, only to have the whole thing ripped out from under me.

"Maybe I can take out a mortgage on the carriage house," he says. "We'll have to talk to Peter to see if it's legal, but I don't see why it wouldn't be."

"No," I say, trying to gather my voice back together into some semblance of strength. "I can't take your money."

He raises an eyebrow. "It's *our* money. Or have you already forgotten that you just said you'd marry me?"

I laugh. "Oh, right."

"Did you mean it?" he asks, tentatively. "Or were you just trying to piss off your mom?"

"Of course I meant it," I say, placing my hands on either side
of his worried face.

"Good," he says softly. He leans down to kiss me, his mouth
feather light against mine. He deepens the kiss, gripping my hips
and pulling me forward, and I groan a little at the feel of him.

"I warned you about making that noise," he says in a low
voice, and he scoops me up and carries me to bed.

The next morning there is someone at the door again, but this
time the knock is timid, almost childlike.

I half-expect to find a Girl Scout or a lost toddler, but instead
I find Mia, who glances warily over her shoulder before she
even speaks.

"I heard what happened," she says. "I'm so sorry."

"Thank you," I grin. "But it's okay. I'm really happy."

"I kind of figured that." She smiles, and then casts another
anxious glance back at the mansion. "I heard you weren't allowed
back in the house," she says nervously. "I went in after your parents left and packed up what I could. It's in my trunk." She says it
so apologetically you'd think she was telling me she'd lit my stuff
on fire rather than rescuing it.

I throw my arms around her impulsively, wishing hard for a
way to save her though I doubt it exists. "You know you don't have
to stick around to clean up Jordan's mess, right?" I ask. "You could
leave. You could come with us. You deserve better than him."

She shakes her head a little sadly. "I've made my choice," she
says. "But I just wanted you to know... I think you made a better one."

* *

We call Peter to set up a meeting, and he suggests we talk after Jordan's hearing. I agree reluctantly because I'm not sure that I'd planned on going. If my parents are blaming me for this, Jordan is too.

I sit in the courtroom with Nate beside me, thinking about how much things have changed in seven days. One week ago I was here with Ethan, feeling as if my life had ended. Thinking I'd lost the only person I'd ever loved. And now he's beside me. No matter how awful the next hour will be, it pales in comparison to the last time I sat here. I squeeze his hand and when he smiles at me I feel weightless, buoyant, as if we're here to get married rather than to watch my brother get arraigned.

Jordan's bail is set. He walks to my parents and Mia grimly, and never says a word to me as he leaves the courtroom. Nate and I turn to leave and my steps stutter to a halt. Ethan is against the back wall. And there are no words for the look he gives me.

What I did to him at the wedding is, arguably, the worst thing I've ever done in my life, but to have him find me with Nate two days later surpasses it. My behavior is absolutely inexcusable. And I wouldn't change it for the world. Not for a moment do I wish Nate wasn't beside me. Not for a moment am I anything less than overwhelmingly grateful for the pressure of his hand as we walk toward the exit.

"You didn't do anything wrong," Nate says gently. "He knew you didn't want to marry him. He asked the way he did to pressure you, and he deserved what he got."

I know Nate's right, but my stomach twists with dread as we reach Ethan. There is nothing I can say that will make this better. No heartfelt apology is going to fix it.

"I want to talk to you for a minute," Ethan hisses. "Without *him*," he adds, glaring at Nate.

Nate pauses, waiting for a signal from me before he drops my hand and backs away.

Ethan looks at me with disgust. "So the two of you are a *couple* now?"

"Yes," I say, and as bad as I feel about the whole situation it's hard to look apologetic. I'm with Nate now. It's out, and no one can take it away from us this time. And I'm marrying him, which is about as real as it gets.

"And I guess this was going on all summer behind my back?" he asks.

"No, of course not," I tell him. It's sort of true. And sort of not. "I'm sorry," I say, hoping he'll at least hear the sincerity in the words. "About the wedding, about how things ended... I'm just sorry."

"Is that all you have to say?" he snaps. "You humiliated me in front of 300 people, Maura, and all you have to say is 'sorry'?"

"There's nothing I can do to change the way things happened," I tell him. "You shouldn't have asked me in public. You knew I didn't want that. You were just trying to shame me into it."

"You don't think about anyone but yourself," he snarls. "Every decision is only about what *you* want, what's best for *you*."

Nate, sensing the increased hostility, comes back to my side.

"Who am I supposed to be thinking of when I'm making a decision that will affect the rest of my life?" I demand of Ethan. "You? Your parents?"

"Why don't you ask me who you *shouldn't* be thinking about, Maura? Because it shouldn't be *him*!" he yells, looking at Nate. "No matter how many times we all tried to set you straight, you went right back to him, didn't you?"

The chill in my spine puts me on alert. I grow still as the room around me grows chaotic, as Nate's arm wraps around my hip and pulls me into him protectively, as the bailiffs begin moving toward us. "How exactly have you all tried to set me straight?" I ask.

"Do you know how many times I warned your grandparents about the two of you? Your grandfather would never listen. If he hadn't died you'd probably still be fucking Nate out on the beach where anyone could see you!"

The rage I feel is lethal, so intense that I don't want to waste my energy yelling. I'm saving it to wound. "It was you?" I ask, frighteningly calm. "You're the one who told my grandmother?"

"Yes," he sneers. "And all summer I had to put up with your good-girl routine, knowing what a little slut you were in high school."

Nate releases my waist and instinctively I step back, because I know what will happen next. When Nate's fist connects with Ethan's jaw, I'm not even vaguely surprised.

And he's part of what took me away from Nate, so I don't feel all that guilty.

Peter waits for us. He waits while the bailiffs rush to pull Ethan and Nate apart, while Ethan insists he wants to press charges for assault and the bailiffs ignore him. Finally we walk away, and I kiss the bruised hand that holds mine as Peter leads us to a conference room.

"Well that was interesting," Peter laughs as we sit. He looks at our linked hands. "I guess you two figured it out then."

"Figured what out?" I ask with an edge to my voice. It's beginning to feel that everyone alive was somehow complicit in my grandmother's plan, but I never dreamed Peter would be among them.

His brow furrows. "That you were my spies?"

Nate and I look at each other in surprise.

"It was *you* who told us when they were tearing down the walkways?" he grins. "I had no idea you were so devious."

"And you were the person who staked it out." I smile, but Jordan's involvement has made the victory a little hollow.

"I'm sorry about your brother," Peter says.

I'm sorry too, in a way, but in another I am not. Maybe this will be a turning point for Jordan. Maybe the specter of prison will make him realize it's time to be happy with what he has.

"You had some questions about the terms of Daniel's will, is that correct?" he asks.

"Yes," says Nate. "I know I can't sell the carriage house unless the Pierces sell their house too, but what about taking out a mortgage on it?"

Peter shakes his head. "I seriously doubt you can get a mortgage on a property that's entailed in that way."

Our faces fall, and Nate squeezes my hand. "Then we'll come up with something else."

Peter looks back and forth between the two of us. "Uh, why on earth would *you* need money, Maura?"

I explain the situation, and both Nate and I sit for a moment, deflated, while Peter continues to look confused. "Maura, just because Nate can't take out a mortgage doesn't mean *you* can't. That would give you more than enough to live off for quite some time."

I laugh sadly. "I'm no expert on real estate law, but I'm pretty sure I'd have to own some property in order to take out a loan on it."

His face goes from befuddled to astonished. "Maura, you *do* own property. You own the mansion."

I laugh again. "No I don't."

"I administered your grandfather's will. I think I'd know," he says. "You must know this. You signed all the documents."

"Peter, I don't know what you're talking about. I never signed anything."

"They couldn't have…" he begins, and then trails off, aghast. "If you're saying your parents forged your signature, it's not just unconscionable, it's illegal."

He pulls a copy of the will out of the folder in front of him and hands it to me. I see my name, my grandfather's signature, and watch the document shake a little in my hand.

"This can't be right. What about my grandmother, my parents, Jordan? I'm the *last* person it should have gone to."

"I think your grandfather felt differently," he says. "Your grandmother is allowed to remain there until her death, but he always hoped that it would end up with you and Nate. That's why he specified in his will that the carriage house must pass to Nate in the event of Mary's death."

"But we were just teenagers when he died," Nate says. "He couldn't have known we'd end up together."

Peter smiles. "You weren't even teenagers. He wrote this will when Maura was 10. I advised him against all of it, but I couldn't dissuade him. He said he just knew."

I look over at Nate through a film of tears, and smile when I see that his eyes, too, are suspiciously bright.

CHAPTER 40

We leave the courthouse a little shell-shocked.

"Are you okay?" he asks.

"Yeah," I say. "I just learned I own a mansion worth millions of dollars. Hard to be down about that." My voice, despite my words, is a little flat.

He looks at me speculatively. I know what he's thinking: that it has to hurt, knowing how far my parents would go to deceive me. And I suppose it does, in a way, but the truth is that I'm not really surprised. Jordan always came first — not just the firstborn, but the most important. They admired his ability to make a big splash, to draw a crowd. In their minds he deserves everything, and I deserve the debris that trails behind.

"Your parents never deserved to have you for a daughter," he says.

I smile a little. His loyalty means more to me than anything they could ever give or take away.

The only surprise today — the one I can't wrap my head around — is my grandfather. We pull into the driveway, and both of us stare for a moment at my grandmother's house. No, *my* house.

"Why do you think he did it?" I ask.

Nate shrugs. "You were always his favorite."

"I wasn't his favorite," I laugh. "*You* were."

He smiles and shakes his head in disagreement. "Honestly, I

just don't get it. He had to have known what a shitstorm it would cause to give you the house. Even if he'd wanted to make a point to everyone, I don't think this is how he would have done it. That wasn't his style."

"I know," I murmur. "That's what bothers me. He must have had a reason for giving it to me. And I'm not sure I'll ever know what it was."

I think about it all afternoon, while Nate is at work. I reach into my memory and try to pull forward even the tiniest snippet of conversation that might explain things. I find nothing.

"Grandpa, why didn't you say something?" I sigh. It feels like I'm failing him, whether I mean to or not.

I bike to the store and start dinner when I get back. I've got the music up loud so I don't hear Nate until the door slams. I turn my head from the stove to find him, arms stretched high over his head as he grips the frame of the door. His shirt rides up enough to display a mile of toned stomach, the sparse trail of hair below his belly button. For just a moment I feel a shot of something so heady it could knock me off my feet. Something that goes beyond lust, although that's there in spades as well. It's an almost unbearable thrill: he's here for me. He's mine.

"You cooked? I never thought I'd see the day," he says.

I smile. "You know, I'm not completely incompetent."

He chuckles, coming up behind me, his hands on my hips and his voice low against my ear. "Believe me, Maura, I know how competent you are." My tank slides up and his hands follow its progress.

"Other than in bed," I laugh, but the sound is a little breathy. "Dinner will be ready in just a minute."

"I just worked for six hours," he replies. "And not for one

minute of those six hours was I thinking about food." His hands cup my breasts, as his mouth moves to my neck.

The spoon slides from my hand.

Hours later we are still in bed, remnants of our reheated dinner on his nightstand. Our plans are beginning to take shape: Peter is looking into the mortgage, and until then we'll use Nate's savings and whatever he can earn working construction. He's going to leave his equipment down here until he's established enough to start up his own business again, so really it's just a matter of dealing with the jobs he's already taken on. I lay beside him while he makes a list of everything he needs to complete or hand off before we leave.

"I hate that you're so swamped this week," I tell him. "Is there anything I can do to help?"

He looks at me and bursts out laughing.

"What?" I cry indignantly. "I might be useful."

"Do you know how to lay a roof? Work a table saw? Hang drywall?" he asks.

"Well," I equivocate, "maybe not as well as *you.*"

"Maura, have you *ever* done any of those things?" he laughs.

I grin. "Not exactly."

"Yeah, that's what I thought."

"You know what I *am* good at?" I ask.

His brow raises and he looks at me with sudden interest.

"Filling out college applications," I say.

He sighs and drops his list on the floor. "Not where I hoped you were going with that."

"I could fill one out for you."

"I could fill one out for myself," he replies. "If I had any interest in going back. Which I don't." He gets out of bed to brush his teeth, which I assume is his way of telling me the conversation is over.

The conversation is so *not* over.

He wanted to be an architect too badly, and for too long, to have his interest in it seemingly evaporate. But I know it's something he's sensitive about, so I have to tread lightly. Admittedly, not my forte.

He comes back and sets his alarm for an hour I can only describe as painful. "Oh my God," I moan. "Tell me you're not planning to go in that early. And before you make some comment about people who don't work for a living, keep in mind that I stalked you all summer so I know what time you normally go in."

For some reason that pleases him. His smile is almost shy. "Well, you see, there's this girl I kind of like," he says, climbing into bed. "And if I want to go to Michigan with her, I've got to do about a month's worth of work in four days."

I pull him toward me, wedging my knee between his, as my lips brush his neck. "She must be spectacular if you're going to all that trouble."

"She's okay," he says, his mouth tipping up at the corner.

"I bet she's *brilliant*."

"I don't know about 'brilliant', per se," he replies. "'Literate' or 'employable', maybe?"

He gets a pinch for that one.

"Super hot?" I ask, rolling him on his back and climbing over him.

He shrugs, pulling my shirt over my head. "You know, looks aren't everything. She has a good personality."

I smirk. "Her good personality seems to be having a *sizable* effect on you. Take it back."

His laugh turns into a groan as I slide over him. "I take it back," he says. He reaches up, pulling my mouth toward his, suddenly earnest. "She's the prettiest girl I've ever seen in my life."

On Wednesday night he insists on going back to North Shore, despite the fact that he wasn't home for a single hour of daylight. That day we spent here together when I was with Ethan felt indulgent, forbidden. It's hard to believe it happened so recently, and it's hard to believe how much has changed since then.

He takes a piece of the funnel cake he's eating and pops it into my mouth.

"You've got powdered sugar here," he says, pressing his mouth to the side of mine, heedless of the swarms of people moving around us.

"You put it there," I smile.

"Irrelevant. Some here too," he says, his breath brushing my upper lip. He tips my chin toward him and captures my mouth lightly before pulling away. "You have no idea how much I love being able to do that in public."

He's wrong. I know exactly how much he loves being able to do that. It still feels like a miracle to me too.

We go sit on the beach, hidden by the darkness, and I lean against him. "Thank you."

"For what?" he asks. I can feel him smile against my neck.

"For this. For taking me out tonight when you have to be so exhausted."

"I'm trying to get as much time in with you as I can. Once school starts you'll be busy and I have no idea how long it will be before I'm able to set my own hours."

"*Or*," I suggest cautiously, "you could go back to school."

He stiffens, his jaw setting like I knew it would. "I can make as much as an architect once I'm up and running again," he says.

"It's not about the money," I argue. "I don't care what you do for a living or how much you earn, but I want you to love what you do. And you always wanted to be an architect."

"One of us has to work, Maura," he warns. "Especially if that mortgage doesn't come through."

"Okay, but assuming it does…"

"Assuming it does, I'm still not going back."

"Why?" I demand. "Why are you so set against it? I'll never bring it up again if you've got a good reason. Maybe you started studying architecture and discovered you hated it, and if that's the case…"

"I didn't hate it," he says, pinching the bridge of his nose.

"Then what is it, Nate? Why not go back?"

"That's not my world, Maura," he sighs. "It's yours. I spent so much time listening to you and your grandfather that I kind of forgot that."

"What are you talking about? In what possible way was it not your world?"

"Not everyone goes to college. Most of the kids who grew up down here didn't. Your brother is an asshole, but the shit he and his friends used to say to me was kind of true. A kid like me had no business dating a Pierce and going to UVA. It just took everything that happened – us breaking up and me losing my scholarship – to realize it."

I hate my brother in this moment. I hate him with the kind of blinding, momentary hatred that makes people act violently. I hate him enough to hope he goes to prison, to hope he has just a little of his charmed life stripped from him. I turn away from Nate because I don't want him to see my face. I need to master this thing in my throat that's strangling me.

"Look," he says, placing a hand on my shoulder to turn me toward him. "Don't get pissed. I know…" His words falter to a stop and he blinks in surprise. "You're *crying*? Why?"

I cover my face as he pulls me into his chest. "We did this," I whisper. "Me, my brother, my friends. All these assholes down here from Charlotte. We did this to you."

"Don't ever lump yourself in with them," he demands. "And no one did anything."

"We made you doubt yourself," I rasp. "How could you possibly think they were right? You're a hundred times smarter than any of those boys. You're a hundred times too good for me. But you somehow only see what they wanted you to see."

"You're biased, Maura," he murmurs against my hair. "I love you for it, but you're biased. Look, whatever happened, it all turned out for the best. We're together and it's behind us."

"It's not behind us. You gave up your dream and you're *still* giving it up, and for the wrong reasons."

He lifts my head from his chest, kissing a tear off my cheek before he finds my mouth. "Maura, life isn't a fairy tale. In the real world, not every wrong is made right."

But this one could be, I want to cry. This one could be fixed so easily. I say nothing. He knows how I feel and at a certain point I will need to stop assuming I know what's best for him. Maybe that time is now – I'm not sure. I lay my head against his chest heavily, and in the silence he seems to guess at my thoughts.

"I love that you want so much for me," he finally says. "Let's just tackle one thing at a time."

On our last day he works and I pack. I'm not sad to be leaving, though I wonder if he is. This is home for him, but for me it's just one more place where history clouds vision. Where people look at us and insist we don't belong together, blind to all the things that actually matter.

When he gets home from work I have my answer. I see his face when he walks in, when he looks at the suitcases and few boxes I've packed, sitting by the door. I see unhappiness there but something that troubles me more. Uncertainty.

It's the first moment it's occurred to me, all week long, that he might have a change of heart. That perhaps this week felt like some magical interlude because that's all it was for him. A week to revisit who we were. A week to bask in a sleepy daydream of what we could have been.

He goes into the kitchen, opening the refrigerator and staring inside blindly, his mind elsewhere.

"I cleaned it out," I explain, feeling the blood drain from my face. "It would've all gone bad."

I want to ask him what he's thinking but I don't, because I'm a coward. Because I can't stand for him to do this to me now. A week ago, I could have left without him. Now I'm not sure I could. I busy myself with the last open suitcase, and when I turn back, he's watching me, something haunted in his eyes.

"Are you okay?" I ask.

He looks away, as if I've caught him thinking something he didn't want me to know. "I need to swim," he says, avoiding the question. "You want to go?"

We walk to the beach in silence. He grips my hand tightly, in the way he might if it were our final night together. With every step away from the house I expect him to stop me, to explain what's going on, but he doesn't. When we reach the shore he runs ahead to dive into the water. He's halfway to the sandbar before he turns back to look for me, still standing where the water barely hits mid-calf.

I wait for his devious, lopsided grin. I wait for his standard threat – *get in or I'll throw you in.*

But instead he walks back toward me, wordless and unsmiling.

"What's the matter?" I whisper as he reaches me. His wet hands push through my hair, bringing me closer. His palms frame my jaw as he looks at me, searching for words.

He doesn't answer, and that worry in my stomach curdles and tightens into a hard knot, allowing my fears to play themselves out. If I leave without him I'll be destroyed. But I also can't stay with someone who doesn't care enough about me to go.

"You're not coming with me," I whisper.

For a moment he looks appalled, and then his face breaks into the first smile I've seen all night. "Did you really think I'd back out?" he asks. "Of *course* I'm coming with you."

My body goes boneless with relief and I sink against him. "You looked so unhappy when you came home, and I could tell there was something you wanted to say but you were nervous."

I feel a rumble of laughter in his chest. "Maybe you need this as much as I do then."

"Need what?" I ask.

"More," he says simply.

I look at him wide-eyed. *More?* We're living together. What more is there?

"I feel like I've spent my whole life waiting for you," he explains. "When we were kids I spent every school year scared you wouldn't come back, in high school I was scared you'd get sent away. Then we were apart, and when you finally come back you're with Ethan. I've spent my entire life scared of losing you, and I just want to know it's behind us."

"Of course it's behind us..." I begin.

He shakes his head. "I need more than that and so do you. I need to know that no one is taking you away from me again, and based on how quickly you thought I'd change my mind, I think you do too."

I can offer him a thousand words of reassurance, but I know they'd be insufficient. "It will probably just take time, Nate," I say. "We just need enough time away from here and away from my family to trust that nothing's coming between us."

"Or this," he says, dropping to his knees in the surf.

I stare at him, for a moment, uncomprehending. And then it dawns on me as he grabs my hands.

"I had this whole plan for how I was going to propose," he says. "But it involves waiting, and I just can't wait. I want you to be my wife. I want to know it's permanent this time."

I smile, feeling my whole body filling with something so light and all-encompassing I could float away on it. "Of course it's permanent."

"Just answer the question," he growls.

I raise a brow. "You didn't actually ask me a question."

He rolls his eyes but he's trying not to laugh. "God, you're such a lawyer already. Will you marry me?"

The second I tell him 'yes' he's back on his feet and scooping me up like he's going to throw me in.

"Are you seriously throwing me in right after proposing?" I demand.

He shakes his head. "I'm still trying to get over the fact that you're going to be my wife," he says, brushing my forehead with his mouth. "I'm not throwing you anywhere for a little while."

We leave for Michigan in a slightly different style than I'd originally planned – in a decade-old truck with our few worldly belongings tied down in the back. Nate's meager life savings are the only thing standing between us and a homeless shelter when we arrive.

I'm not nearly as stressed by this situation as I should be. I look over at him, his profile as he drives – strong jaw, soft mouth – and I feel that nothing matters as long as I have him.

I look at the ring on my finger, the one that belonged to his grandmother, the one he set aside for me nearly a decade ago. I take off my seat belt.

"What are you doing?" he asks sharply.

I had no idea he was such a fiend for automotive safety until the past week.

"Just this," I say, sliding over, pressing my mouth to his cheekbone.

He tries to look stern but I see a small smile peek through. "Fine. Now put your seat belt back on."

My mouth moves to the lobe of his ear, to his neck. In a short amount of time I've learned, or relearned, his triggers. The things he can't resist. The things that will make him go into work late, leave a bar early, or – possibly – pull off the road.

"Maura," he groans. "Seriously, you have to stop. We have eight hours of driving before we reach the hotel, and I can only take so much."

I slide back to my seat reluctantly. "You know we don't have to stay in a hotel tonight. We could just sleep in the car."

He shoots me that lopsided smile. "Stop freaking out about money. Just because we aren't rich doesn't mean we're destitute."

"I know. But what if something goes wrong with the mortgage?"

"It'll work out," he says, grabbing my hand. "I'll make it work."

And I believe him, just like I did when we were small and he told me he'd protect me from sharks. I believe him against all reason and logic. Or maybe I simply believe him because I believe in the part that matters most – he's beside me and he's mine. Always.

CHAPTER 41

FIVE YEARS LATER

The call comes late, so late I probably wouldn't have answered at all if it wasn't coming from the south. I know, without even looking at the number, that it won't be a member of my family. My parents have called me three times since I left. Each call begins with the clear expectation that I will show some contrition for the decisions I made, and when I don't they grow angry. They don't regret their actions – they regret only that I was so impulsive and selfish, as if the preservation of our family's social standing was well worth any sacrifice I may have been asked to make.

This is a call that should have come from them, but does not. It comes from Peter, informing me that my grandmother has passed away. Yet another reason the call didn't come from my parents, who still feel the house should have gone to Jordan.

Peter asks what I want to do with the house. I probably should have already thought this through, but I really have no idea. Before I hang up, he stops me. "I know things ended badly here, Maura. But when you make a decision about the house, keep in mind why your grandfather wanted you to have it."

"What do you mean?" I ask. I've thought about this often, my grandfather's mysterious gift.

"You know your grandfather hated how insular things are

here," he says. "He thought you, and Nate, might be the ones who could change that. You could make this a real community, not just a place for rich folks to pass some time."

"Why are you only telling me this now?" I breathe.

"To be honest, I was worried you'd feel like you had to stay put," he says. "And I thought you needed to get away from your family for a while. Get some perspective."

Except our lives are here now. We're *happy*. So many good things have happened in this place, a web strung of tiny, beautiful memories that tie us together.

"I don't know," I demur. "I think changing the Cove is a bigger task than two people could take on."

"I got the birth announcement," he says, changing the topic suddenly. "Congratulations."

"Thank you," I smile, looking across the room at my little pink bundle and her exhausted father, who have fallen asleep together in the rocking chair, as they are both apt to do.

"Can't be easy to take care of a new baby and work at a big firm at the same time," he comments.

"I'm still on leave, but no, it probably won't be easy," I sigh. The truth is that working at a big firm has been far less glamorous and far more grueling that I once envisioned. And the thought of leaving my little girl to work 60-hour weeks is killing me.

"Did I tell you I'm getting ready to retire?" he asks.

Peter is typically a decent conversationalist, but tonight I can barely keep up with the change of topics.

"No, I hadn't heard," I say.

"We could use a good lawyer down here, Maura," he says. "And I guarantee you it's a lot more relaxed than working at a firm. Nate must be nearly done with his master's degree. Tons of new homes going in at North Shore. Architects have more work than they can handle."

I laugh. "You're kind of a pain in the ass. You know that, right?"

"I'll stop," he chuckles. "But I'm looking at this birth announcement and thinking your grandfather was right about a lot of things," he says. "Maybe you should have a little faith."

Nate climbs into bed with Mary Rose still tucked into his arm like a football.

"Who called?" he asks groggily.

"It was Peter," I say, and that rouses him. I tell him what Peter has said, watch the way his face lights up when I mention the beach, like a homesick little boy.

"What do you think?" he asks. I know he's stayed away for me. I know he wants, more than anything, to go back.

I think about the house. I think about Mary Rose and the other children we'll someday have, running through the wet grass of the side yard in their bare feet, blooming in the salty air. I see myself sitting on the porch with Nate on a summer night, listening to their distant laughter.

It's an image, I'm guessing, that my grandfather once had too.

Nate waits for my answer, his trust and his loyalty absolute. I look at the little girl in his arms who reminds me so much of him, and his mother. We've created something my family can't take away, no matter how hard they try.

I press my lips to my daughter's downy little head, and then to Nate's own. And then I tell him it's time for us to be the people my grandfather hoped we'd be. It's time for us to go home.

ABOUT THE AUTHOR

Elizabeth O'Roark lives in Washington, DC with her 3 children. *Undertow* is her first novel. For a chapter of *Undertow* from Nate's perspective, or to sign up for the mailing list, visit her on Facebook at Elizabeth O'Roark Books.

Printed in Great Britain
by Amazon

36845649R00155